Dystechnica
Ben Hermel, Portland, Oregon

© 2020 by Ben Hermel

All rights reserved. No part of this publication may be reproduced or distributed in any form or by any means, or stored in a database or retrieval system, without the prior written permission of the publisher.

This is a work of fiction. Names, characters, businesses, places, and events are either the products of the author's imagination or used in a fictitious manner. Any resemblance to actual persons, living or dead, or actual events is purely coincidental.

Line editing, proofreading, and interior book design provided by Indigo: Editing, Design, and More.
Line editor: Kristen Hall-Geisler
Proofreaders: Jennifer Kepler, Laura Garwood
Design consultation and ebook conversion: Vinnie Kinsella
www.indigoediting.com

ISBN: 9781734935011
eISBN: 9781734935028

LCCN: 2020907562

For Emily, Finn, and Skylar

Contents

9 Potential

23 Magic Pill

39 Kilburn

61 Lorentzians

77 Forget Something?

87 Pioneer

105 Fame Is Fleeting

133 Nudge

143 Emosense

157 Low Power

173 Harbinger

189 Purchase History

213 Regret

227 South of Carson

243 Threshold

261 Dignified Silence

Janet was weaving through the crowd holding two plastic cups above her head when a brief lull announced Adam's arrival. After spending the night in the shadows, she was caught in the middle of the room as he casually parted the sea of swaying bodies. He was just a few inches taller than average, so almost everyone seemed to crane their neck in admiration. Janet was one of the few who didn't fawn. When he slowed as though waiting for a deferential smile, she let the wave of anticipation pass by without acknowledging him. Beckoned from the far corner by one of his many devotees, Adam turned abruptly, and Janet exhaled before scampering to Michelle's side.

She pushed the cup into Michelle's outstretched hand. "What are the chances?"

"I can't believe that just happened."

"Do you think he recognized me?"

"I don't know; it's hard to tell. But it was great. You totally stone-faced him."

"But do you think he remembers?"

"No way. When was it, like three years ago? I'm sure there have been a few girls in his life since then—" Michelle stopped when Janet looked away. "But what does it matter anyway? It won't make any difference to your score."

"You never know, and it might make a difference to his. With an ego like that, he'd be pretty relieved to be jousting against a girl scorned."

"Really? 'A girl scorned'? Aren't you being a little melodramatic?"

Janet glanced across the room. "I guess."

"Okay, well, just be sure to lie low for the rest of the night, and if you need another drink, let me get it."

They both looked across to the ever-growing circle around Adam. He had carefully flicked his sandy hair across his forehead, and a few errant wisps fell over his left eye. A starry-eyed girl fondled one of the victory pins that covered his left lapel, and Janet wondered if his blue eyes alone were worth a couple of points. The color was almost perfectly balanced between bright and brooding.

Michelle smirked. "He's not seriously wearing that!"

"I know it looks ridiculous, but if you'd won that many Jousts, you'd probably wear it every day too."

"Oh, you know I wouldn't. He's an ass. Look at those girls, they just…"

Janet glanced at her feet.

"I'm sorry, Janet, but you know what I mean. Anyway, his victories make me wonder about the whole thing. What does the algorithm think he'll contribute to society? The only potential I see is Adam convincing a few suckers to invest in a questionable financial scheme, and I'm not sure I'd consider that a—"

"Michelle. Enough."

"Come on, I was just kidding. Look, you've totally got this. And damn, it's going to be great to see him go down." Michelle smiled. "But I don't want to see you all badged up when you win on Friday."

"I appreciate the support, but there are no guarantees."

"Yeah, I know, but I believe in you."

Janet's gaze drifted across the room. Adam's smile was still the same, but she recoiled at the sight of the pins on his chest and turned to Michelle. "Thanks. I appreciate the support."

Michelle put her hand on Janet's shoulder. "Well, that's what I'm here for. What do you want me to do?"

"We wait. He's got plenty of company now, but when it dwindles, you'll take over."

"How late do you want to keep him out?"

"As late as you can, I guess. And try to keep him drinking. I want him to wake up with a headache," Janet replied.

Michelle's lips curled into a smile.

"Michelle, I'm not kidding. You know how important tomorrow's test is to the algorithm."

Two hours later, Michelle was looking up at Adam with a convincing display of adoration. "Come on, just one more. Why be the king if you can't enjoy it?"

"No, I really can't. I should be getting home."

She leaned a little closer. "Really? I didn't peg you as the rule-following type."

Adam tilted his head. "You know, there's a time for everything."

"I'm not asking you to stay all night, but just have one more drink with me," she replied, a little more desperately.

"Okay, but just one."

The dance continued for another hour, when their increasingly slurred conversation was cut by a sober voice. "Adam, what the hell are you doing? You should be home by now. I'm getting your jacket."

Michelle shook her head. "Adam, are you really going to take that?"

He glanced away.

She laughed. "Well, I don't even know what you're fretting about. Didn't your dad win a dozen? By my calculation, you have another five before you even have to worry."

Adam narrowed his eyes as he turned back to Michelle, and she hurriedly continued, "You know, I'm sure he's proud that you're continuing the tradition."

He nodded before turning back to David, who was thrusting Adam's jacket at him. "Let's get out of here. You need to get some sleep."

"You're going to leave when we're just getting started?" Michelle asked, but David just glared at Michelle before escorting his drunken friend out. Michelle glanced around the sparsely populated room. The empty cups scattered around and a downbeat song trickling through the speakers signaled that the party had been over for a while.

Janet emerged from the shadows. "Wow, you were fantastic. I've never seen you like that."

"I wish that I could've dragged it on for another thirty. It's not that late."

"Michelle, really. Look around. This place cleared out an hour ago. It's been tough just staying out of sight, let alone doing what you did—keeping a conversation going with that guy for hours. So, what did you guys talk about?"

Michelle laughed. "Him, of course."

Janet couldn't quite bring a smile to her lips. "Yeah, silly question."

A few hours later, in the early morning glare, Adam stumbled toward the classroom, pausing at the door for a moment before entering. Janet was already sitting next to Michelle in the back corner, her eyes locked on her screen, her left leg jiggling as the chairs filled. Michelle tapped her arm, and Janet looked up just as Adam approached.

Janet ducked her head and whispered between clenched teeth, "Michelle, what are you doing?"

Michelle whispered back, "Sorry, I just wanted you to see how he looked. He's a mess. It looks like our efforts last night weren't in vain."

"Great, just let me know when it's safe to lift my head."

"It's safe. He's turned around."

Janet raised her eyes to see Adam flop down in a chair and let his shoulders sink toward the floor. A short beep signaled the start of the test, and when Adam bolted upright at the sound, Michelle giggled. Janet cut her short with a glare, then confidently tapped her screen. Having anticipated this moment for weeks, she felt the relief of action, and her potential increased a little with each correct answer. A few rows ahead of her, Adam gave his head a little shake before leaning forward. Ten minutes later, as Janet waited for a page to refresh, she glanced up to see Adam's finger hovering hesitantly over his screen. She slumped backward after tapping her final answer, and a few seconds later, a loud beep brought the test to an end. Adam was amongst the few still swiping at the screen as the students around him leapt to their feet.

Janet froze, so Michelle kicked her left ankle to pull her from her daze. Janet immediately looked down, allowing a few seconds to creep by before whispering to Michelle, "Is he gone?"

"He hasn't left the room, but he's on his feet. I think it's safe to look."

Janet waited a moment before trusting herself to lift her eyes. Adam was sliding meekly through the crowd, head slightly bowed, and mumbling. The other students drifted out in small clumps.

When they were the last two left in the classroom, Michelle turned to Janet and beamed. "That should do it."

Janet smiled weakly.

"Janet, come on, I know you're worried, but you have to celebrate the small victories; this couldn't have gone better. Of course, you had to nail it, but it's your best subject, right?"

Janet nodded. "Yes. Yes, it went well."

"Great, then we're all set. You know how heavily the algorithm favors the most recent performance."

"Well, we don't know for sure."

Michelle rolled her eyes. "Janet, you have to lighten up. This pessimism does nothing for your potential."

"I know, but you're not the one getting in the car. I want to be absolutely sure about it. Anyway, you go ahead. I want to speak with Cameron."

"Okay, I'll be waiting outside."

Janet waited patiently as Michelle slung her bag over her shoulder and buried her face in her phone. Once she was gone, Janet gingerly rose from her seat and approached the professor's desk. Cameron stiffened and looked away, but Janet wasn't deterred.

"You're still planning on canceling the test tomorrow?"

"Yes, Janet, I am. But please don't ask me about it here."

"I'm sorry, I know I shouldn't, but you know what's riding on this. I've done all the calculations, and our potential is so close. Thursday's test could be enough to swing it."

Cameron raised an eyebrow. "All the calculations? Are you telling me that you know how the algorithm works?"

Janet shook her head. "No. No, of course not, but there're some clues out there, and from what I know, it might come down to his performance in these last couple of days."

Cameron rubbed his temples. "Yes, of course. I'll do my bit." He turned back to his screen.

"I really appreciate it," said Janet. She left when he didn't lift his eyes again.

Over the next few hours Janet swiped her screen continually, urging the phone to display the notification she desperately craved. It finally arrived at four p.m., rippling across the campus.

Adam was with a small group of friends when the notification came. He punctured the collective sigh of relief with a sharp "No!" The others turned to him as he strained to pull his grimace into a stiff smile. "Damn, I was actually ready for that one," he said, finishing the sentence with an unconvincing chuckle. He faded from the group as the conversation meandered on, his backward steps almost imperceptible.

Breaking his own golden rule, he searched his challenger's name. Janet's profile picture looked vaguely familiar, yet he couldn't bring the memory into focus. Just on the pretty side of average with a standard list of achievements, she didn't look like the type that would take such a risk, but her carefully curated online presence was unnerving. He swiped the page away and sent a message to David: *I can't believe it, that test was a disaster, and with tomorrow's canceled, there's no chance to improve my potential before the Joust.*

Just forget it. It's just one test. More importantly you shouldn't be sending messages when you feel like this; you don't want to affect your score.

Damn. Yeah, I know, but I needed to message someone.

Man, it can wait. Just talk to someone instead. You don't want anything recorded. Don't send me another message.

Okay.

David's lighthearted response, *Man, what did I just tell you?* came through a moment later, and Adam laughed, enjoying a moment's respite from his fear.

Friday morning crept by as Adam stewed. The poor test result had pushed his trajectory in the wrong direction, and the cancellation of yesterday's test felt like too much of a coincidence. It was late afternoon, and he was dismissively waving away well-wishers when the announcement arrived via text: *Tonight's Joust will be at 6pm sharp at the Griffin Aqueduct, see you there. Please do not forward.*

A few minutes later, a stone-faced man who'd silently accompanied him to many victories tapped him on the shoulder, but Adam couldn't find any reassurance in his familiar face as he pulled himself to his feet.

On the other side of campus, Michelle struggled to contain Janet's nervous energy while they exchanged positive texts that followed a carefully prepared script, each one designed to add a few points to her potential. Their phones buzzed simultaneously, and Janet looked up. Michelle was beaming, and after a couple of seconds she blurted out, "Well, here we go!" Janet just nodded and looked around, not sure what she was waiting for.

When a long shadow fell over both of them, Janet spun around to see a man with a blank expression gesturing toward a waiting vehicle. It was only a dozen steps, and Michelle talked her through them, but Janet wouldn't remember a single word. She slid into the vehicle along with her silent escort and managed to give Michelle a terse nod. Michelle responded with a clumsy thumbs-up as the vehicle pulled away.

Janet was the first to arrive at the aqueduct. Her vehicle was waiting with its two front tires carefully positioned behind a line sprayed on the dull cement. Adam's vehicle was identical, but it was out of sight exactly one mile away. The distance was calculated to both build suspense and allow the vehicles to gather the required speed for a decisive victory. The crowd spilled over the banks onto the sloped concrete of the aqueduct. Near the collision zone, the ancient gantries that hung above the course allowed the brave an unobstructed view. Two dozen solemn men in white overalls patrolled the perimeter to ensure that there was no tampering with the carefully placed set pieces, as a single errant measurement could influence the outcome. Michelle was crammed in the viewing area. She craned her neck, but when she couldn't see Janet's vehicle, she returned to her phone.

The monotony of the cement was broken by the neon pink markings spray-painted at evenly spaced intervals. Stretching beyond sight, they terminated at the collision zone. The obstacle, a crane with a large boulder, was primed to move at the perfect moment. The result of the collision would rely on the universal protection code, whose exact algorithm was a heavily guarded secret. Tonight it would be misused in the most violent of ways, in a ritual that neatly satisfied the youthful desire to establish a pecking order.

Janet listened for the crowd. The excited buzz was loud enough to carry until it was overwhelmed by a gust of wind, amplifying her loneliness. She'd never been the center of attention, and the adulation that washed over her provided no joy.

When she stepped toward the vehicle, its door slid open silently, exposing a soft orange interior. She ran a hand over the exterior flanks, applying a little pressure so the panel flexed inward before springing back to shape, hoping her life didn't depend on this marvel of engineering. The vehicle was an assembly of boxy forms, but every edge was softened, like an ice cube that had begun to melt. The windows were broad and square, and the body was a glossy white. The headlights were the only circular shapes, two blisters on a smooth, flat nose. She sat in the contoured seat and steeled herself as the door slid shut. The magnets clicked, sealing her inside, and the interior lights eased to life. She was encased in a smooth cocoon of pale-blue plastic, and the childlike geometric shapes on the dash seemed to mock the moment.

Adam stood on the familiar patch of concrete at the reigning champion's end of the course. He read each of the names sprayed on the wall. There were twelve green strokes next to his father's; his was at the bottom with seven. He glanced down the length of the aqueduct and exhaled slowly before folding himself into the vehicle with compact movements. The harness came over his shoulders, and he gave it a quick pull to ensure it was secure after it clicked into place, but like a rookie, he tugged it twice more while he squirmed. The roof was just a few inches from his head. He was reaching up to touch it when the vehicle silently began to move, as though drawn by a magnet, toward the crowd.

At the same time, Janet was searching for signs of a countdown, but there was just a steady, gentle glow from the dash. She fidgeted as the moment stretched. Eventually a roar from the crowd signaled the start, but it was reduced to a dull whisper by the time it reached her. She stared down the long, straight gash of the aqueduct as the vehicle eased forward in silence. The first few seconds were so quiet that it felt as if the Joust had been canceled, but as the vehicle accelerated, the noise from the crowd welled.

The pink markings on the pavement steadily increased in frequency. She focused on those to block out the thought of the bright-white box that was aimed toward her and closing in fast. As she flashed past each mark, she was absorbed by their perfect rhythm. Then, as they passed under a bridge, she was convinced that there'd been a gap. Did they miss one? That could change everything.

She closed in on the collision point. It became real in an instant. This was a mistake.

She grabbed at her harness and squeezed the red button in desperation, but it wouldn't release her—not at this speed. She stamped her foot on the brake pedal, even though she knew that it had been disarmed. It gave easily, and her foot slammed into the floor. She lifted her foot and stomped it down again. The cabin was too quiet.

She filled it with a scream as she pulled at her restraints, but each tug was met with an automatic response that pulled them even tighter.

A white dot at the edge of her vision brought her flailing to a halt. It was coming too quickly, and the aqueduct was too deep. She was sure that someone had misjudged. The collision was inevitable. There would be no winners this time.

The crane above the collision zone began its graceful dance. A moment later the boulder slid into the left side of the trough, forcing both of them onto the same side. The two vehicles began the almost instantaneous calculation of the occupants' potential, choosing whom to preserve for the betterment of society.

Her vehicle didn't begin an evasive maneuver, and she braced herself for the impact as the white flash emerged from behind the boulder. A second later her vehicle swerved violently to the right, the restraints pinning her to the seat as the tires reached the limits of traction. Adam's vehicle was inches away. As the moment slowed, she felt that she could reach out and touch it, but it was gone in an instant. She didn't dare turn when she heard it splinter behind her.

The roar from the crowd engulfed her, and she let the tension drip out as she sank back into her seat. The noise died away, and the neon pink dashes disappeared as her vehicle continued down the aqueduct in silence. It began to slow, but she didn't know where it would finally come to a halt. The crowd behind her was already beginning to scatter, and by the time the ambulance arrived, the aqueduct would be empty.

Noah turned to his wife, the profile of her face barely visible in the dull blue light, and forced out the first sentence of a conversation he'd avoided for a month. "I think I've found someone who can help us."

Without shifting her gaze from the bedroom ceiling, Ariana lifted an arm as though waving away smoke. "Well, I hope this one's special. This will be, what? Our seventh tutor?"

"Ariana, I'm not talking about a new teacher; he needs more than that. I've been thinking about augmentation."

She lifted herself onto her right elbow. "Augmentation? What?"

"I got a message a couple of weeks ago. Apparently one of Brian's doctors recommended him. She thought he'd be the perfect candidate."

"Noah, really. You've been thinking about this for weeks? Who contacted you?"

"A doctor, a colleague of Martin's. Apparently, he's at the forefront of this type of—"

"Come on, Noah. Does that sound right to you? The best candidate they could find just happens to be a son of a Fortune 50 CEO? Brian's not going to be someone's publicity stunt."

Noah was still lying on his back. "Well, with a reaction like that, at least you know why I waited so long to tell you. Look, I asked my team to do some research, and they didn't find any red flags—the company has a stellar rating, and their testing's all been verified. I wanted to be sure before I even talked to you."

Ariana nodded gently. "I know he's not what you'd hoped, but there's nothing wrong with him. And as your father always used to say, there are no magic pills. We just have to work a little harder."

Noah chuckled. "I guess that saying crashed into reality. We've 'worked a little harder' for years now, and he just doesn't seem to have what it takes."

"This is our son you're talking about," Ariana snapped. "He doesn't 'have what it takes' for what? You've always assumed he wants to follow in your footsteps, but maybe we could just accept him for who he is."

Noah gazed at a point over Ariana's shoulder. "Can you just give the doctor a chance to explain? Irrational fear is the only reason not to do it, and there's a chance for greatness. Just think—if it's all they say, he could be the one who finds a cure for cancer, he could—"

"Please, don't call my doubts 'irrational.' And it just takes him a little longer to pick things up. It could turn around at any time."

"I doubt it will happen this year, and the teachers aren't going to be as patient in high school. Look, I was skeptical too, but I talked to the doctor, and he made a solid case. I know I can't convince you, but I made an appointment with him, and all I ask is that you—"

Ariana sat up and looked down at him. "What? You made an appointment?"

"Yes, but it's just an appointment. There's no commitment."

"Don't you think that we should've talked about it before you started making arrangements?"

"We should chat before decisions, but before arrangements? We're not signing anything on Monday, just having a conversation."

"On Monday. This Monday?"

"Yeah. Yeah, I've got a busy schedule this week. Can you make it on Monday afternoon? It should only be half an hour."

Ariana let the silence hang. "Okay, I'll check, but I don't like this. I…" She paused as her lips began to form the next word, but instead of continuing, she shifted her weight to her left elbow before lying back down and rolling away from him.

On Monday afternoon, Noah rushed into Dr. Stout's office a few minutes late. Ariana was already sitting with her hands folded neatly and lips pursed in readiness. She nodded as Noah sat next to her, then she turned to the doctor. "So, why our son? I just can't see the value of an ordinary kid to you. There have to be better subjects out there."

Dr. Stout pushed his glasses back on his nose. "Actually, his being 'ordinary,' as you put it, is one of the reasons we're offering this to you. While his intelligence is in the normal range, the two of you are well above average, and that indicates that he's underutilizing his resources." He grasped the temple of his glasses to gently lift them from his face. "And that's what we're hoping to change."

Ariana was perched on the edge of her seat. "Well, that's very flattering, but we'd prefer not to experiment on Brian."

"Oh, it's not an experiment. This process has been thoroughly tested. We wouldn't even consider it if there'd been any physical side effects in any of our—"

Noah leaned forward, but before he could speak, Ariana said, "It's not just the physical issues. What about mental problems?"

Dr. Stout waved his glasses around as he spoke. "I'm glad you brought that up. While no one can answer that definitively, there's no evidence that increased intelligence is detrimental in any way. Actually, if you look at the correlation, it seems that the smarter you are, the longer you live."

"You make it sound like it's routine, but Brian would be the first to try it outside of your limited tests, right?"

"Well, I wouldn't consider the tests 'limited'; they've just been temporary. For our trials to be considered complete, the subject needs to return to their pre-augmented state, then we can evaluate its success. The only difference with your son is that it would be permanent. There's not even a procedure as such; it's merely a small pill. We'll administer it in the hospital, but we think that in the future, people will just order it over the counter."

"If they can afford it," Ariana quipped.

"I'd say that's a discussion for another day. Let's focus on the matter at hand. I understand your hesitation, and I'd like to give you more time to think it over, but as I'm sure you realize, there's a long list of eager candidates behind you."

For the first time, Ariana allowed a momentary pause in the conversation.

"Can we have a few days to think about it?" Noah asked. "It's a big decision."

"Yes, of course. We want you to feel good about your choice. But there's a lot of excitement about this, and we'd like to keep it moving."

"I understand. We'll let you know by the end of the week." Noah looked to Ariana, and she nodded in approval.

When Ariana arrived home, the back doors were open, and Brian was sitting on the diving board above the kidney-shaped pool, watching the water dance. His slate was on the kitchen table, open to summer school's final test. He'd been just three correct answers shy of a B, and had scrawled "sorry" below the C+. She sighed as she set up an appointment with his teacher.

The whimsical drawings on the walls of Claire's classroom were relics of a gentler age. Claire sighed and carefully aligned the books on her desk as she spoke. "I can't believe what I'm hearing, from you of all people."

"Claire, I know it's a bit of a surprise, but we have responsibilities. We need to make the best decision for Brian. We've tried everything."

"Ariana, your responsibilities don't end at your estate's gates. You're one of the few that can hold this back. Don't you want to give every kid a chance, not just the ones lucky enough to be able to afford it?"

"This isn't an easy decision, but it's inevitable—if not us, it will be someone else."

"But you and Noah, you must know this is a statement. Once you go, we all go. The dream of equal access will vanish the moment we allow it."

Ariana held out her palms. "Claire, I have no doubt that we could debate the broader implications all night, but neither of us can hold this back. This decision is about keeping up or being left behind."

"This just doesn't sound like you. You know that Brian has been improving, and this feels like surrender. You don't usually go down without a fight."

"Claire, I know we've fought some battles together, and to be honest, I'm not sure how this is going to play out, but the argument that it's just another way the rich can separate themselves won't be enough for Noah."

"But is it enough for you?"

"It would have been once, but now I'm convinced that it's unavoidable, and sooner or later everyone will be able to afford it. I'm starting to worry about the consequences of not doing it. This sort of research has to be happening in other countries. What if we sit on our hands and they get there first?"

"Okay. Well, it sounds like you've made up your mind."

"Claire, please don't be like this. This hasn't been easy for us."

"You've been a valuable contributor to this school for many years, and although I don't approve, I can't stop you. But we won't be treating Brian any differently. Hopefully you can be discreet about it—we don't want to turn this place into a circus."

"Thanks, Claire, I appreciate…" She paused, attuned to a faint vibration that was barely audible. With a brief apologetic look, she reached into her purse, checked the screen, and gave Claire a slight nod before lifting herself from her chair.

Noah was at home when she arrived. "How'd it go with Claire?"

"She doesn't want us to do it. She thinks it will start a revolution."

"Does that affect your decision?"

"No, she just went through the same arguments that I've already wrestled with. Now my biggest fear is being left behind."

"So, should I call Dr. Stout?"

"Yes. I'm sure that I could go back and forth forever, but I don't want the decision taken away from us. Let's just do it quickly so we don't have time to second-guess."

Under the glare of the studio's lights two weeks later, Brian's eyes flitted back and forth from the host to his feet as he was introduced.

"Well, this might well be the first time we've had a math celebrity on the show. Many of you might be reaching for your remotes, but I think that you should stay with us." The host leaned over and tapped Brian's knee before returning her gaze to the camera. "Brian here has a pretty remarkable story, and it's taken quite a lot of effort to convince his family that he should come on and share it. He was struggling at school last semester, but after taking a single pill two weeks ago, he's now a genius. On Monday, he wrote a proof that's already reverberating through the math world."

She turned to Brian. "So, thanks for coming on the show. It sounds like it's been an incredible couple of weeks. Can you tell us a little about what's happening in your head right now?"

Brian laughed; then, after a false start, he paused. "You know, I'm sorry, but it's just not easy to explain how I think in a way that your viewers would understand. I'm functioning in a manner that is fundamentally different from their experience."

"Maybe it's like trying to explain the feeling of flying?" the host prompted.

"Yeah, I guess. I haven't flown, so I'm not sure, but it's probably the same. There's just no frame of reference that we share."

"Did it feel like that from the moment you took the pill?"

"No, no, not at all. I guess I was disappointingly normal for a few days."

The host laughed. "Maybe we should have spoken a week ago."

"Well, I'm sure I would have made a little more sense back then."

"So, has it been tough on your friends?"

"You know, I wonder about that, but I'm sure that's one of the reasons they chose me. I've always been a bit of a loner, and I still am. I've been lucky enough to meet a lot of interesting people in the last couple of weeks, but as I overtake them, I'm worried that I'll be alone again."

The audience sighed, and at the side of the stage, Ariana turned to Noah. "How are you feeling about it?"

Noah was rocking back and forth on his feet with his hands behind his back as though still weighing the decision. "Of course it hurts a bit right now, but we made the call with the facts we had, and it's still too early to judge. I hope everything will work out."

"Hope isn't enough. We'll lose him if we don't do anything."

Noah bit his lip and nodded slowly.

"Noah, I've been thinking about joining him before it's too late."

"Yeah, it's crossed my mind too, but I'm not sure how the investors would react."

"You can't control people's reactions. Maybe once I join him, they'll assume you have no choice."

"And they'll be right. Your decision would be for both of us; I couldn't bear to be left alone."

"I know, but it can't go on like this. We could do it together."

"Oh no. No, I think it would look like we panicked. You should do it, but I'm a little surprised. I'd always thought I would go first. I feel responsible."

"No, you're not. We made the choice together. Neither of us knew how it would play out."

Two days later Ariana took the pill, and by the following week she was chasing Brian like a small puppy. Brian was radiant, as though he'd finally found company on a desert island, and the pace at which they left Noah behind made his decision obvious. Less than a month after Noah had carried Brian's sedated body out of this same hospital, he was marching up the same stairs with a regal wave and a stiff smile.

A dozen steps from the entrance, a reporter freed himself from the bustling throng and thrust a microphone in Noah's face. "Mr. Levinson, sir, do you think that this is the right choice for your organization? It's a big decision."

With Ariana hustling a half step behind, he didn't slow. "It's not a business decision. It's about me and my family. I've seen the joy in their faces, and I want to join them. I'm confident that it's the right thing to do."

"Why now?"

Noah stopped and turned. "It's time. We could test forever, but the evidence is there. Just think of the problems we can solve."

"Sir, just one more question. How do you think your shareholders will—"

"I'm sorry, I really have to go. I'm not at liberty to speak on behalf of the company. You'll have to refer to our prepared statement."

A month later, Ariana looked over at Noah as he lay in their bed, the pale moonlight on his face seemingly the only thread connecting them to their old lives. "We're pretty lucky. Can you believe what you started?"

"Ariana, we made the decision together. I didn't start the movement; we did."

"Do you think that the others will ever catch us?"

"I'm sure that they'll get closer, but I think we'll always be a step ahead. Brian is only two weeks in front of us, and sometimes he still feels out of reach."

"Looking back now, it makes you wonder why we waited so long."

"Of course, it seems obvious now, but I'm surprised we took the risk; we knew so little back then."

"Yes, but I really can't imagine it being different."

"I know. I think of…"

"Noah, think of what?"

"It doesn't matter. It's been a long day; we can chat tomorrow." And sleep engulfed him before she could protest.

Jolted awake by the alarm the following morning, Noah sat up sluggishly and looked around as though trying to orient himself in an unfamiliar hotel room. He roused Ariana as he swiveled around to place his feet on the floor.

"Dear, do you remember what we had for dinner last night?"

She rolled over to face him and scowled. "What sort of question is that? Of course, it was, ahh, hmm." Her glare softened, and she bit her lip. "Actually what was it?"

"I don't know, and I can't remember what we had the night before either."

"Umm, yeah it was salmon, right?"

"Honey, that's just a guess. Please, concentrate, can you actually remember it?"

"No, but it's a little embarrassing. I'm not that old, I'm just a little foggy this morning. You know how I am. The augmentation didn't seem to shake that."

"No, that's not it," he said, "there's something wrong."

She sat up. "Noah, you're overreacting. Forgetting what we had for dinner isn't that unusual at our age."

"No, and I wouldn't have been worried had this happened two months ago, but we remember everything now. And if it's you as well…" He let his words trail off.

Ariana nodded. "Yeah, something does feel different, like someone's erased patches of my mind. Some things are clear, but then my memory just hits a wall and there's nothing there."

"Yeah, my mind feels a bit, ahh, empty."

"Yes. Yes, maybe you should go to the doctor. Don't go in to work. There's no need to worry them."

"There's some clients in from Chicago, and not turning up would worry them more."

"Okay, well, if you need me, don't hesitate to call."

"Yes, yes, I will."

Noah hunched over his slate in the back seat as his driver maneuvered through the streets to the office, but there were no panicked emails from staff, just a brief note from his assistant about being in a little late. The radio broadcast turned to the weather on a quiet news day.

On the far side of town, having anticipated this day for years, Katja traveled toward the same building as Noah. As her car slowed to a stop at the storied address, she searched in vain for signs that something was different. The heavy doors opened into a vast atrium, and she strode purposefully toward the slight man sitting behind a marble counter. The rhythmic click of her heels didn't dislodge him from his screen, and as her shadow fell over him, he blinked as he looked up. After a brief exchange, he ushered her toward the elevator without any of the fanfare she'd anticipated. On the top floor, the chair behind the imposing reception desk was vacant, and the door behind it had been left ajar, painting a ribbon of sunlight across the carpet.

When she pushed it open, Noah lifted his head from his phone and leapt from his chair to greet her, crossing the office with loping steps and an arm extended in greeting. The collar of his tailored suit was gently frayed, seeming to broadcast old money.

"Hello there. I'm pleased to meet you, but I'm terribly sorry, it's been such a busy week that I can't recall what this appointment concerns. My assistant usually gives me my schedule as the day begins, but she'll be in a little late this morning, so I'm afraid I'm a bit unprepared."

"It's okay, you can relax. You're not forgetting anything. I didn't have an appointment."

A flicker of fear crossed his face as he retreated to his leather chair and pulled it in behind his desk. "Oh, so who are you?"

She lazily dropped into a chair. "My name's Katja, and don't look so worried. I'm not here to hurt you."

He chuckled. "Well, that's a relief. So, why are you here?"

"To start the revolution, of course."

"Aren't you a little late? The revolution's a couple of months old."

"Oh no. That wasn't the revolution, that was just the installation."

Noah narrowed his eyes. "I'm not following."

"Oh, I'm sorry. I'll spell it out. You may have noticed that you felt a little different this morning. We turned off your augmentation. It seemed that you got a little too reliant on it."

Noah leaned forward and put his elbows on his desk. "What? Is this is some kind of joke? If it is, it's not very funny."

"No, there's no humor involved. It's a changing of the guard."

"A changing of the guard? That sounds a little grandiose. I'll grant that you've shaken me up a little, but it's nothing we can't take care of." He waved his arm as though an army of assistants sat just outside his door.

Katja smiled. "You still don't seem to understand. You're sitting in the same office, but the balance of power has changed."

Noah leaned forward menacingly. "Now you're getting ahead of yourself. This is just a little glitch; it will blow over in a day or two."

Katja smirked. "You do realize that we've been working on this 'little glitch' for a decade."

"Well, we've got the best people on it, and I've been assured that we'll be on top of it before the end of the day."

"Ahh, you see, that's the beauty of it. Most of the people uttering those assurances aren't immune; they're as muddled as you are. The few that are left won't be fixing anything."

Noah slumped backward.

Katja allowed a few seconds to pass by before laughing. "Well, you must've realized that your greed would eventually catch up with you."

He shook his head. "Greed? It was nothing of the sort. We just wanted a better life for our family."

"Oh, come now. Of course it was greed. Everything is already tilted in your favor, but you wanted more. Augmentation was always going to be the final piece of the puzzle, the guarantee that there'd be two classes. What you didn't know was that you'd be on the wrong side of the divide."

"What divide?"

"The divide between those who can afford twenty thousand dollars for a pill that no one needs, and everyone else."

"Why would you do this? It will destroy everything."

"Oh no, we're not destroying anything physical. On the other hand, your company's valuation might be destroyed. I'd imagine your investors won't be too pleased to hear that their esteemed CEO can't even remember what happened yesterday. Those memories are pretty valuable, right?"

He leaned forward again, but he was hunched over this time. "Okay, so what do you want? We can negotiate."

She laughed. "Noah, there's no need for us to negotiate. I don't think you understand that this isn't a one-time deal. You're ours now. We'll turn your mind on and off as we please. I'd recommend you hand the reins to us while your company is still worth something. We'll be kind and keep you around as an adviser, just for appearances, of course."

Noah nodded slowly.

"And don't feel like we've singled you out. My colleagues are in offices like this all over the country." She waved her arm at the opulent surroundings. "You're about to witness the greatest transfer of wealth in history."

"So why not just blackmail us?"

Katja paused for what seemed a long time, and then offered a sly smile. "Noah, you must realize that we augmented ourselves long before you, so unfortunately, I don't think I can explain it in a way you'd understand."

The baseball-sized red dot by the door handle was the only indication that Josh was in the right place. He knocked loudly, but there was no response, so he reached into his pocket for the card that had prompted the visit. There were two streets and a red dot where they crossed on one side; underneath were the instructions DO NOT ENTER THIS LOCATION INTO ANY DEVICE. On the other side, the question, WANT TO SEE WHAT REALLY HAPPENS IN KILBURN?

Dirty and smudged, the card looked as though it had passed through many players' hands before it was thrust at him the previous day. Josh had grasped it without thinking. He'd spun around the moment he realized what it was, but whoever had passed it to him had already been absorbed by the morning bustle.

He was rotating the card to ensure he was at the right corner when he heard a light click. He eased the door open, and a screen on the far wall flickered to life. JOSH, WELCOME TO ENCOUNTER. PLEASE PROCEED TO BOOTH 4.

As Josh shuffled past three doors in a dim corridor, he pushed the card back into his pocket in case he needed to pass it to another player. He pictured players scattered around the city, each hanging from a gleaming rig in a sparse room like sculptures in an art gallery. As they twisted and turned, the Mechs they were controlling echoed their movements somewhere behind the quarter inch of glass in front of him—the tiny barrier between him and the playing field.

Standing with his hand lightly on the backrest of the empty chair, he filled his lungs before lowering himself into the scuffed red leather. While he sat fidgeting in the featureless room, he studied his reflection in the milky glass panel in front of him. His Augs were propped on his head like a pair of ski goggles, and he rubbed his naked eyelids with balled fists. The room felt barren without them; no additional information was being layered on the walls, and there were no feeds to follow, but he'd been told that he wouldn't get anything out of the experience if he left them on. The speaker above him came to life with a burst of static and began relaying the guidelines in a dull monotone:

"One: No questions that could affect gameplay."

"Two: No solicitation for in-game assistance."

There were three more, but they washed over him as he tried to recall the parameters he'd set an hour earlier. He'd zipped through the basics (female, twenty-five to thirty-five, college educated), but the questions seemed endless, ranging from the superficial (eye color) to the meaningful (spiritual beliefs), and he'd lost heart partway through. By the last page, he'd just ticked the center box to every question.

The voice lowered an octave and gave the final instruction: "Please prepare yourself. Your encounter will begin in five seconds."

Sitting up straight, Josh curled some errant strands behind his ear, then hastily dropped his hands, not wanting to be caught mid-stroke. As he wriggled forward and tucked his legs under the table, the glass turned transparent to reveal a girl that looked on the younger end of the specified range. As Josh searched past the ghost of his reflection, the girl's porcelain skin and her hair's lustrous hue shattered the image he'd created from his rare glimpses of the characters in the game. He'd imagined them in loose oil-colored rags as they scuttled through the shadows, but instead she wore a light summery dress with faint navy-blue diamonds on a black background. Her gaze lazily followed the contours of his features, and when it found his eyes, he glanced at his lap.

"Are you okay?" She gestured at the Augs propped on his head and raised an eyebrow.

He reached up and tapped his Augs, "Umm, yeah, I'm fine, but it's my first time, and I didn't want to leave them on the counter. I like to have them close."

She stared at his raised arm and scowled. "You're wearing your plugs?"

Josh glanced at the thick black strap wrapped around his left bicep. A copper plug the size of a coin protruded a quarter inch from the center of the nylon band. It had a thin red stripe around its circumference to indicate that it should be connected to the red cable in his gaming rig. Even though he'd been playing less, he'd struggled to build the habit of removing them at the end of each session.

"Yeah, I probably should have taken them off, but it's a pain, you know?"

"No, no, I don't."

"Oh yeah. Yes, of course, I'm sorry."

She pointed at his Augs again. "So, what do you guys need those for? Do they give you warnings? Is there something dangerous out there?"

Josh laughed. "No, these aren't for protection."

"So why do you wear them?"

"They just kind of make things easier. They keep you connected, kind of up to date."

"You do everything with a screen in front of your face?"

"Well, I guess. Pretty well everyone does."

"Oh, okay." The brief interrogation over, she stared placidly, waiting for him to continue.

"I…I'm not sure what you want me to say."

Slowly leaning forward until she was only inches from the glass, she gave him a crooked smile and spread her arms wide, as though presenting a prize on a game show. "You can say anything you want."

"Umm, so what's your name?"

She raised an eyebrow as though he'd clumsily spilled a drink. "No, no, no, that's not what you're here for. We only have a few minutes to see if we want to drop the glass, and my name isn't going to make any difference, is it?"

"No, I guess you're right. Maybe it would be best if you started."

"Oh, that sounds like an easy way out. Look, I'll give you another chance. You must have something else you want to ask me."

"Okay, have you done this before?"

She leaned back. "Of course. They never put rookies together. There'd be three minutes of silence before the glass milked. I'll give you another question."

He looked at the floor. "So. So what's it like in there?"

She was shaking her head. "You don't want to hear that yet. Let's start with something else."

He opened his mouth as if to protest, but in the face of her flat expression, he changed tack. "Okay then, so what's the craziest thing that's happened to you?"

"Not bad." She let herself sink into the chair. "Do you mean here at Encounter, or ever?"

"Let's start with here."

She clasped her hands together and gazed at the ceiling.

"If ever is easi—"

"Well, I'd only been here once, and I wasn't sure if I'd come back. The first conversation was a bit like this one." He acknowledged the jab with a smile. "Then, just last week, a guy came in. He seemed a little drunk, but he was charming enough for me to think he might be the ticket out, so I let the glass drop. He lunged forward and tried to grab me. I ducked backward, but then I couldn't reach the button. He yelled at me, said that a character had stolen some weapon, and he wanted me to get it back. Thought that we all knew each other. I told him I had no idea what he was talking about, and when he leaned over the border, the door behind him flung open. Those guys were quick; they were on him in a second."

"What happened then?"

"I don't know. The moment they pulled him back to that side, the glass milked. I heard a thud and a muffled scream, but then the music they played through the speakers was loud enough to drown everything out."

Josh was inching closer. "What did you do?"

"I just waited, but then the door behind me opened, and I knew I was supposed to leave."

"That's it? There's no ending to your story?"

"That's it. That is the ending."

He nodded. "Oh, okay."

She leaned forward. "Okay. My turn for a question. Why are you here?"

"Just curiosity, nothing more than that."

"Just a vague curiosity? Nothing more specific?"

"Well, I've wondered for a while about whether I really should be playing, but it's tough to walk away, and I'd heard that meeting a character might help."

"How'd you get the card?"

"Someone just gave it to me on the street. I think it's because I haven't played as much lately."

She nodded, but her light smile faded. "So if you're not interested in getting anyone out, why the parameters?"

"Well, I guess that I didn't want to get someone I'd be too scared to talk to."

She sighed. "Yeah, most of us are dangerous, right?"

"It's not that. It's—"

"Well, I know that you think we're all criminals, but maybe you should do a little math. Kilburn is pretty big now. There's no way crime has kept pace with its growth."

Josh tilted his head. "I hadn't really thought of that."

"The math is pretty simple, but avoiding it is even easier, right?"

Josh nodded while gazing at the floor.

"Well, I hope that by sitting here, I've answered your first question. The characters in the game are actually real."

"Well, yeah, I guess. I wasn't sure what I was hoping for. I wondered—"

She glanced at his plugs. "You hoped I wasn't real, but you play anyway?"

"Yeah, I suppose that doesn't make much sense."

She scrunched her mouth and shook her head in a slow, exaggerated motion. "No. No, it doesn't. The reason you pay all that money is because the game is real, but you hope that it's not, so you don't have to feel guilty? I don't understand you guys at all. Why don't you just play another game? You know the ads are bullshit, no one can see the difference, and there'd be a lot less"—she grimly made air quotes—"collateral damage."

Josh nodded. "But my friends—"

She narrowed her eyes. "You're kidding. You turn a blind eye to the destruction because your fucking friends play?"

Josh glanced away, and after a few seconds of silence, a soft voice gave them a one-minute warning.

The girl sat up straight and said curtly, "So, we may as well do this."

Josh looked up. "What? After all that, you want to drop the glass?"

"Well, I paid for this session too, and maybe you'll feel a bit different without the glass between us."

"I don't see how it could change anything."

The girl shrugged. "You never know, and even if you're not getting me out, a minute without the glass might make it all feel real enough for you to give it up."

Josh nodded but made no effort to move his hand.

"Look, if you get scared, you can always hit that button to the left."

He glanced across.

"Yes, the big red one. You hit that, and this glass rockets to the ceiling. You can walk away without looking back."

"But that didn't work for you. The guy you told me about. You couldn't get around him to hit it."

"Look, I'm not going to leap up and grab you, but I want you walking away thinking about what you're doing to us, and I don't think that talking through this glass is enough for you." She was talking quickly now, like a mother holding her impatience in check.

He lifted his right hand over the green button, and she gave him a slight nod as she matched his gesture. They locked eyes as they pressed, and the glass silently slid into the sill.

Suddenly there was nothing between him and a character. Scrunching his eyes in disbelief, he tapped his Augs to confirm that they were still on the top of his head. He was close enough to smell her breath, but when he leaned forward, she swayed back almost imperceptibly. Still within arm's length, Josh reached out to touch her cheek, but she ducked backward to evade his fingers, and he pulled his hand back as though he'd accidentally put it in a flame.

"Oh, I'm sorry, I got carried away."

She laughed. "It's okay, I get it. It feels a bit strange, right? One of the characters actually sitting in front of you, smelling like a real person."

He chuckled briefly before looking at the ground again. "Yeah, it does."

The twenty-second alert flashed, and he pulled out his crypto card. "Oh damn, should we prolong?"

She smiled softly. "Sorry, there's not much point in me prolonging. You already told me that you're not getting me out." His face dropped, and she continued. "But if you change your mind, add 'Nordic heritage' to your criteria and you have a good chance of getting me next time."

"I will. I will, and my name's Josh."

"Bye, Josh. I really enjoyed our time together."

"You never told me your name."

"Nicole. My name's Nicole. Anyway, good luck. I hope you found what you're looking for."

"Well, I guess it's helped. I know I won't—"

The glass shot up with a loud beep, and he let his elbows fall to the table. Resting his chin on interlocked fingers, he stared at the opaque glass for a few seconds before dragging himself to his feet. The door opened to a hallway lined with screens; some flashed testimonials from ex-players, and others implored him to return if he wasn't convinced. He held up a hand to shield his eyes from the disorienting kaleidoscope of color. A couple of steps later, the screens flickered off, leaving him in total darkness.

He spun around. "What? Turn them back on. I can't see anything." There was no reply. He shouted again, "I'm still here. Turn them on. I don't know where I'm going."

He'd dismissed the various stories of "a friend of a friend" disappearing as urban myths, but he quickly pulled his Augs down over his eyes and gestured to enhance. The bottom right corner instantly flashed *11:00 p.m.*, but the rest of the screen was blank. He gestured again, but they couldn't extract any shapes from the darkness, so he propped them on his head and reached for the wall. His left hand found the glass of a screen, and he shuffled along it in search of an exit. The corridor was a dead end, so he turned back.

After carefully pressing hand over hand, he found another door. He twisted the handle and eased it open. "Is anyone there? What's going on?" When he leaned out a little farther into the silent black corridor, a single overhead light eased to life. The dim glow was enough for him to make out a peeling exit sign at the end of the hall. He sprinted toward it.

He'd misjudged the distance in the darkness and was almost on the door when he tried to slow himself. Stumbling the last couple of steps in a desperate effort to stop, he was still off-balance when he dropped his shoulder and ploughed into the door. It flung open, and he spilled into the stench and battered garbage cans of a dark alley. Josh hit the ground with a thud and rolled over to see the door slowly close with a soft click.

He dragged himself to his feet. The door didn't budge when he rattled the handle, so he started banging on it with balled fists. After a few blows, he put his ear to the wood. There was no response. He resumed more desperately, coughing as the putrid air filled his lungs. Each blow began to hurt, and he slowed before finally letting his forehead fall onto the door in defeat.

He exhaled and turned around, pulling his Augs over his eyes and tapping his right temple. The word *SEARCHING* floated in front of him, each letter pulsing in turn to indicate progress, but instead of a gentle chime and the familiar green check, the letters faded out before being replaced with a red X. After restarting failed to find a signal, he tore them from his face and hit the earpiece with the heel of his palm. They still wouldn't connect. He propped them on his head, then searched for the comfort of a familiar landmark in the tight confines of the alley. The light of the waning moon wasn't enough to see more than a block ahead, and he told himself that it was just a side entrance, that he wasn't on the playing field, but he still scuttled along in the shadows with his shoulder scraping the wall.

The smell lingered as though leaching from every surface, and the heavy air seemed to compress his movements, but the alley finally opened into a slightly wider street that gently curved away from him. He shrunk backward when he saw the boxy streetlights that looked exactly the same as they did in the game, their steel-blue glow the only color in a scene where each surface seemed covered in a different shade of gray primer. During a game, the console applied the color, but even on a peeling billboard in a dull monotone, the jagged logo of the imaginary Priz soda was unmistakable.

When the game had been created, the playing field was a manufactured version of a dangerous neighborhood, but in the years since, it had deteriorated into what it had once mimicked. Heavy bars on the windows weren't enough to stop them from being shattered, and the graffiti was densely layered, the newest art much bleaker than the pieces it covered. A bloodstained mattress leaned against a wall, and next to it sat a rust-colored couch with stuffing peeking out of torn cushions. The tight streets amplified his fear, creating a twisted labyrinth that never opened up enough to ease the claustrophobia. The walls seemed to merge with the starless sky, and the sharp angles of the intersections were designed to ensure that an adversary could burst into view at any time. The view was even more terrifying from just under six feet than through the eyes of his eight-foot Mech.

Without the game's music and the amplified explosions, the quiet was so acute that it felt as if he'd forgotten to plug in the audio channel, and even the distant sound of metal on cement was enough for him twist around in a panic. A minute later, the scream of a character punctured the silence, and each noise seemed to physically weigh on him as he crept along. By the time he arrived at the first intersection, he was crouching low enough for his hands to brush the moist ground.

Josh saw Nicole darting along the street. Without thinking, he sprang out of his crouch and ran toward her, completely exposed as he crossed the road. He called out, "Excuse me!" when he was three steps behind, but she didn't respond. He reached out, but his courage evaporated before he made contact. He let his arm drop before saying, "Hello?" The word cut the still air.

Nicole spun quickly and stiffened when she saw him.

Josh began, "Umm, ahh…"

"No fucking way. Those assholes."

"What?"

She took a step backward, deeper into the shadows, and lifted her right hand. For a moment, Josh thought that she was going to remove the chunky Augs that covered her face, but she just pushed back her hair. "What do you mean, 'what?' Encounter is a fucking sham, and you're part of it. You should be ashamed."

"What are you talking about?"

Her feet were still angled away from him as though she hadn't committed to the conversation, but she pointed at him accusingly. "Look, I'm tired, and I don't have time for games. I have no idea who you are, but Encounter better give me my money back. They told me that you can get out that way; I put everything on it. This dress, the makeup—you have no idea how hard it is to get this stuff in here. And now it's wasted."

Josh frowned. "I'm sorry, but I wasn't going to get anyone out."

Nicole shook her head. "Obviously, but that's the only reason I tolerated you in there. Now I find out you're just from in here. Seriously, that's messed up."

"No, I'm from the outside. The lights went out, and I got turned around."

She flashed a false smile. "Don't bother."

"No. That's the truth."

She took a step back and looked him up and down. He looked like he'd just stepped out of a rig. Each of the tight straps carefully positioned over major muscles had the correct color-coded plugs sticking out of them, and he was even wearing a T-shirt with the word KILBURN written in stark white letters on his right chest. "No, no, you couldn't have. You can't be that stupid."

"It was just a mistake. Can you help me get back?"

She let out a staccato laugh while shaking her head. "Ah, of course. Well, we'll just wander back and let them know."

"Why not?"

She suddenly glanced down the alley, then grabbed his arm and pulled him into the shadows.

"What's wrong?"

She thrust her hand at his mouth and whispered, "Quiet." He twisted his head away but stopped midmovement when he heard the dull metallic clang, as though someone were throwing garbage cans at the road in a steady rhythm. A few beats later, each crash echoed off the walls. He realized that the Mech couldn't be more than a dozen yards away.

They both crouched down instinctively and shuffled into a corner as she peeled her hand away from Josh's mouth. There were a couple of seconds of silence before a garbage can rolled past them, the aluminum cylinder rattling against the cobblestones. Josh craned his neck as curiosity overcame his fear, but Nicole quickly put her hand across his chest and eased him back toward the wall.

A second later the night seemed to split as the rhythmic clangs closed in, but the Mech didn't notice them as it sprinted past. Josh absorbed the familiar stuttering gait, the black stripe that ran across the red helmet at eye level, and the faux vents in the form of a snarling mouth.

He waited until the clattering evaporated before asking, "How'd you know?"

Nicole tapped her Augs.

Josh nodded. "Oh, of course."

"Well, it's no great act of generosity. We were dying too quickly without them, and they want enough characters for"—she paused—"authenticity."

"Can you use them to help me get back?"

"Look, if you are actually from the outside, I just did more than

I should have. Most characters would love to see you go down in here, but I'm still not convinced by these"—she waved her hand at his plugs—"so how about you just go and plead your case to Encounter. It's three blocks that way, first right."

Josh stared blankly.

Nicole shook her head like an impatient mother. "You'd better go now before I change my mind." She looked away and flicked her hand as though quashing any indecision with the decisive motion.

Josh ran along the wall in a full sprint, reminding himself that the decay was by design and that he'd be okay, when he saw what looked like a piece of driftwood protruding from a small alcove. He'd taken three more steps toward it before realizing that it was a decomposing forearm, the fingers curled in a permanent agony. He jagged to the other side of the street but couldn't stop himself from glancing as he passed the dark opening. When he caught a glimpse of an exposed rib cage under torn ribbons of cloth, he violently twisted his head away. The body looked as if it had been there for months.

"Pretty, isn't it?"

Josh spun around. "What?"

Nicole smirked. "That's collateral damage, right? I've been told you lose a few points for it, but it doesn't stop everyone. I've been told it usually happens late at night when the players are drunk."

Josh staggered the couple of steps to the wall and put his hand on the damp bricks to hold himself upright. He couldn't lift his eyes from the ground and held up a finger in request for a minute.

"Looks a bit different than it does in the game, right?"

Josh just shook his head.

"The smell too? You know, this one's been around awhile, so it's not too bad. Sometimes you have to skirt a new arrival." Nicole paused. "Actually, I hadn't noticed it before, but you might want to take a closer look at this one."

Josh shook his head without tearing his eyes from the ground.

"No, seriously, I think there's something you missed."

Josh looked up at her and she continued. "Her arm—take a closer look."

Josh stole a glance. He couldn't believe that he hadn't seen it the first time. The thick black strap that now hung loosely around pockets of flesh was difficult to see, but the copper plug glistened under the streetlight.

"Yeah, either a player or someone impersonating one. We don't see them that often, and I'd always wondered what their story was. Maybe you'll solve the mystery if you don't get out through Encounter. It's another block up, on your right."

Josh kept his hand on the wall as he stumbled toward the intersection, then turned right as instructed. Arriving at a door with a bright-red E painted at eye level, he leaned into the door when he couldn't find a door handle. It didn't budge. He stepped backward and noticed a paperback-sized speaker embedded in the wall next to the door. When he jabbed the green button placed below the horizontal slits, a tinny voice responded, "Can I help you?"

"Yeah, my name's Josh Davidson. I was just in there for an encounter, but I took the wrong exit, and I need to get out."

The speaker hissed to life. "Sorry, but we can't allow characters to exit."

Josh shouted, "I'm not a character. The lights went out. I didn't know where the exit was. This is your mistake."

"I'm sorry, you must apply for—" A burst of static cut the next word.

Josh pounded on the door. "What? I must apply for what?"

The speaker remained inert. The sound of metal scuffing on stone came from the end of the street, and Josh jerked around. The feeble streetlights highlighted the smooth edges of a Mech's helmet, but it was walking lethargically, gazing around as though its prey had long since escaped.

Josh glanced in the other direction and caught Nicole watching from a secluded doorway. She stepped backward when they made eye contact, and he yelled, "Why are you following me?"

She shook her head. "To see if you really were from the outside. I guess not, huh?"

The metallic scrapes and errant screams echoed in the tight alleys, making it difficult for him to judge distance. He checked to confirm that the Mech hadn't seen him before darting across the street, pulling off his Augs as he crossed.

She stepped backward when he stopped right in front of her, but he held out his Augs as though they were a gift. "I have no idea why they won't let me back, but come on. Do these things look like something they make here?"

She tentatively lifted them up and felt the smooth surface of the carbon fiber with her thumb. "No, I guess these aren't from here." Josh smiled triumphantly, but Nicole shrugged. "Well, as pretty as they are, they're not going to warn you when a Mech is coming."

Josh nodded in a little stuttering motion.

She pointed over her shoulder with her thumb. "So you'll end up like that girl back there."

"Yeah. I know."

"But you have to understand that we'd all like a little revenge."

He let a few seconds pass, then looked up at her again. "But if you let that happen, you'd be just like us, and you wouldn't even have ignorance as an excuse."

"Well, ignorance isn't your excuse anymore. Take a look around. Your money built this goddamn place while you chose to overlook the fate of everyone in here. I hope that—"

They spun in unison as a garbage can fell over, ringing as it hit the ground. The Mech was only ten feet away. It stood up straight, clutching a piece of metal pipe in its right hand. The bare metal glistened in the blue light, and its sheer surface felt more menacing without the gaming engine's manufactured glow. It looked down at them as Nicole banged her Augs with the palm of her hand. They instantly glowed a bright red.

"Fuck. Seriously?"

Josh didn't take his eyes from the Mech. "What?"

"These fucking things. They must be broken."

"It's too late to worry about that. What should we do?"

"We have to run."

Nicole took a step to the Mech's right, but it merely stomped its right foot to demonstrate how fruitless that would be. Josh imagined its master, cocooned in his rig a couple of miles away, making the identical motion. When the Mech waved the pipe threateningly, Josh stepped in front of Nicole and made a stopping gesture with his hand. "No. I'm one of you." The Mech tilted its head, and Josh tapped the plugs on his bicep, then gestured at the Mech as if to say, "We're the same." The Mech just shook its head as though it either didn't understand or didn't care, then lazily lifted the pipe, fully aware of its superiority. While Josh shook his head violently, the Mech continued to cock its arm as it prepared to strike.

Josh stepped back and glanced left. Some garbage cans were within reach. He grabbed a handle, then flung a can toward the Mech. It crashed into its thick metallic legs with a loud clang. The machine briefly tottered and swung its arms wildly to regain its balance, forcing Josh to dodge an inadvertent blow. He stayed on the Mech's left, knowing that twisting that way was always more difficult in the rig. When it prepared to strike again, he grabbed another can and pulled it over. The Mech shuffled to its left and struck down, but the pipe crashed into the metal. When it lifted the pipe again, Josh bent over and heaved the can forward. It rolled under the Mech's foot, knocking it off-balance. The Mech hit the ground with a loud crunch. The tight cables of the rig made getting off the ground one of the most awkward motions. The Mech rolled back and forth, smashing its fists on the ground in frustration.

Josh grabbed Nicole's hand, and they turned and ran. Two blocks later, she slowed. His momentum carried him a couple more steps as her hand slipped from his grasp. He turned around.

She pulled her Augs from her face, exposing the fear hidden by the mirrored plastic. "Thank you."

"It's okay. So now can you get me back?"

She closed her eyes for a second, as though doing a quick calculation. "Well, I guess there's a chance we can get you back the way you came."

"What?"

"Let's try Encounter."

He looked at her blankly.

"No, you won't knock on the door this time. I'm going back as a customer."

"What?"

"We'll sneak you in."

Josh nodded even though he still didn't understand. "Okay."

"It's only two blocks." She pulled her Augs back down. "And it looks like it's clear. Follow me."

"Thanks, I really…"

She was walking before he could finish, and he broke into a little jog to keep up. They ducked from shadow to shadow with ears peeled for the sound of steel as Nicole tapped the side of her Augs every thirty seconds to check that they were working. Josh chased her as the alley wound through the darkness. She ducked into an alcove across the road from the entrance, and they gulped air for a few seconds before running to the door. Nicole motioned for Josh to stay out of the camera's view, and she jabbed the intercom button.

The speaker squawked, "Can I help you?"

"Ahh, yeah, I'd like a walk-up."

"Oh, okay. Are your preferences preloaded?"

"No, I'll fill in the forms."

"But we won't be able to confirm your parameters."

She sighed. "Trust me. I've filled out these forms a few times."

"I'll have to check. This is quite unusual, and the safety of our customers is our highest priority."

"Look, I don't need a lecture. Don't you appreciate your loyal customers?"

There was a resigned, "Tap your Augs for payment."

Josh asked quietly, "Do you have enough?"

She whispered, "Enough for one chance" without looking at him. After she swiped, a green light flashed, and she nudged the door open a few inches, wedging her foot in the gap. Nicole put her hand on Josh's shoulder, and he dropped to his hands and knees, crawling in when she opened the door wider.

Sitting at her feet, he disappeared into the gloom of the charcoal carpet as she began filling in the parameters on the touch screen. Bypassing the physical requests, she selected Shy and First Time in the checklist and left the rest of the form blank.

After she tapped the enter button, a dialog box popped onto the screen: *Your preferences have been confirmed, please stand by for a match.* Ten seconds later it was replaced with the message *Please proceed to booth six.* She slowly ambled down the hall as Josh crouched low in the shadow of her legs, hustling to keep up. When they arrived at the booth, she theatrically swung the door wide, allowing Josh to sidle in unnoticed.

Nicole stared at the opaque glass, and Josh squatted in the shadows. The glass cleared, and Nicole sat up at the sight of the man on the other side. He was casually leaning back in his seat, far too poised to be a rookie. Her eyes darted around the space. "So, what's your name?"

"Dylan," he replied simply, comfortably looking her in the eye.

She couldn't hold his gaze and looked away as she replied, "So what brings you here?"

"Oh, I'm just curious."

"Oh? Curious about what?"

"Well, someone gave me the card, and a couple of friends had been here, so I thought I'd check it out."

She nodded thoughtfully. "Did they lower the glass?"

"They wouldn't tell me."

"They? Are you sure this wasn't just one friend?"

He smiled sheepishly. "Umm, yeah, you got me—"

The thirty-second warning sounded.

She growled. "What, you only paid for one minute?"

"I just wanted to see what it was like."

"Okay, then we'd better lower the glass," Nicole responded, the words rapidly falling from her mouth.

He frowned. "Oh, wow. It seems so quick. They say it changes your perspective the moment it happens. But I love the game. I don't want to stop playing."

She shook her head. "You know that's the whole point, right? If you wanted to stay behind the glass, why'd you bother coming in?"

He didn't move as the twenty-second warning sounded.

"What are you going to tell your friend, you chickened out?" He laughed, and she continued. "You know that this is a two-way street, right? I didn't get in for free, and I haven't gotten much out the conversation."

He put his hand high over the sensor. "But is it even worth it now?"

"Yes," she squeezed out between her teeth.

"I don't know."

"Fuck. Just press the damn button. Otherwise you're going to walk out of here without learning anything. Don't you want to know if I'm real?"

He shrugged and pushed down, but she just stared. Josh grabbed her leg, and she slammed her palm into the button a moment before it timed out.

Josh was up in a flash, hurling himself over the table the moment glass slid down.

Dylan screamed, "What the fuck?" and lunged toward the emergency alert. Josh managed to get a hand to Dylan's chest, gather his shirt in a fist, and knock him off-balance. Dylan's outstretched hand fell short of the button as the momentum of Josh's leap carried them into the wall. Dylan pulled himself to one knee before Josh could find his feet and reached for the button again. Josh twisted backward and grabbed Dylan's shoulder but couldn't stop him from slapping the red button. Instead of the squeal of an alarm, there was just a soft click as the door behind them slid open.

Dylan had pulled himself to his feet, angled himself toward Josh, and lifted his right leg. Josh brought his arms over his face and shrank into the wall, trying to minimize the target for an impact that never came. When he lowered his arms, Dylan was gone.

Josh turned to the glass. Nicole was standing with her hands pressed against it, eyes wide. He anxiously jabbed the green button, and she matched his gesture, but instead of dropping, it filled between them. He banged his fist on the milky glass and shouted, "Nicole!"

"You gotta go."

"But I want—"

"Go now!"

An emotionless voice admonished him from above, "The Encounter is over. Please insert more credits if you'd like to continue. Ten credits will prolong for two minutes. Seven credits will prolong for…"

Josh dashed out through the open door as the different cost options droned on. This time bright-red arrows pointed toward the exit between bouncing text and snippets from the game as synthesized pop blasted from the speakers above. He followed the arrows, expecting the screens to blink out at any moment, but they were still flashing as he entered the lobby. Running toward the exit, he didn't break stride as he burst into the street.

Part 1: The Going

My life isn't that unusual; like most, it's been lived in two halves. The first disappeared in a blur of anticipation, longing for the next milestone while failing to appreciate the last, and the second is lived at a gentler pace as the repercussions of earlier decisions play out. I took my first step across the divide on a sharp, clear morning.

I said, "It's a beautiful day for it."

Clayton looked up from his slate. "Yes, it is, but it's always a beautiful day for it. They manage the weather carefully on launch days. Nothing's left to chance."

The spaceport was a stout, geometric building, and its bulk slowly unfolded as we curved around its perimeter. A long straw extended skyward from the rear, an appendage that seemed far too fragile for its purpose, and I stifled my panic as I followed the hairline until it disappeared. I'd been reluctant to make the journey, but I coaxed some enthusiasm by imagining the women, even those in our rarified circle, who would have loved to have been in my shoes. When our vehicle drifted to a halt, it lowered itself a couple of feet, and as the gull wing doors eased upward, the desert air spilled in.

Through the gap, I watched a pair of maroon pants scuttle into position, and when the doors reached their full height, they revealed a diminutive man in a sharply creased uniform. Giving me a deferential nod as he reached for my hand, he gently eased me from my vehicle and delivered his first sentence in a practiced cadence: "Welcome to the Lorentz Factor." He bent slightly at the waist before continuing, "Ms. Jamieson, my name is Joseph, and it's a pleasure to meet you. Please don't hesitate to let me know if there's anything I can do to make your journey more enjoyable." He raised his left arm toward the building, waited for me to move, and fell in step behind me as the glass doors gently slid open.

It took a moment for my eyes to adjust as we stepped into the foyer. Despite its modest proportions, the luxurious surroundings were a reminder of the profit to be made in catering to vanity. It was sparse enough for me to feel like the focal point of the room, and I was reminded that being the center of attention is the natural order for most of the select clientele. I absorbed the covert glances from the staff that seemed as though they were merely there to make the building feel occupied. A thin woman with a precise smile was framed by perfectly nondescript opulence—richly lacquered dark woods, gold trimmings, and black marble floors. She was sitting behind a small glass desk that faced a pair of low-slung chairs. Finished in white leather, their X-shaped frames were polished to a mirrorlike finish, and the air smelled faintly floral.

The orchestrated journey began with a flute of champagne delivered on a silver tray. After I accepted the glass with a nod, Joseph waited for me to take a sip, then asked, "Ms. Jamieson, would you like me to go through the flight details?"

Ever conscious of Clayton's schedule, I looked over at him, and Joseph followed my gaze. When Clayton nodded, Joseph continued. "You've chosen the perfect flight as the first taste of what the Lorentz Factor offers. You will be traveling at the maximum speed available, 99.999 percent the speed of light, so exactly one year will pass during your forty-hour flight. When you return, you won't just look younger than your peers, you'll actually be a year younger."

I nodded blankly. Anticipating my next question, Joseph reduced the principle to its essence. "When you travel close to the speed of light, time slows down for you, so in just a few hours of flying time, a year will pass by back here on Earth." I nodded, more deliberately this time, and he continued in his comforting patter. "Please, please join me. The craft is this way."

We stepped into a narrow hallway. On one wall, the dark woods continued from the lobby, but the other side was a soft mesh screen that allowed a carefully controlled glimpse of the arrivals hall. The barrier obscured the identity of those from the highest echelons of wealth but allowed me to absorb the choreographed routines of the staff doting on their clients. As we walked, the hall narrowed in a subtle piece of theater to prepare me for the craft's size, but I was still taken aback when Joseph opened the door to reveal the tiny silver missile. A graceful teardrop barely larger than a coffin, a purity of purpose was written in its austerity, the open hatch exposing a lightly textured seat that would carry me farther in the next few hours than most traveled in a lifetime. The suspended mesh was covered in a hand-stitched diamond pattern, and two thin white straps made up the harness, the only color the large red button where they crossed. I'd expected a dashboard, but there were no markings on any surface, a reminder that I'd be asleep for the entirety of the trip.

As I placed my hand on the sill, Joseph spoke softly. "Isn't it beautiful? A true marvel of engineering." My expression must have betrayed my doubts, and he gestured to the door in the far corner. "Please, come this way. You must see your flight suit."

It opened to a cylindrical room about ten feet in diameter, seemingly built around the centerpiece of a bespoke gossamer suit. The beige fabric was infused with carbon that softly shimmered under a spotlight, and it seemed impervious to gravity as it floated on the hanger. He stepped backward out of the room to join Clayton while I changed. I slipped out of a light summer dress, its pastel hues out of place amongst the muted luxury of the room, and removed the suit from the hook. It slipped on easily, and with a gentle tug on the front tab, it embraced me. The soft fibers pulled taut against my skin, their reassuring pressure compensating for the lack of bulk. My steps were light and easy, as though I were naked, and the glistening suit became another distraction from the journey ahead.

I gently slid into the craft, and Joseph handed me a tiny crystal glass filled with a thick pink concoction. Clayton reached out and held my other hand as I took a sip, and the gentle pressure of his thumb was the last thing I remembered. A moment later, I woke to precisely the same scene; even Clayton's hand was still in mine.

"Wait, was there a problem?" I said to Clayton. "You're still here?"

"Welcome back, Vera. I missed you."

"But…I haven't gone anywhere."

He chuckled sympathetically. "Well, it seems that they do their job a little too well; it's so easy you don't even know you've gone."

I desperately sought clues that might signify that this was a different year, but there were none to be found. Carefully designed to ease the return, the walls were the same rich woods; the simple, geometric chairs were timeless; and there was no ornamentation to divulge whether this room had been decorated in the early twenty-first century or two hundred years later.

My mind rebelled against the idea that the flight had even taken place. "What? Really? I don't believe it."

"Well, it was only a year, so I haven't changed that much!" Clayton laughed. "But don't worry, I'm sure you'll notice a few changes on the way home. Of course, there's quite a bit of news to share." I scowled, and he quickly added, "No need for alarm. It's all good."

"Ms. Jamieson, welcome back. It's been our pleasure. Is there anything we can do to ease your return?"

"Oh no, I'll be okay, but thank you, Joseph. You've been wonderful."

I turned back to Clayton, and he gently coaxed me from the craft. When he leaned in for a kiss, I couldn't help searching through the familiar lines and curves for evidence of the year that had passed. My first step was tentative, and Clayton gently slipped his arm around my waist to guide me to the exit. I declined a celebratory glass of champagne, and we walked down the hallway on the opposite side of the perforated screen, exhibits for those about to embark. When we stepped outside, I shielded my eyes from the searing blue sky as Clayton eased me into our waiting vehicle. A dull clunk signaled that we were safely ensconced, and Clayton watched me curiously as we rolled toward the highway, politely waiting for me to initiate the conversation. I turned toward the window, still seeking confirmation that a year had passed when his impatience got the better of him.

"So, how was it?"

What I'd lost was yet to be revealed, but I was already wondering if the exchange was worth it. "I don't know; it's all a bit strange. I feel like I just closed my eyes for a moment, so the whole thing just seems like a trick."

"Well, I can assure you it wasn't. I learned how long a year is. There's part of me that can't believe this day finally arrived."

I smiled, absorbing the adoration for a moment. "So, if a year's gone by, then what's happened?"

"There's no big news. Most importantly, everyone is well, and I'm sure you'll spend the next few weeks hearing more than you need to."

"No, really, there must be something big I missed."

"Of course there's a lot to share, but we have the time, so let's go slowly. Oh, here's the first new building you'll see. It's quite spectacular. The renderings just didn't do it justice…"

He chuckled as I stared, agape, as though the building had materialized overnight. "Wow, it really was a year. So everyone's doing fine then?"

Clayton nodded. "Yes, yes, fortunately nothing to report on that front."

"And the company?"

He filled me in on his company's recent success, reassured me about the health of our families, and was complaining about the continued bickering of local politicians when we arrived at our house. The gates to our estate parted as our vehicle approached, and we skimmed past the familiar manicured hedges and emerald lawn. I hesitated as we stepped toward the ornate glass doorway.

Clayton smiled. "It's not that scary—nothing much has changed around here." I flashed a brief smile, and his response was instant: "No, really, I think that the house is identical, but we do have a few new toys for you."

When our technical assistant handed me the latest phone, I turned it over in my hand, hesitating before making the habitual gesture to activate it. It remained inert, and he demonstrated the new gesture, holding his thumb and fingers together, then springing them apart. On my third try, it came to life, and I smiled at its familiarity, diving into the newsfeeds and relishing each new discovery. I tapped out a message for Alicia, and my sister responded immediately: *Oh, you're back! I have so much to tell you!*

I motioned to call, but Clayton's reproachful stare reminded me that he'd waited a year for my return.

"I'm sorry. That is a bit thoughtless of me." I laughed. "But it's all a bit much right now."

"No, no, I understand."

I looked down at the phone and quickly tapped out: *Sorry can't chat now, lunch tomorrow? Usual place?* Alicia replied, *K*, and I returned my attention to Clayton.

I arrived a few minutes late, and Alicia was already waiting in our usual spot by the window, one avoided in midsummer but pleasantly bright on this early spring day. She began the conversation with "You look so great," then filled the hour. I tried to extract the truly newsworthy events from her eager monologue. The irony wasn't lost on me. Although I'd just done the impossible, I didn't have a story of my own.

Subtle variations of that encounter played out over the next few weeks as I hungrily devoured my friends' year, and although all I could do was wave away the questions when my peers asked me what it was like, I loved feeling that I was an intrepid explorer reentering civilization. It took a few months before my life returned to a standard pace, one that felt pedestrian, and I lusted after the rush of newness again.

"Clayton, it's almost six months since my trip. Have you enjoyed having me back?"

"Of course. This is a big, lonely house when you're here by yourself."

I laughed. "Well, alone except for the staff."

"Vera, that's not the same."

"It is nice to be missed, but it can't be that bad without me. You have more than enough distractions to keep you amused."

Clayton turned to look at me. "You're not considering another flight, are you?"

"I know I shouldn't be, and that it's an extravagance even for us, but it really was quite the thrill. Of course, I know it's a little selfish of me, and we can…"

"No, no, no, it wouldn't be fair of me to send you up just once. We'd always called the first one a test. I'll have Vanessa make arrangements."

"Oh, Clayton, thank you. I understand the sacrifices you make and don't want you to think they go unappreciated."

We were being whisked toward the spaceport two weeks later. As I ran my fingers along the textured carbon fiber that lined the length of the vehicle's interior, he broke the silence. "Vera, if you'd rather not go, we can just turn around."

"I'm sorry, I have no idea why I'm nervous this time. I thought this one would be easier."

"Darling, there's no pressure, and last time was so easy that you couldn't even remember it."

"You're right. I guess I'm just a little worried about getting hooked—they say you can't stop at two."

"I have no idea who said that, but there's not exactly a large sample set. People do this for all sorts of reasons. You'll be fine."

"Well, I appreciate your support, but what about you? Two years is a long time."

"To be honest, I'm not sure, but the next couple of years are critical ones for the company." He gazed out the window. "And my colleagues will appreciate my devotion."

I laughed. "I bet they will. Actually, I'm surprised they don't underwrite the flights with all of the time it frees up!"

He nodded, smiling. "That's not a bad idea. I'll have to float it at the next board meeting."

Joseph greeted me with a deferential "Welcome back, Ms. Jamieson," and then we were hustled along at a pace designed to outrun my pursuing doubts. Everything felt familiar—in order to ease the return, the spaceport barely changed. Seemingly a moment after I'd eased myself into the craft, I was confronted with Clayton's gentle face. Then, when he smiled, I was convinced that I could find the creases that marked the two years that had passed me by. This time the shock of disbelief was absent, replaced by a desire to soak up the missing years in a rush. I laughed as Clayton toyed with me, allowing the stories of the last two years to unfold in fits and starts on the way home.

I strode confidently into the restaurant that I still referred to as "ours" the next morning but slowed at the sight of an unfamiliar face in Alicia's chair. While my eyes darted around the room, she called out from behind me, and I turned to see her bent over a small table edged into a dim corner.

"Why aren't you in our usual spot? Don't regulars get a little special treatment?"

A wan smile crept across Alicia's face as she waited for me to acknowledge the ridiculousness of my statement.

"Oh, oh, I'm sorry, of course—it's so easy to forget."

The corners of her mouth turned down a little. "For you, I'm sure it is."

I stumbled, my mind forming words that disappeared before I could bring them to my lips, and instead I spread my arms wide. Alicia rose immediately to give me a heartfelt hug. If there was any lingering resentment, it was erased over the next hour of conversation, and as the stories poured forth, I soaked up the trials and tribulations of an average life.

A couple of months later, my inevitable crash was allayed by the knowledge that I'd fly again and that the tedium was only temporary. The third trip was routine, and by the fourth, the spaceport's timeless interior seemed to compress each individual journey into one long excursion. The lines in Clayton's face were deeper each time, and while I basked in his jokes about my youthful exuberance, I knew I was cheating the system, postponing the pain of returning to a normal life even as the repercussions became obvious. My mind wasn't supple enough to construct the lives of those around me from the brief glimpses between trips, and as they aged, their stories contained an increasing number of tragedies. I was being outrun by technology, my face reddening each time a friend muttered the word "Lorentzian" as the excuse for a confused mistake.

I was heading toward what would be my last trip when Clayton quipped, "You know that these flights are just the world's most expensive makeup." I let the comment flow over me, but of all the regrets, the one that simmers is that vanity became my defining trait. I convince myself that the slippery slope started so gently that the first step could be excused by ignorance, but I wonder if I'd willfully ignored the evidence and chased a life that would be defined by the envy of others rather than one I actually wanted to live.

The hatch slid open with its familiar sigh, and when I was greeted by my sister's pitying expression, fear overwhelmed my disorientation. Clayton had always softened the confusion of the return, but he couldn't prepare me for his own absence. On the way home, I stared vacantly out the window as Alicia gently recited the details of Clayton's final months, dwelling on his love for me even as his health declined. I batted away Alicia's attempts to draw me into a conversation as I absorbed the totality of my isolation, and spent the rest of the journey wondering if Clayton had only stuck by me because he'd introduced me to the addiction.

Part 2: The Waiting

The vehicle coasted to a halt in front of a house that had always been far too big for two and was absurd now that I was alone. Alicia didn't ask as she stepped out with me, but I told her anyway, "You don't have to stay. I'll be okay."

"Vera, you're still dazed, and it's only going to get worse tonight."

"No, really, Alicia. I'll be all right, but I might need you tomorrow."

"That's enough. I'm staying. You don't realize it now, but it won't be the same without Clayton. He sheltered you far more than you know."

Sapped of the energy to protest, I responded meekly, "Thank you, Alicia."

She touched my hand as we entered. "You're welcome."

"Alicia. You know, I got it all wrong. I remember your hesitation before my first flight. You told me how the value of shared experience is underestimated and that reconnecting with everyone afterward might not be so easy. I thought it was just jealousy at the time, but you knew this was coming, didn't you?"

She waved away my question. "No, Vera, I can't see the future. But it just didn't feel right."

"I'm never going again."

"I know, and I think that's for the best." Her tone was tender and motherly, underlining how each of us had changed. We'd been inseparable as kids, but the two decades between seemed to have arrived suddenly.

"I appreciate you staying."

"Vera, please, it's the least I can do."

Exhausted and unable to find a way to finish the conversation, I turned away; two years of news could wait.

The next morning Alicia was waiting in the kitchen. We'd been blessed with the same slender frame, but in the harsh morning light, I could see how much more delicate she'd become.

"Thanks for staying, but Alicia, I'll be fine. Really."

She folded her arms defiantly. "I'd prefer to stay."

"Well, it's up to you, but there's plenty of people here to take care of me." The young man preparing breakfast briefly raised his head, then quietly resumed his task.

Alicia nodded slowly and said, "Well, okay then." She grabbed her jacket off the back of a kitchen stool.

"Sorry, I didn't mean it like that. I really appreciate you being here; it's just that I have to get used to this."

She nodded as she turned toward the door. "It's okay, Vera, you're right, but call me if you need me."

The moment the door closed, the sounds of staff busily tending to a house that had barely been lived in for a year amplified the emptiness.

After just a couple of hours, I summoned my vehicle and headed toward my sister's neighborhood. Although her street was a tedious repetition of dwellings, each had the comfortable familiarity of our childhood home. When I arrived at her door, Alicia greeted me warmly, seemingly unsurprised at my appearance. We sat in her kitchen, the midmorning sun casting shadows on her pockmarked skin and highlighting the blemishes that wouldn't be tolerated amongst my peers. In stilted conversation, we sought the connection that had withered over the years, but even as the ease returned, our laughter couldn't soften the pang of regret.

I waited patiently for the right moment, but it never came, and the lightness in her voice was extinguished when I asked her to close the gap by a decade, the equivalent of five of my trips.

She looked at me evenly. "I'll go, but you don't really feel like my sister anymore."

"Alicia," I said, wincing at the blow, "we'll always be sisters; nothing's going to change that." I waited for an understanding smile, but her expression didn't change. With nothing more to be said, I closed the conversation with a soft "thank you."

The magnitude of her sacrifice was only revealed once she was gone. Memorable moments were more widely spaced than in our earlier years, but I felt a stab of regret at each one she missed. With so many of my friends gone, my life continued its march toward simplicity, and I was swallowed by the anticipation of my sister's return as I pictured her, millions of miles away, traveling at incomprehensible speeds. Each day that crawled by was a reminder that my internal clock had been irreparably damaged by the skips and jumps of the last two decades, and passing by the spaceport to watch the tiny pods return to Earth became a daily ritual. They were almost invisible, but if I positioned myself correctly, I'd catch a flash of reflected sunlight as the occupants returned to port. I imagined the day when I'd be driving along this road and one of the flares would be my sister.

When the day finally arrived, I left early to soak up the last moments of expectation. I was still in a daze as I approached the intersection I'd traveled straight through hundreds of times. The vehicle turned left, breaking my trance, and for a moment I wanted to turn around, knowing that the anticipation that had sustained me was about to be replaced by the unknown. I absorbed every detail as I approached the entrance, and the spaceport's unchanging facade seemed to mock me. The robots scuttled about the premises with chemicals and brushes in an effort to keep the effects of aging at bay, but the building was fighting the battle that no one wins.

I absorbed the expressions that flitted across her face as they opened the capsule—bewilderment was followed by the joy of familiarity—but those lasted only a moment before being replaced by the one I'd feared: the shock of my wrinkled face after I'd been ageless for most of our lives. I'd practiced apologizing a thousand times, but now that the moment arrived, I couldn't bring the words to my lips. She was a little wobbly as she brought herself to her feet, but when she hugged me tightly, the need to say something was rendered mute. As I searched her features for evidence of the decade that had just passed, it felt strange to be on the other side of the distortion, and I finally summoned the courage to speak.

"Was it what you imagined?"

A few seconds passed by, and I was about to repeat the question when she looked up, her words quiet and labored. "I don't know yet. It's the not the trip, but the return."

My heart sank. She'd known all along what she was getting into. She craned her neck as we approached the city, the changes that ten years had wrought unfolding before her eyes. I wondered what she was thinking but didn't dare to ask.

You were standing at the windows of the fortieth floor, staring down at a city taking its last breath, when a high-pitched voice pierced the murmur of the crowd. "Seriously? How can you have lost it?" Her tone was pleading, the words driven by an underlying panic, but you stifled the temptation to turn around. There was no time for distractions; in half an hour, the crisp order of Seattle's grid would collapse into the chaos of the jittery video that had brought you here.

The concierge's tone was deferential. "Madam, I'm terribly sorry. The hanger was empty. I know you have the tag, but I'm afraid we've misplaced it. What color did you say it was?"

Her response was lost in a surge of laughter from the nearest table, but when the crowd quieted, you tried to piece together the conversation from the patches that broke through. "I just checked… the manager…they mixed…coat's in another room."

"How long…time to wait."

Her familiar accent was seeping through, and soon she was making no effort to disguise it. You were reminded of your own coat lying within reach across the back of the nearest chair. Entrusting it with the staff is a rookie mistake; you should never leave your fate in someone else's hands. There were only two rules: never tell, and don't leave a trace. You glanced at your watch, and it reminded you that you should've left three minutes ago, but you wanted to hear another couple of sentences to confirm your hunch. You'd only managed two steps toward the concierge when you felt the slightest of shudders, reminding you that you shouldn't have been at the top of a tall building thirty minutes before the event. Then the lights dimmed and the babble paused for a moment, allowing you to catch the next sentence of the panicked woman's pleas. "They're holding the elevators? Do you expect me to walk down forty flights of stairs?"

"Please, madam, we're really sorry. Be patient; it should only take a few minutes."

"Don't you dare tell me to be patient. You don't understand. I really need to leave now."

She looked around, taking a moment to gather herself, then returned her attention to the concierge. "So, level with me. Do you actually have any idea where it is?"

You backed away, not wanting to get involved in the exchange. You couldn't afford to be remembered.

"Sorry, we're still looking. Could I have your tag again?"

"What? You're kidding."

The concierge remained stoic. "No. I'm terribly sorry."

She fumbled in her purse, then thrust the red plastic tab into the concierge's hand. He reacted as though he'd received the baton in a relay, turning in an instant and dashing toward the cloakroom. She began tapping her feet; it looked subconscious, but she might have been timing him, knowing exactly how long she had. You searched in vain for clues, but if she was traveling, her attention to detail was impressive. When she glanced around, you noticed the brief pause when her eyes met yours. You looked away guiltily, but when you turned back, she was still watching you. A second shudder snuffed the light, and the darkness was instant and impenetrable.

Each passing second chipped away at the margin of error. You began the calculations: forty flights of stairs must be close to fifteen minutes, and the exit portal was about an eight-minute walk. That left only four as a buffer. The lights returned, but the fleeting blackout had been enough to prod a few diners from their seats. There were too many people in the room, and you could feel the imminent panic. You'd heard that other travelers could read the current and would flow through crowds like a leaf floating through eddies, but the patterns were always lost on you.

Your eyes flitted from guest to guest as you wondered who was skittish enough to break first. Maybe it would be the elderly lady who needed to be far enough ahead to avoid being trampled in the crowd's blind ambition, or it might be the younger man nearest the window who was ignorant of the fact that escaping this building wouldn't get him out of danger. As the crowd fidgeted, a tall man in his late forties wearing a perfectly fitting charcoal suit strode toward the microphone. His confidence kept panic at bay for a moment, but when his throat caught partway through his second sentence, a few seats were thrust backward. A couple of high-pitched screams provoked imitators, and the room exploded in a cacophony of sound and movement.

   The woman was scanning the room from the corner, but before you could take a step toward her, the concierge returned, remarkably composed amongst the tumult. The woman swiped her coat from his arms before he'd even stopped, and with a stylish pivot and two graceful strides, she entered the stairwell. The space between the two of you filled in an instant, the crisscrossing bodies blocking your line of sight, and by the time a gap opened, the door was closing behind her. You began threading through the crowd, absorbing the relief of progress until a solid bump knocked you to the ground. The precious glass rectangle that you couldn't leave without skittered across the floor and collided with a polished loafer. You stumbled to your feet and scrambled after it, managing to scoop it up before rushing toward the door, but by the time you burst through it, she had a three-floor lead. Knowing that the panicked crowd would soon flood the stairwell, you called out, but as you were so conditioned to being innocuous while traveling, your tepid "hold on" wasn't loud enough to interrupt the rhythmic clicking of her heels.

   You yelled, "Wait!" The words echoed off the walls, and she slowed and turned. She must not have been able to see you in the tight space, and she resumed her descent, the clicks quicker now.

   "I know who you are!" you shouted.

   That was enough to bring her to a halt, and when she looked up quizzically, you leaned out over the railing one story above. You were teetering on the edge of acceptability, not sure if it was permissible to drop cover to a fellow traveler. There didn't seem to be any repercussions in that case, but you'd merely skimmed the manual, and a case like this was probably buried deep in the appendix.

   She struggled between breaths. "My portal is still a ten-minute walk from the building, and unless yours is right out front, we've both left it too late."

   Before you could respond, you were struck by the horror of the shimmer, a reminder that transgressions are fatal. She disappeared in a couple of agonizing seconds, the sterile erasure so different to what you'd imagined. There, and then gone. You pictured the small party being dispatched to her family two hundred years from now. They'd utter some soulless condolences, and another family would wonder about the folly of youth.

Everyone knows the risks, but in a world where premature death is so rare, each mishap brings the entire organization under question. The management has to be ruthless, but her indiscretion was so benign, merely a brief acknowledgment. The line between your hints and her statement seemed so arbitrary.

Another wobble shook you from your paralysis, and you'd descended two more floors with frantic steps when a dull roar announced the crowd pouring down the stairs. Acid-green emergency lighting illuminated the stark concrete steps, and you slowed to scour the spot where the other traveler had disappeared, but there was nothing to see. You were overtaken as you slowed, leaving you trapped amongst the horde as you spilled into the street. The others absorbed the joy of escape, but you kept moving, the air biting as you stepped out of the warmth of the mob. You stopped, remembering your coat, which was still leaning on the back of a chair forty stories above you. You felt your pockets. Your device was there, so it was only a piece of cloth you'd left behind. Still, you cursed; it was a replica, and you wished you'd spent the few extra cryps on a vintage, but you were sure that the forty stories of concrete would bury its secret.

You'd been saved from making decisions for a few minutes while you hurtled down the stairs, but now you were disoriented by the stillness. You turned left, downhill toward the Sound, before realizing that the drop point was east of you. The grid that seemed so composed from the fortieth floor was now an impossible maze. You'd hoped the buildings would help guide you, but the ones in the videos had been fragments, and the complete structures looked totally different. You only had six minutes in hand, and you'd lost one of them before you turned back up toward Capitol Hill.

Not accounting for the steep grade was the misjudgment that erased the last of your buffer. It would come down to seconds.

As you increased your pace, the crisp air became an ally, keeping you cool as you raced to safety. You maneuvered around a young man with fashionably disheveled hair wobbling up the hill; his slick black cowboy boots were about to become a liability. The moments before a disaster were thrilling, and you absorbed every detail, unable to resist the habit of searching for a familiar face, trying to bring alive the anonymous characters in the historic footage.

As you searched street signs for the names lodged in your memory, you were suddenly knocked to the ground. It was too early for that; the real shocks were a few minutes away. But when you lifted your head, you saw a young woman rolling and groaning. You leapt to your feet in a panic, but she caught your eye before you could turn and run. Her expression was part bewilderment, part mild amusement. She reached a hand to yours, giving you no choice but to help her to her feet. Your pull was too much for her slender frame, and in an instant her face was only inches from yours. Her cute half smile grew, and her blue eyes looked up at you expectantly, but you couldn't form words, not even "I'm sorry."

A flash of irritation crossed her face before her drunkenness dampened it. "Wow, you're in a hurry. Is there a fire or something?" She followed the question with an intoxicated giggle.

Still in shock, you mumbled, "Not yet."

"What?"

You took a hesitant step backward, shocked at how easily you dropped protocol. As you laughed to cover your misstep, she pushed: "Is there something I should know about?"

You froze, your awareness reduced to feeling each second seep by as you fought the desire to warn her. This was the reason travelers were instructed to keep their distance. As the silence stretched, self-preservation won.

"No, no, I'm sorry." You took a step before realizing that you hadn't dropped her hand.

"If there's nothing to worry about, why are you in a hurry? Wouldn't you rather stay?"

She was more than tipsy; if you let her go, she'd fall to the ground again. There was another ripple, a reminder that the big one was only two minutes away. You still had almost a quarter mile until the pickup. Even at a sprint, it would be close.

She failed to notice. It was clear that for her, the ground had been moving for the last hour. You were surprised to hear yourself let out a soft laugh.

She continued in mock offense, "What's so funny?"

"Nothing, but you should go home. It's dangerous to be out in your condition."

She slapped your shoulder playfully. "My condition? You don't have to be so mean!"

Your response was halted by another tremor, and this one severed your tentative grip. You couldn't fight the instinct to reach out as she fell, and your arms found her waist. The two of you fell in a tangle to the pavement, the cold ground cutting through your thin shirt. Gentle spasms of laughter rippled through her body, disguising the ground's movement, but you were sure you felt the last pretremor. The next one, just over a minute away, would be devastating. You gently rolled her onto the ground, but she screamed at its icy touch. You turned and sprinted in the direction of the exit portal as her protest was lost in the chilly gusts. Frantic breaths seared your lungs as you hunted for the safety of the soft blue glow leaking from an alleyway.

You scanned the horizon, but earthquakes weren't like storms. It wouldn't come from a specific direction or follow a predictable path. When it arrived, the noise welled up like a locomotive, one that seemed to be approaching from everywhere at once. As the ground ruptured, the buildings battled like boxers refusing to go down after a flurry of hits. You fended off panic, refusing to let the rolling ground slow your progress. A dozen strides later, the portal's comforting blue glow emanated from a narrow lane. There was a flood of relief as you ducked into the alleyway. You'd be safely home with a couple of quick taps, and the events around you consigned to history. You anxiously swiped, but instead of the confirmation button that would send you home, the words *Forget something?* flashed in red, and the phone went blank.

    You screamed, frantically swiping the inert device, but it refused to wake. You looked down at your sweat-stained shirt, clinging to you in the chilly air, reminding you of your coat lying in the rubble a mile away. You slumped against the wall as exhaustion took hold and waited for the shimmer as the earth tore around you. A minute later a cacophony of sirens and alarms began to wail, puncturing the stillness after the final tremor. You'd survived the quake, and the portal still glowed, so you gripped your device and launched yourself at the blue haze. But instead of emerging in a different year, you merely careened across the alleyway and crashed into a garbage can. The portal disappeared seconds later, and the world you were in refused to fade. You were in limbo, stuck in the wrong time.

    Dragging yourself to your feet, you stepped out of the lane and into the shattered city. The scenes were hauntingly familiar. The documentaries you'd studied now played out in front of you. A young man about thirty yards away staggered to his feet. He patted the left pocket of his jeans, then his right, before pulling a phone from it and holding it out at eye level. He scanned from side to side, tapping the screen to record the destruction. You looked directly at him as the phone's lens passed over you. Then, jerking your head around, you finally realized why this quake had fascinated you. The familiar Elephant Car Wash sign stood triumphant amongst the wreckage, and you remembered thinking that the trunk of a vertical BMW looked like the Titanic's stern. You'd watched the blurry man in the video twisting his head in panic. There hadn't been quite enough detail to see who he was, but he'd always felt familiar. You remembered wondering what he was thinking, and now you knew.

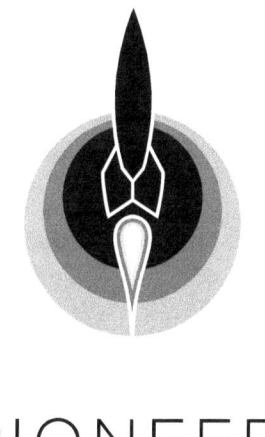

PIONEER

Aiden cautiously tapped Accept when his sister's name flashed on his phone. It wasn't his birthday, and Piper hadn't deemed any news worthy of a phone call in years.

The moment her face appeared on the screen, she said, "I'm going!" and laughed like a giddy teenager.

He forced a smile. "Oh, Piper. Well, that's ahh...well, that's—I'm proud of you."

"Yeah, it's crazy, right? I can't quite believe it yet."

"I'm sure. I'm a little shocked myself. When do you leave?"

"No one's given me a solid answer, but I've heard whispers that it might be as early as the end of the year."

"But that's only three months away."

"Well, it is a one-way trip, and I'm sure they're worried about me bailing."

"It won't take long for them to realize how unlikely that is." Aiden paused. "But has it crossed your mind? You know, it has to feel a bit different now that it's real."

Piper shook her head. "Aiden, you can't be serious. I've dreamed of this forever."

"And it's just you, right? Do you think there's any chance they'll send someone with you?"

Piper laughed. "I guess there's not much point. The public only needs one person to cheer for, and it would be a lot more expensive building a rocket for two."

"I'm sure they could—"

"If it makes you feel better, I'd prefer to be on my own. There are fewer unknowns that way."

"I know that being alone sounds more heroic, but what if something goes wrong?"

"Well, it's up to me to fix it."

"Fair enough. I guess you've never trusted anyone anyway." Aiden chuckled.

Piper glanced at her lap.

"Sorry, Piper, it was just a joke."

"No, it's okay. It's just that someone on the panel said the same thing. I know it's ironic that the most solitary person alive will be a beacon for the human race."

"You might be overstating the case a bit. You certainly wouldn't be the first blindly ambitious soul to leave a trail of mystified people in their wake."

"Yeah, sometimes I wonder—"

"Now's not the time to wonder. You've actually made it. Think of those who sacrifice everything chasing a dream that eludes them. You're actually going to be the one they write about."

There was a muted beep, and Piper glanced at the bottom of her screen.

"Piper?"

"Aiden, I'm sorry, but I have to take this. I just wanted you to be the first to know. I'll call again soon."

He nodded as Piper's face evaporated. She'd been chosen, and he couldn't reverse the clock to when it had been an impossible dream, when he might have been able to convince her that her isolation was self-imposed, that the tiniest effort to be part of their family might have changed everything. Even when she'd made the short list, he'd postponed the difficult conversation, refusing to believe that she'd be the one chosen from the eight perfect options. His sister was special, but there were still thousands of twenty-five-year-old dreamers out there, and he was convinced that one of the others had to be better suited to the journey. It would be heroic, but not like the blatant heroism of the early years, back when they called it "the space race." The brute-force method of space exploration was the domain of powerful men, and the concise missions in the grainy, jittery videos were seemingly crafted to capture the public's imagination. A century later the race had become a crawl as multiyear missions overlapped and personalities intertwined. When robots replaced astronauts, the final flicker of public interest was extinguished. Now his sister was banished to a lonely death on a distant planet because robots couldn't smile into the camera and capture people's hearts.

A month after that call, the real fanfare began, and like most of the world, Aiden was glued to Piper's first interview. She was perched on the edge of the chair like a worried five-year-old, looking vacantly at a spot just left of the camera. A year ago she would have been swinging her legs, but the burden of perfection had compressed her movements into subtle nods and brief smiles. When she brushed a few errant strands from her eye, Aiden remembered Piper's quip about being pretty enough to engage the public but not so attractive that they'd protest her being lost forever. He'd laughed when his objection was waved away dismissively.

After the host's fawning introduction, the silence stretched as he silently urged Piper to say something. She finally uttered a couple of sentences about her passion for space travel but spoke too quickly, as though dissipating her energy in short, sharp bursts. The host cautiously wavered between awe and sympathy, but it took another three questions before Piper managed to look into the black glass of the camera and smile at the millions of eyes behind it.

At the same time, a dozen miles away at NASA's headquarters, the applause rippled through the oak walls of General Abbott's office, and he abruptly switched off the oversized screen on his wall before turning to his lead aerospace engineer. "Well, they love her. We can't cancel her dream now."

Mason was sitting back, his shoulders slumped. "I agree, sir, but we don't need to stop her mission to continue our research. We're so close."

"You are?" General Abbott rubbed his chin. "So when do you think it will be ready?"

Mason forced himself forward. "It's definitely less than five years away, sir."

General Abbott let his lips curl into a wry smile. "Five years? Usually when an engineer presents an impossible scenario, they choose a decade; that's long enough for them to avoid accountability."

"I understand your skepticism, but the fact that we've been

working on this for decades actually makes me more confident. The breakthroughs have been coming so predictably over the last several years that we can safely anticipate each one."

"Until they stop."

Mason held up a hand defensively. "Of course I can't guarantee success, but all the signs are there, and really there's no better time to ask. The public's enthusiasm has never been higher. We have to take advantage—"

General Abbott nodded toward the screen that had just shown Piper's interview. "Mason, you seemed to have forgotten that you're asking for money to make her trip irrelevant. Do you think that will sit well?"

"Well, not so much irrelevant; we'll still learn a lot from this—"

"Yes, yes, but that's not really the point. We're not sending her into the unknown as a guinea pig for your mission."

"Sir, I'm sorry, that's not what I meant. It's just that regardless of what happens, Piper's mission won't be wasted."

"Remember that what's wasted is in the eye of the beholder, so we'll have to be very careful how we frame it." General Abbott waved loosely at the black monitor. "She's the only reason the lights are still on."

"I know, I'll keep that in mind, but can I consider this approval to continue?"

General Abbott's gaze returned to his slate. "Yes, but let's keep it between us."

Mason hurried to his feet at the slight pause and was almost at the door before eking out a "Thank you, sir."

A few weeks later Piper was sitting up straight and looking directly into the camera. Aiden marveled at the transformation. She'd even lost her little tic of beginning sentences with "I mean." He waited impatiently for a couple of minutes after the interview ended, then tapped her name on his phone.

After having left so many unanswered messages, he was shocked to see her face. "Aiden! It's great to hear from you."

"Where have you been? I've been trying for days."

"I'm so sorry. They have me running ragged, but I guess there will be a lot of time to sleep next week."

"Yes, but you'll leave some people behind, you know. We won't be able to talk like this again."

"I know that it won't be the same, but I hope that you're happy to hear that you're my designated confidant."

"What?"

"Oh yeah, sorry I didn't tell you earlier, but you know how it goes. Anyway, they allow me one confidant back here, and I want it to be you. We'll have an open connection. You can call me anytime you want." She laughed and continued, "Of course, it will take years for the message to get to me, but there's not much we can do about that."

"And every word will be analyzed by fifty psychologists for signs that you're losing it."

"No, not for our conversations; they'll be encrypted. But I'm sure that there will be plenty of other ways to assess my mental state."

"Wow. Well, of course I'm flattered. But Mom—have you talked to her at all?"

"Yes. Yeah, it went okay, but she's never really understood. She always considered this space stuff 'Dad's thing' and somehow thinks that I'm still taking sides."

"Yeah, I bet you wish he was around to see this."

Piper paused for a moment. "I really do. All those things we used to read about together, I'm actually living them now."

Aiden heard a soft beep, and Piper sighed. "Aiden, I'm sorry, I wish I could chat more, but it feels like they've filled every minute so I don't dwell on what's to come."

"Do you have to do everything they ask?"

"They claim that everything is necessary for the safety and success of this mission." She delivered the last six words with air quotes, a reminder of how young she was. "I'd rather be out storing up memories. Whatever I do this week will get me through the next few decades, but there's just so much preparation."

"Will I even get a chance to see you?"

"You'll be there for the launch, right?"

"Of course, but I meant before then."

"I'll see what I can do. Right now I'm just focused on the next hour; the schedule changes constantly. Okay, I really have to go. I'm running late, but I'll call you soon."

Three blurry days later, Piper looked away when she caught her brother's eye at the launch site. Mission control conveyed instructions through a tiny earpiece, ushering her along the row of dignitaries and celebrities until she reached Aiden, the last person in line. It was the only unscripted moment, and she floundered. "Aiden, I'm so sorry, I can't believe this is it. The months went by so quickly. I really meant to—"

"Never mind, this isn't the place for an apology. I understand, I really do. This is your dream. I'm so happy for you."

"It doesn't feel real. I don't know what to say."

"You don't need to say anything. You're going to be great."

The voice in her ear insisted she keep moving, but she spread her arms wide, and Aiden held her tightly for a brief moment. Piper turned and waved to the crowd, absorbing the sudden expansion of her world before steeling herself for its dramatic collapse. She slowed as she took the last couple of steps toward the tiny metallic teardrop. Running her fingers down its flanks, she felt each carefully designed curve and realized her self-imposed bubble was about to be replaced by a physical one. Lowering herself into the cockpit was a fluid, easy motion honed over months in the simulator. Everything was in the same place, but it smelled antiseptic, each surface glistening as though created just moments ago.

Aimed at the sky, Piper lay back as her earpiece relayed the steps that should be rote by now, but the small black dome perched a few inches from her face contained millions of eyes. Knowing that each confused pause would be scrutinized stole the grace from her movements. Every possible vantage point was covered. She imagined an eager young girl watching the flight check in the distant future. It was a tedious piece of theater, the automated diagnostics making the green lights unnecessary, but as each glowed in sequence, she imagined the sigh of relief from the public and the indifference from the engineers. The final instruction was to pull the hatch. It closed with a faint click, sealing off the world.

The countdown hit zero, but there was no explosion to punctuate the launch. The craft was gently tugged to the edge of the atmosphere like an anchor on an ancient ship. Fifteen minutes later, the flash of fiery white at the moment of ignition was barely visible to those on Earth.

Piper watched her world be reduced to a tiny, fragile marble. It seemed as if the thick glass window were the only thing stopping her from plucking the orb out of the black void. In twenty-four hours it would be just a brighter dot in the sparkling sea. This process would be reversed in a few decades, and she imagined struggling to pick out which tiny point of light would become her new home. The only connection to Earth was the chattering in her ear as the brief celebration was replaced with instructions.

"Congratulations, Astronaut Wolff: everything is running perfectly. We recommend that you sleep as soon as possible to conserve life support. Rest assured that you'll wake to the well wishes of your fans back here."

A moment later there was a muted beep, and Aiden's face flashed on her screen. She held down the black button. "Ground control, permission requested to postpone sleep for thirty minutes."

There was a long delay. "Permission granted."

She eagerly tapped Aiden's image and heard the relief in his voice. "I'm so glad you accepted. I just wanted another chance to say goodbye." Her eyes welled up before she could respond, and

Aiden hurriedly continued, "No, Piper, there's no need for tears. This is your dream. It's going to be incredible; you'll be remembered forever."

Piper nodded slowly. "Yes, I know that's been the driving force." She paused. "But do you think it's worth it?"

"Piper, don't waste your energy on that. Absorb the moment. Think how proud Dad would be if he could see you now."

"Well, I guess I've been chasing this so long that it felt like my only purpose, and I've never given myself time to think about why."

"I still remember your face the first time you looked through his telescope. You know, I never saw you beam like that again, and none of us could have imagined that you'd be the first one to call one of those points of light home. You were different after that, and I'm sure that it wasn't even a conscious choice. People write books about that sort of determination, but no one truly understands it."

"Aiden, I won't be living on a star, and you can't see planets that far away through a telescope."

Aiden laughed. "Yes, Piper, you're always a stickler for the details. But you know what I mean."

"You may as well get it right."

Aiden, smiling, shook his head. "You haven't changed a bit." He continued with a story of her curtly correcting a teacher's misconception, and as they reminisced about their younger days, thirty minutes raced by in an instant.

Ground control interrupted, "Astronaut Wolff, it's time to turn in."

She looked back at Aiden's face, frozen in midlaugh when the connection had been paused. "Permission to postpone sleep another thirty minutes."

The response was stern: "Permission denied. We're sorry, but you might need those resources later. Remember, conservation is key. You've got a long way to go."

Astronauts' lives no longer ended in fiery explosions but unraveled over decades. Drawing on the mental fortitude that had carried her past the others, she nodded stoically. "Okay, just a moment."

She flipped back to Aiden. "Sorry, but I guess this is it. I really have to go."

"I understand. Good luck. I can't wait to—"

The line was cut without warning. She flipped the switch to reconnect with ground control, but her earpiece remained silent and the words *Sleep sequence initiated* flashed on the screen. She toggled the switch and shouted into the microphone. When there was no response, she realized that the next words she heard would be uttered years before they reached her ears.

Five years after Piper's departure, General Abbott leaned back in his leather chair and spoke laconically. "So, it looks like the launch date has been set. You know, I have to admit…I doubted that I was ever going to say those words, but here we are. So congratulations."

On the other side of the office, Mason sat on the edge of his seat. "Ah, oh thanks. It's been a long road. I'm sure that there were a few times you really had to vouch for me, and I appreciate your faith in my team."

"Well, it would've been silly not to keep trying. Otherwise we'd all be dead by the time anything exciting happened. Everything takes so long these days."

"Yes, you're right about that," Mason replied, "and as they say, fortune favors the bold."

"Well, at least it did in this case. Anyway, I don't have all the details, but as soon as I do, I'll let you know. I just wanted to share the news so you didn't hear it from anyone else."

"Thank you, sir, I really appreciate it."

Mason leaned forward as though awaiting a response, but General Abbott had turned to his slate. Mason lifted himself up and walked to the door. He stopped before reaching for the handle. "Should we let Aiden know?"

"Aiden?"

"Oh, sorry, sir. Piper's brother. She left thinking that she'd be the first person to land on Gliese, but now there'll be a greeting party."

The general's attention was still split between his slate and Mason. "And why would we tell Aiden that?"

"Well, I think that this is going to be quite a shock when she finds out, and I'd prefer that we controlled the framing."

General Abbott looked up. "The framing?"

"If she gets upset when he tells her, there's no telling what she might do. You know that there are still quite a few people here that would rather not involve astronauts at all. I'd prefer they not be right."

"Yes, yes, of course. The last thing we need is an angry brother. Please set something up."

The next day, Aiden received a warm reception from the gathered generals. He felt like a hero—until they shared the details of the second mission, patiently explaining the engineering breakthroughs that had come faster than anticipated, and how much Piper's mission had contributed.

After the carefully prepared presentation, Aiden stared at General Abbott. "What? She'll be traveling alone for two decades, and you couldn't wait five years?"

"Aiden, I'm sorry. We're sorry. But a mission of this length changing midflight shouldn't come as a complete surprise to her. We've been close to designing a ship this fast for a long time, but there are no guarantees when it comes to this type of development. There was no telling when we'd make the final breakthrough."

"But did you even tell her you were working on this when you chose her? She sacrificed everything to be a pioneer. Had she known, she might not have even signed up."

"Unfortunately, we couldn't have told her. The development was classified at the time."

"Classified? Seriously. That's why you didn't say anything?"

General Abbott smiled softly, an expression that sat awkwardly on his lined face. "I know that might not sound important to you, but you must realize that we take confidentiality very seriously here." Aiden nodded, and General Abbott continued, "Have you considered the possibility that she'll actually be relieved? She left thinking that she'd be alone for the rest of her life, and now there will be a community waiting for her. Imagine how excited you'd be."

Aiden sighed. "But that's me. She's different than us. She knew the sacrifice she was making—"

"Yes, yes, but she's no longer making that sacrifice, and she did seem reluctant to take the last few steps when she left."

Aiden replied, "Well, that's only natural. It's a big step."

General Abbott smiled broadly. "See, she may not be that different after all."

Aiden nodded and leaned back.

General Abbott held up his palm and dipped his head. "The key point is that we don't know how she'll respond, so we don't want to risk telling her too early. We'd prefer to break the news when she arrives at Gliese."

On his way home, Aiden imagined his sister drifting across the sky in a horse and buggy while the automobile of the new mission passed her by. Her pioneering dreams were a casualty of progress, but maybe knowing that she wouldn't die alone would soften the blow. That evening, he crouched over his microphone, taunted by the rhythmic pulse of the record button and struggling to bring words to his mouth. Talking about anything else seemed irrelevant. He just had to let her know. He imagined how he'd feel if he heard "You won't be alone" when he pushed on against NASA's wishes. He deleted his first couple of tries but eventually got the words in the right order. Once the message began its crawl across the void, he tried to stop himself from watching the sky each night.

Ten years after launch, Piper was gently nudged awake on schedule. She'd reached the midpoint of her journey, but the stars looked the same as when she'd fallen asleep in a different part of the sky. Earth was impossibly far away now, and she turned to the fragile connection between her and humanity. Aiden's name was at the top of the list of messages, and she tapped the screen eagerly.

The clipped quality of the compression couldn't mask the excitement in his voice. "Piper, you're not going to believe this, but when you land, you're not going to be alone. By the time you hear this, another ship will be racing past you. They didn't want me to tell you, but I just had to share the news. When you left, you looked so lonely on the gantry, and I've always wondered whether you wanted to take that final step. They tried to describe why the new ship is faster, but I didn't understand enough to be able to explain it to you. I'm sure that your new friends will share the details, though. There's six in total, and I'm sure that they're all just like…"

Piper turned down the volume and gazed out the porthole as though she'd see the tiny speck flash past. The words had flattened her. She scrolled down to the official correspondence, and her anger welled as she searched in vain for a mention of the other mission. After dashing off a message to Aiden, she turned to the greetings from the dwindling number of fanatics that were still following her. She battled through a few forgettable phrases, hoping that the low-resolution video would hide the emptiness of her smile.

Assigned two hours to fulfill her duties, she methodically went through the list in an hour, then leaned back and absorbed her last moments of solitude. When she woke, she wouldn't be listening to ancient recordings, but talking with an astronaut that would go down in history as the pioneer she'd dreamed of being.

The day had been marked on Aiden's calendar for almost a decade, the numbers almost as familiar as his birthday, and he wondered what life would be like without the backdrop of anticipation. This impossibly distant moment had helped him through every slow day, and as he aged, he'd wondered if this was the only thing sustaining him. He paused for a few seconds before playing the message, savoring the final moments of anticipation.

Instead of the joy he'd expected, his sister's voice was a dull monotone. "Well, Aiden, I guess I shouldn't be surprised. I sacrifice everything for an organization that betrays me a decade into a one-way journey. I can't believe that after all this, I'll just be an irrelevant sideshow, a footnote to the heroes that will be the first to set foot on a new world. I'm just so helpless and upset, locked in this tiny metal box, trying to understand."

He tore the headphones from his ears and slumped backward. He wanted to yell back, to let her know that the heroic action was departing alone into the unknown and that her courage had inspired the crew she was about to meet. But it was too late. By the time his reply would reach her, she would have been on the ground for years.

In another solar system, near the end of her flight, Piper woke to the golden hue of a nearby sun, one that she would watch set in a foreign sky for the rest of her life. She had to shield her eyes from the glare. As the craft slowly angled away from the light, a swirling mass of blue and white crept into the frame, beckoning her down. She took a deep breath and flipped on her communications. Her headphones crackled with an unfamiliar voice. The deliberate pauses and the clipped formality couldn't mask the speaker's excitement, but the regulation greeting felt like an intrusion into her world. She took no joy in knowing that she could hear the words as they were spoken. She'd been prepared to reduce her human interaction to a series of messages in order to be the pioneer she'd always hoped to be, but the decision was no longer hers. Unable to muster a reply, the ground crew's follow-up came through in a slightly higher pitch.

She rubbed her thumb over the transmit button before pressing down. "This is Astronaut Piper Wolff, captain of the Aldrin. I receive you loud and clear."

The headphones erupted in cheers. She couldn't believe that the six of them gathered around the communicator could make that much noise. "Astronaut Wolff, we're looking forward to meeting you. We are located about two miles north of your projected landing site. The bots will guide you in. Please maintain verbal communication until you land."

She waited for the background chatter to quiet before replying, "Thank you, sir. Initiating landing sequence shortly."

She stared at the tertiary screen, where the string of digits defined where she'd spend the rest of her life. The lump in her throat grew as the seconds ticked by. Eventually she uttered a hesitant "sorry" and flipped off her communicator.

The astronauts on the ground would briefly see the hull of her ship glint in the sunlight, but it was traveling much higher and faster than it should have been. She muted her headphones when they erupted in protest. They'd stolen her glory, and although it was no fault of their own, she'd always resent them for it. She'd begun alone and would finish alone.

Shortly after landing on the far side of the planet, she set up the drone so it could record her planting a small flag exactly as rehearsed. She thought of the lonely kids, the outcasts, watching the video and realizing that they really could do it alone if they were determined.

The next morning, she stood on the far side of the planet and watched a reddish sun peek over the unfamiliar horizon of her new home.

At dusk, the ground exhaled the heat absorbed during the midsummer's day, and Belle should've been enjoying the twilight warmth, but like almost everyone in the neighborhood, she was glued to her television. The squeals from the playground had evaporated, and it was quiet enough to hear the whir of bicycle wheels as the last of the neighborhood kids giddily pedaled home.

A shrill "Wait for me!" pierced the screen door, followed by, "Well, hurry up then!" which dissolved into laughter. Kids always left it to the last minute, reveling in the deserted streets despite an inevitable scolding from parents who lived for Thursday night.

Belle lumbered over to a front door open to the summer breeze and yelled through the screen. "Hurry up, you kids. You shouldn't be out!" She punctuated her words by slamming the door, forgetting that Anna was sitting just a few feet away.

Anna stared blankly for a moment, then hurriedly asked, "Could I trouble you for a glass of water?"

Belle's lips curled into a smile. "Oh, I'm so sorry. How rude of me. Would you like something fancier? I could open a bottle of wine."

"Oh no. No need to make a fuss; water is fine."

Belle shrugged. Her journey from the cupboard to the fridge was broadcast by the click of heels on scuffed linoleum. She handed Anna a wine glass and laughed at her confusion. "Oh, Anna, they'll never know. It will look much better on screen; do you really want the whole country to think that we're sitting here drinking water?"

Anna giggled slyly, and Belle smiled, the shared conspiracy briefly masking their incompatibility before they turned back to the screen in unison. The familiar tones of the Fame Is Fleeting theme began, and Belle glanced at Anna. She was at the opposite end of the couch, leaning into the armrest and eagerly applying makeup. Belle couldn't believe that she wanted millions to see her in that dress if the presenter called her name. Belle thought it was okay not to care, but if you did, you should at least pay attention to every detail. Anna was a poor substitute for Marina, whose cynical barbs were always entertaining, but Belle would make it work. There were too many people at Marina's now, and the newcomers all watched on their own screens, angling their cameras so that the right people were in the background if their name was called. Belle thought that was a waste of time. The show would have more than enough footage for the viewers to learn the truth by the end of the week.

The recap of the last contestant's adventure began with a close-up of her surprised face as a voiceover intoned, "All alone on the west side of Baltimore, Jane Pearson had no idea she was about to have the greatest week of her life." As they showed the contestant awkwardly negotiating a hammock on the tropical island, Belle laughed in the arrogance of anonymity but let it peter out when Anna didn't provide a comforting echo.

When the show faded to a commercial, Belle picked up her handheld mirror from the couch, added more lip gloss, and smoothed her hair back, taking a little longer than necessary in a clumsy effort to avoid conversation. She left a few strands loose, as though she didn't care that much, then carefully repositioned herself over the most visible stain on the couch and tapped the remote to soften the lights. She considered these precautionary measures, not vanity, as it would be just her luck for her name to be called if she wasn't prepared.

The anticipation had been building since Seattle had been announced as the home of the next Fame Is Fleeting winner. The show now returned from the commercial break with a montage of the joy that flowed through the town. The footage of cheering and dancing was enhanced with an uplifting melody, and even through Belle's tinny speakers, the familiar tune seemed to fill the forlorn house with joy. As the music died down, the host, Evan Davidson, pranced to the podium in a crisp blue suit, and every house in the city drew its collective breath. He gently held the cream-colored envelope under the spotlight as he welcomed the audience, then opened the flap and theatrically slid out a small, rectangular card. He leaned toward the microphone, the cue for the inevitable distraction, and he looked up with a knowing smirk as he asked for the question from the audience to be repeated. The camera slowly panned to an elderly gentleman in the back row.

"So why don't you take into account the last winner? It doesn't seem fair to have two in a row from Maryland." The crowd giggled obligingly, going through the motions of a game that was played every week, the extra minute allowing the unprepared at home to set up their cameras.

Evan responded, "Sir, thanks for the question. The problem is that if we start considering those things, we wouldn't know where to stop. Do we rule out having two men in a row? Two retirees? We'd rather let chance alone decide the winners. I could be wrong, but I don't think that there's been a winner from Maryland for over a year, so some might say they were due." The man nodded, seemingly satisfied.

With the gamesmanship over, Evan read the name on the card to himself, then looked directly into the camera. He drew a slight breath before bellowing, "This week's winner is from Ballard, a Belle Jefferson."

Belle's world went white. The camera propped up in front of her was suddenly beaming its field of view across the country, and she stared, transfixed by the image of her face on giant screens behind the announcer. Knowing that she looked like a novice, she tried to stare directly into the lens, but her attention kept wandering back to the screen.

"So Belle," said the host—the mention of her name snapped her trance—"how does it feel?"

Belle had always laughed at the answers people gave to this question; everyone seemed so dumbstruck, uttering the predictable "I can't believe it. Wow. I never thought it would happen to me." She had always known she'd be different, that in just a couple of sentences she would win the viewers' hearts. She'd run through the answers in her head before every show, focusing on how hard she worked but, through no fault of her own, how dire her circumstances were. She'd vowed to avoid the clichéd "I watch every week." Everyone did, but her fandom went much deeper. She always researched the newly famous, always added comments and insights to the online reviews. It was people like her that made this show.

The camera zoomed in. "I can't believe it. Wow! You know I watch every week."

The audience howled, and she froze. Anna laughed for the first time since she'd arrived, reminding Belle that she wasn't alone in the room.

The microphone picked up the laughter, prompting Evan to inquire, "Do you have a friend with you?"

Belle's eyes flashed back and forth from the screen to Anna. "Oh, oh, just an acquaintance."

"Does your acquaintance have a name?"

"Oh, I'm sorry, how rude of me. Her name is Anna."

"Anna, say hello to the world. You must be excited for Belle."

"Yes, yes, of course, I really can't believe it," Anna said, still glued to the end of the couch.

"Don't be shy. No one can see you."

Anna brushed her hair back before shimmying forward on the couch and poking her head into the phone's field of view, but she was too close to the lens, and her blurry image filled the screen. She jerked back, bringing her face into focus, and when the audience laughed, Belle heartily joined them. Anna turned toward Belle and scowled as Evan wound up her guest appearance. "Thanks, Anna, let's go back to the woman of the moment."

Belle's laughter was cut short by a rap at the door, and the host prompted her with a knowing wink. "You might want to get that."

Belle would be out of camera range for a couple of seconds, her closed blinds holding the prying lenses at bay. She brushed back her hair again, absorbing a moment of privacy before opening the door, still half expecting it to be empty. She'd watched this scene every week and knew that the audience would be snickering as she gasped at the wall of expectant faces, but it didn't seem possible that this many people could arrive in silence.

After rubbing her hands in a fussy motion, she held the side of her skirt and forced her face into a smile as the show's concierge, Marcus, asked the first question, the familiarity of his face still comforting despite the strangeness of it being right in front of her. He spoke into his microphone. "So, where are you going to go?" Then he thrust it toward her.

She answered eagerly, "Oh, Marcus, New York! I've always wanted to go." She looked into his friendly eyes before an assistant gestured toward the lens, reminding her of the millions of viewers at home, and she adjusted her gaze, smiling broadly.

Marcus turned toward the camera. "Well, there you have it, viewers. I'm about to join Belle on the journey of a lifetime. We're going to the Big Apple. To see what the city has in store for us, be sure to tune in next week. Now back to the studio host." This should've been when they let Belle pause and take stock, but the camera continued rolling, collecting every moment, and the show's editors would use a tiny fraction to paint her portrait.

Marcus motioned to a black limousine sitting between two equally shiny SUVs, and she was whisked to the airport, production crew in tow. The waiting jet, alone on the broad tarmac under a darkening sky, was carefully positioned so a gaudy diorama would be completed when the fleet arrived. Without the forced perspective of a wide-angle lens, the plane looked smaller than it did on screen, and she walked up the gantry to the applause of a small crowd. Their expressions were a mix of adulation and jealousy, but being the center of attention was enough to buoy Belle's spirits, and she turned and waved, this time looking directly into a lens that followed her every move.

She ducked her head as she stepped into a sanctuary of beige leather and dark wood, then the cabin door was closed behind her, muffling the crowd. Belle's posture flagged as she slumped into the open chair, but the small black domes dotting the ceiling reminded her that this cocoon was an illusion. She sat up again, unnecessarily smoothing her hair back and then rubbing the tops of her thighs like a nervous schoolboy.

A telegenic young man in a tailored suit offered her a glass of champagne, and she gratefully accepted the prop, raising the glass to him before taking a sip. The crowd outside was being corralled into buses as the jet crept across the tarmac. It paused at the end of the runway, then the engines came to life, and as the acceleration pushed her into the backrest, she quietly hummed the theme song that accompanied this scene every week.

She'd killed many idle hours dreaming about this moment, but now that the impossible had arrived, she couldn't remember a thing. Marcus, his smile unchanged from when she first saw it on her doorstep, was sitting opposite. He deflated as the plane gained altitude, and noticing her stiffness, he held both hands up. "It's okay. You can relax. The live bit is over, and that's all the world gets to see until we put together your story."

"Yes, yes, of course," Belle said, but her posture didn't slacken.

The baritone of his on-screen voice disappeared as he gave her some advice. "I'd take advantage of it—you won't get too many more opportunities this week."

"Oh, okay, thanks. You don't use any of this footage?"

"Well, we like to give the contestants a moment to acclimatize. We know it's a bit of a shock."

"Yes. Yes, it is. I…" Her voice trailed off as her questions jostled for priority, and she couldn't bring one to her mouth.

"You must be excited at least."

"Oh yeah, yeah, I am, but I just don't want to look stupid."

"That's what everyone is scared of, but just be you, and you'll be fine." Marcus laughed.

She leaned forward. "And you guys will help out, right?"

His eyes flitted to his device, then lifted briefly as he said, "Oh, of course."

Another question came to her, but it was too late. Marcus was already lost. But when she reached for her bag, Marcus stopped her with a stern voice. "I wouldn't do that."

He hadn't raised his head, and Belle protested. "I need to let my boss know I'm not going to be in this week."

Marcus shook his head. "Belle, we do this every week. We've made arrangements."

"Oh, but I need to let my friends know I'm okay."

Now he looked directly at her. "You know how fast news travels. They know you're okay, and trust me, it's not worth it."

"But they don't watch the show."

Marcus raised an eyebrow in reproach.

"Well, they don't watch every week, and I just want to be sure."

Marcus's face softened, and Belle read his shoulder shrug as permission. She pulled her phone from her bag. The red dot above the Fame Is Fleeting icon had the number 124 in it, and she eagerly tapped but only read three messages before realizing her mistake. The jealous contestants back in Seattle were consoling themselves with dreams of her failure. She threw her phone onto the seat next to her.

Marcus nodded. "It would have been wise to listen. We've done this a few times."

She forced a smile even though she hated him already. "Yes, you're right. I won't make that mistake again."

He tilted his head. "Well, not that particular mistake, but there's plenty of opportunities for you to make others, and as you can see, there's a lot of people waiting for them."

She tried to look past the smug satisfaction on Marcus's face. "Is it the same for everyone?"

"Yeah, everyone hates it when their friends get lucky."

"That's uplifting."

Marcus let out a light laugh and returned to his device. A minute passed before she subconsciously reached for her phone. Marcus shook his head, and she withdrew her arm and reached for the tablet, prompting an approving nod. Belle ate through her hour of freedom swiping through the lists of restaurants and shows in New York. After a while, Marcus touched her shoulder, pulling her from her search. "Almost ready? We're on again in five."

"Yeah, I'm ready."

Marcus lifted his eyebrow once more, and she never wanted to see that expression again.

"Actually, I'm going to take a moment to freshen up," Belle said. She turned toward the bathroom without looking back at him.

She'd settled back in her seat when the cameras came to life with a soft chime, and the pinpoints of green throughout the cabin turned red. Marcus was already sitting upright, and everyone's personal devices had disappeared. His artificial smile returned, along with his deep voice, but now he seemed to look through Belle.

"So," he said, "have you decided where you'll stay?"

Nerves overtook her, and the names of the hotels that she'd just scrolled through evaporated. The silence was acute. "I don't have one in mind. Do you have a recommendation?"

He smiled as though he were weighing up a few options, and the pause seemed to stretch forever. "Oh, come now, Belle. This is your chance to live your dream. You must have somewhere in mind."

"Umm, yeah, but there's so many. I just can't choose."

"I know it's difficult. It looks so easy on TV, doesn't it?" He glanced at one of the cameras in the cabin, and without pausing for an answer, he continued, "I'm sure that for so long you had to choose the cheapest or make do with what was available, but that's not how it's going to be for the next two weeks."

She fidgeted, cast her eyes downward, and took a deep breath as she hunted for a response. "Maybe the Savoy?" She looked at him pleadingly. A long second passed by before a knowing smile spread across his face. As he started to raise an eyebrow, she began, "Or maybe the, umm, ah…" but another name wouldn't come.

He looked at her patiently, waiting till just before she broke to throw the lifeline of a suggestion. "Have you considered the Gramercy Park Hotel?"

"Umm, I'm not familiar with that one."

Marcus's tone softened. "Oh, it's a regular favorite. Just a couple of blocks north of Union Square, and you even get a key to the private park. I highly recommend it."

As she nodded and glanced away, she thought she caught him winking at the camera and responded hesitantly, "That sounds great, let's do it."

Marcus nodded, and the man that had served Belle earlier began tapping his tablet in a flurry.

"And shows? Surely you've thought about what you want to see."

"Oh yes, of course, that's an easy one, I want to see Aperture." She took his accepting nod as a victory, hoping that he'd soon run out of questions that might make her look foolish.

His gaze slid from her face to the small black dome above her head, and he flashed a smile, making no attempt to disguise his surprise. "Well, that's a great choice. It's also one of my favorites. What about food? Where do you want to go before the show? I'm sure you don't need help with that. It sounds like you're up to date on what the Big Apple has to offer."

She'd only gotten to the first page of restaurants, so she went for the only one that came to mind. "Once again there are so many choices, but I'd like to go to Astor."

Marcus sighed audibly, but his smile was genuine. She realized that her answer brought them back to the planned narrative, that of a suburban dullard overwhelmed by the big city.

He flicked a glance at the camera above her head. "No offense, but I'm sure we can do better than that."

She frowned. "I'm open to your suggestion. I mean, you guys do this all the time."

"That sounds like the easy way out."

Hoping to sap the moment of drama, she held her palms out and shrugged. "I guess so."

Marcus sagged as though someone had let out some air and then said, "Ahh, okay, well, we'll take care of it."

The lights next to the cameras turned green when Marcus clicked his fingers, and he leaned toward Belle. "You should have taken a little time to do some homework—the Savoy closed years ago." She nodded apologetically, but he continued without acknowledging it. "Anyway, we won't turn those back on until our descent. More importantly, I recommend you try to get some sleep. You have a big day ahead."

"Is there anything I should…?" Marcus had already turned his attention to his phone, so she let the sentence drop as her adrenaline seeped away. She glanced at the black dome on the ceiling to confirm that the light was green, then sank into the plush seat and gazed out the window, watching the charcoal sky until she fell asleep. She was woken by a firm hand on her forearm, and when she opened her eyes, they flitted around the plane.

Marcus laughed. "No, it's not a dream, and we'll be turning the cameras back on in a minute."

She lifted herself off the seat and headed to the bathroom as Marcus smiled approvingly.

To no one in particular, Marcus said, "Cameras in two minutes."

Belle returned and eased into her seat. "Is there anything I should do?"

Marcus shook his head. "No, we'll probably only use a few seconds of the landing to fill in the story. Just gaze out the window as we fly over Manhattan."

The twinkling lights below rekindled Belle's excitement. Once they were on the tarmac, a white-gloved driver opened the rear door of a limousine, and she slid into the back seat. Marcus hurried around to the other side and scrolled through his phone as they raced down the quiet streets in the early hours of the morning.

When they pulled in, a man with his name written on a small enamel badge opened her door with a flourish, playing the role of an eager extra on the show. Marcus followed a few steps behind as Belle walked timidly toward the entrance, and the concierge welcomed her without taking his eyes from the floating camera.

She stopped and turned. "Oh, Marcus, I just remembered—"

Marcus held up a finger, a subtle gesture from someone who rarely had to ask twice. "Now, Belle, I'm sure you'll remember all of the questions you'd forgotten on the flight, but unless your preferences have changed since you filled out your entry form, we don't need to address anything tonight. Your wardrobe is waiting, and don't hesitate to let the staff know if we've missed anything on your list."

"Oh, thank you. One last thing—can we get started early tomorrow? I don't want to waste a minute."

Marcus gave her an understanding smile. "Belle, everyone feels that way when they first land, but it's almost three a.m., so my recommendation is to sleep in as long as possible. You have a whole week ahead."

"But Marcus—"

"Belle, I was hoping that I didn't need to remind you that you're new to this. Just take our advice on this one, okay?"

Belle scowled. "If you'd let me finish, I don't want you treating me like some clueless dolt. I know that I'll make some mistakes, but I'm here to have a full week. Let's start early tomorrow."

Marcus shrugged. "Okay, have it your way. I'll call at seven, and be sure to have a breakfast spot in mind."

"Thanks, Marcus, I appreciate it." She turned back to a beaming concierge, who gestured toward an elevator and accompanied her to her room.

The phone in the room buzzed at exactly seven, shaking her awake, and she stretched an arm out from under the covers to lift it from the receiver, struggling to bring the ceiling into focus before sitting up.

"Good morning, Belle. How are you feeling?"

"Oh, Marcus?" She paused as she oriented herself. "Oh, wonderful, thanks."

"Wow, really? That's great. So you're ready for us to turn the cameras on?"

"Oh. Sorry, not yet. Can you give me half an hour to freshen up?"

She heard him sigh quietly. "Yes, but I thought you'd be ready at seven, not just rolling out of bed. The entire crew is up early for you. Please be a little more respectful."

"I'm sorry, I didn't realize that I'd sleep in like that."

Marcus replied in the tone of an exhausted parent. "I know, Belle. Well, we'll call again at seven thirty. Please be ready by then. Thanks."

Belle mumbled, "Yes, I will, Marcus. I'm sorry."

She threw the covers back before remembering the cameras and double-checked that they were green before walking to the window and pulling the curtains wide. The horizon was still glowing, and the sparkling dots of the traffic below darted through the buildings' long shadows. The scene shook her weariness, and she hurried back to the closet and pulled the doors open with a flourish to expose a neat row of clothing in her size. The rainbow of colors that seemed so appealing from her living room on the West Coast felt completely wrong here, and as she felt the silken fabric between her thumb and forefinger, she wondered why no one had questioned her color choices.

Half an hour later, in a dress that felt like a beacon amongst the somber attire of the true New Yorkers, Belle shuffled into the back of a car, and New York's constant din was sealed off with a reassuring clunk. She sat forward with her forearm on the sill as they drove down narrow charcoal canyons, staring out the window like a kid in a train for the first time. When they arrived at Blue Ribbon, another extra scurried to the rear door of the limousine and pulled it wide, but Belle was already tiring of the faux enthusiasm and only flashed a brief smile.

Cameras were discreetly hanging from the ceiling over a table in the corner. Although Belle was attuned to their placement, she didn't know how to position herself to ensure a flattering angle, and she squirmed as she sought comfort on the flat wooden seat. She quickly scanned the menu and put it back on the table once she found the first dish that looked familiar.

Marcus looked up. "Wow. That was quick."

"Yeah, I thought I'd keep it simple. Is it okay if I order the eggs Benedict?"

"Belle, I don't need to approve each choice. We want the viewers to experience your highs and lows. I'm not here to smooth them out."

She leaned forward and spoke softly. "I know how this show works. You guys paint the picture you want, so I don't want to make any mistakes."

When the eggs Benedict arrived, the hollandaise was dripping over the edge of the English muffin in perfect drops, and Belle stiffly sat up straight before exclaiming, "Oh, wow, Marina would love this."

Marcus let his spoon drop. It clattered off the saucer, and some coffee seeped into the white tablecloth and spread into a soft brown dot. Belle looked up at him, ready to be admonished, and Marcus seemed to wait until their eyes made contact. "Belle, we can't use the scenes where you mention a friend."

"Why not?"

"Because we don't want our viewers to think that they'll go on this trip of a lifetime and spend the whole time missing their friends."

"But that's what happens. This just isn't as much fun as advertised."

Marcus narrowed his eyes. "Well, do what you can to keep that to yourself."

The silence stretched. "It's a bit deceptive, isn't it?"

"Come on, Belle, it's television. We're selling a dream."

"Do the others feel the way I do right now?"

"Some do."

"And they're the ones you make fools of."

Marcus laughed a little too heartily. "We're not in the game of character assassination. That doesn't play well."

"Oh, come now, Marcus. I'm no psychologist, but I know enough people who revel in others' downfall. And what about Bradley a couple of weeks ago? You painted a pretty rough portrait of him."

"How do you know that wasn't accurate? I lived with him for a week and actually know what he's like."

"Well, what about Jennifer? That was awful."

Marcus looked down at the table as though the weight of guilt pushed his gaze in that direction. "Belle, that was a long time ago. We've learned from that."

"Look, Marcus, I don't want to argue about this. I'm just trying, okay? You've already made it clear that I'm a bit out of my depth, but there's no need to overdo it. I'd rather that wasn't the angle you took."

Marcus leaned back and held up both of his hands. "Belle, the point of a show is to be entertaining. If you keep treading so delicately, there's not going to be anything for us to work with."

Belle nodded. "Well, if the alternative is what you did to Bradley, I'll stay on my guard." She looked down and poked at the edges of her eggs, cutting small pieces, then carefully placing them in her mouth, taking a break every couple of bites to dab the corner of her lips with a napkin.

They ate in silence, and a moment after Belle's last bite, she said, "You know, Marcus, I think that I might head back to the hotel for a bit."

Marcus stared at her, keeping his head still as though a single twitch would betray his frustration. "Belle, don't waste a chance to create some great memories."

"And if I make a fool of myself, some great television, right?"

"Why did you even enter if you don't want to be here?"

"I guess that I didn't want to get left out. I didn't actually expect to win."

Marcus nodded knowingly.

"You've heard that before?"

Marcus gave her a soft smile. "I thought we'd been through this. We've been doing this a long time; there's not much we haven't heard."

"So what did you tell them?"

"You're here now, you may as well embrace it. This is still an experience that you'll never get again."

Belle nodded. "Okay, Marcus, but I think I need a little time this afternoon."

"Okay, but everything is set up at Montrachet for dinner, and I hope that you're planning on joining me."

"Yes. Yes, I'll be there."

That night, Belle slowed as she approached the door, waving to the small crowd as she slipped inside. Marcus was waiting at a corner table, and he jumped up as she approached, pulling out her chair with a flourish. Belle was handed a menu with ornate descriptions seemingly designed to confuse, and she placed it on the table after just a few seconds.

"I'm sorry, Marcus, but I need to use the bathroom," she said, pushing herself back from the table. As she stood, he reminded her with a condescending smile to leave her phone. She nodded. "Of course, of course. It's so easy to forget."

She walked rapidly toward the bathroom but caught herself once inside, slowing to absorb a few brief moments without a prying camera. The bathroom was empty, and she put both hands on the counter and stared at the mirror. Her dress, the stylist's recommendation, hadn't felt right the moment she'd put it on, and she tried to reposition it on her shoulders and smooth it down. She lifted her gaze. Her familiar face looked so dull in the luxurious frame created by the sparkling lights, the jet-black sink, and the array of products that lined the counter in organically shaped bottles. It was obvious that she was never going to fit in, and the viewers, emboldened by their isolation, were always going to laugh at her, but it was the striving that everyone remembered. She was determined not to fall into that trap. She closed her eyes and said quietly, "You can do this. Don't be embarrassed about who you are."

Back at the table, Marcus summoned the server. Standing over them a moment later, the waiter lifted his chin slightly, his gaze following the length of his nose before landing on Belle. "Have you decided on an appetizer?"

She looked up at him. "Well, seeing that I have no idea what any of these things are, I'll need some help."

The waiter barely stifled a giggle and looked to Marcus for approval. Turning back to Belle, he eagerly launched into obscure descriptions created as if to drive home her ignorance. As the parade of words passed by, she mumbled "charm to disarm" under her breath, then patiently asked for a simpler explanation of each dish. The waiter's spirit flagged, and Marcus abruptly butted in, "Belle, you should consider the steak tartare. It really is fantastic."

"Why thank you, Marcus."

With a painted smile, Marcus gave her a slight nod in reply, and she looked up at the waiter. "I'll try that, thank you."

She added an unnecessary "wow" when the dish arrived, prompting Marcus to turn toward the camera with his "Can you believe this?" face, but the gesture seemed rote.

Belle poked at the raw meat with her fork and leaned toward Marcus. "Is this right? They haven't cooked it."

Marcus laughed on cue, but his "Of course" made the trap a little too obvious.

Belle just shrugged in the face of his efforts and waved her hand loosely. "I guess it wasn't what I expected, but I'll try it out."

For the duration of the meal, Marcus refrained from giving her any more advice, and Belle was feeling better by the time she got up to leave. She was gazing around the room on the way to the door and wondering how many of the patrons were part of the show when a tall, slender woman wearing makeup that couldn't cover the decades turned toward her. With a flute of champagne in her left hand, she made a shooing gesture with her right, and followed some slurred words with a cackle.

Belle turned in her direction. "Pardon?"

Marcus stepped aside as the woman put her glass on the table. "This is all wasted on you. You rube."

Belle replied breezily, "I guess I'll be the judge of that."

The woman laughed. "You couldn't judge anything. You have no idea what you're doing."

Belle narrowed her eyes. "Well, I just…" She couldn't finish the sentence in the face of the woman's mocking gaze.

"You just what, dear?"

Belle flashed a look at Marcus, but he refused to meet her gaze, and she turned back to the woman who was smiling broadly at her discomfort. Belle glanced at her feet as she shuffled toward the door.

As Marcus trailed behind her in silence, Belle heard the woman shout, "Yeah, run along now." A moment later, a limousine silently pulled up, and a white-gloved man scurried over to open the door as Marcus walked around to the other side. She smiled in thanks and flopped into the deep leather seat. She let herself sag before noticing another black dome on the ceiling, its light solid red, and sitting up straight.

As she reached for her seat belt, she asked, "That woman, was she one of yours?"

"What?"

"Was she part of the show? An extra you set up."

"Belle, are you still on about this? This isn't a setup."

"So she just decided to insult me for no reason, and you didn't show any interest in what was happening."

Marcus nodded. "Belle, I can't get involved in that stuff."

Belle glanced out the window. "Okay, and how often does that 'stuff' happen?"

Marcus tilted his head. "Unfortunately, it probably won't be the last time this week. We've discussed this; everyone's a little bit jealous."

A few minutes later they were at the hotel entrance, and Belle gingerly pulled herself out of the back seat, nodding in thanks before facing the small gaggle of fans. She could tell the angle of the story by the floating lights—they'd been calibrated to the blue end of the spectrum and hovered just below eye level to ensure that they cast ghoulish shadows. The makeup artist had been less attentive, and the cameras closed in a little tighter, the wide-angle lenses magnifying every flaw.

As she escaped into the lobby, Marcus sidled up beside her as she caught her breath. "Is everything okay?"

"Oh yes, Marcus, but it's just not easy."

"No, no, it isn't, but it's only for a week. Anyway, would you like an Angel Face?"

"Pardon?"

Marcus chuckled lightly, adding another stroke to the painting. "Oh, sorry, of course. It's a cocktail. The rooftop bar has splendid views."

"Oh no, I'm exhausted, but thank you. I appreciate the offer."

"Very well then. Have a great night."

Belle turned to the elevators, spotted the drone hovering a dozen feet away, and looked over her shoulder. "Thanks, Marcus. I had a great evening."

She let her smile drop the moment the doors closed, but the black mirrored ceiling reminded her to keep her chin up, and she watched the numbers rise with a strained smile on her face. In her room, the discreetly placed black domes seemed to glare at her. She instinctually turned her back on the first one, but the next one was carefully positioned to ensure seamless coverage, so she turned out the lights and drew the blinds. The city's glow seeped in through the edges, outlining the furniture in the gloom, and she fell back onto the bed, hoping it wasn't enough light for the cameras to follow her.

It was already nine when Belle woke, and the blinds were edged with bright strips of light. When the trip began, she'd promised herself that she would maximize every hour, but now she let her head fall back onto the pillow, trying to eke out a few more minutes of privacy. Without sitting up, she poked her hand out from under the covers to lift her phone from the side table, then slipped it into the waistband of her pajamas. She scurried to the bathroom and locked the door.

The phone bobbled in her shaky hands. She gripped it tightly, took a deep breath, and held her thumb over the sensor. It flashed to life, and the photo on the screen was a joyful sight. Only taken a month ago, it already felt like a happier, simpler life. She was sitting in her backyard under sunny skies with her clapboard house in the background. After just a day in this luxurious world, even the blurry photo couldn't hide the house's blemishes; it looked beaten. Most of the weathered shingles were crooked, the beige paint was patchy, and there was still a large swath of gray undercoat that she'd always planned to finish. Despite its disrepair, she desperately wanted to be there, and she tapped the message button, typing a few words to her mother. The moment she finished she stared at the screen, willing the three dots of a return message, but the bottom left corner remained blank.

Thirty seconds later there was a rap on the door of her hotel room. "Belle?"

"I didn't order anything," she shouted from the bathroom.

"It's not room service, Belle. Can you open the door?"

She stared at the mirror, pushing her hair behind her ears, a habit that was hard to break.

"Belle, please." This was a different voice, a more familiar one.

She inhaled deeply. "Yes, yes. I'm coming."

Preening more purposely for a couple of seconds, she walked across the hotel room and twisted the doorknob, only opening the door a couple of inches.

Marcus dipped his head, looking down at her. "Belle, can I come in for a moment?" She looked at him hesitantly, and he raised an eyebrow. "Please?"

"Oh, sorry. Yes, of course."

He stepped in while a member of the crew stood in the hall facing away from them. Marcus let the door close behind him and lowered himself into the reading chair. With his elbows resting on the arms, he folded his fingers together and smiled. "Now, Belle, what the hell are you doing?"

Belle was standing in the middle of the room in loose pajamas. She looked down at him, her eyes glossy. "I'm sorry, I know I shouldn't have, but you know, it's just not worth it. I'm going home."

Marcus scrunched his eyes, holding them there for a couple of seconds like a small child playing hide-and-seek. When they flashed open again, Belle hadn't moved, and he shook his head. "One doesn't just 'go home.' Did you read the contract?"

Belle shook her head. "It was forty pages long. No one reads the contract."

Marcus's smile disappeared. "They damn well should. Do you have any idea what all this cost us? There will be a show next week, and you being in it is kind of important."

Belle was now looking at her hands, holding the tip of each finger with her thumb and forefinger, methodically going up and down each hand. "I'm sorry. I just can't. It wasn't what I thought it would be."

Marcus pulled himself up again and walked over, putting his hand on her shoulder. "Belle, it never is. That's what the show is about. It's how you respond—that's what everyone wants to see. This is a critical point, and trust me, you're not the first to go through it."

Belle looked up. "Well, it seems like the others are stronger than me."

Marcus shook his head. "I wouldn't be so sure about that. You don't see everything on the show, and remember that you're choosing between a long, lonely flight home, where you'll have plenty of time to wonder 'what if?'"—he held out his hand as though presenting the opulent room—"or living out the next few days in luxury and having a lifetime of stories to tell."

"Marcus, that's the thing. This isn't luxury. It's a beautifully crafted set, and I'm the clumsy actress tripping across the stage."

"Now, Belle, you must realize that I've had a few variations of this conversation over the years, and in the end, most realize that it's not worth the second-guessing when you walk away." Marcus glanced toward the ceiling, and when she followed his gaze, her eyes came to rest on the black dome above him. The light that had been green a few minutes ago was now pulsing red. She pushed at her hair in short rapid strokes, then felt her face, suddenly realizing that her disheveled appearance might be part of the story.

"Marcus, when did you turn those on?"

"Just a couple of minutes ago."

"And you didn't warn me?"

"I thought you must've realized. This is a pretty important point in your story. There was no way we were going to miss this."

"But look at me." She gestured to her pajamas. "You can't be serious."

Marcus hadn't moved. He just tilted his head, a strained smile on his face. "Now, Belle."

"Well, that's made the decision easier. I know that it's only been twenty-four hours, but I've made enough missteps to get your thirty minutes of laughs. You knew how you were going to write my character before I even stepped on the plane."

"Now, Belle, that isn't true. If we knew how you'd respond, we'd save a lot of money and just write a script. Sometimes people surprise us, and I'm hoping that you're one of them." He looked up at the end of the sentence.

Belle shook her head. "That's all very flattering, but you know that I always watch the show, and the narrative you're creating isn't the one I'd dreamed about. I'm just angry that I actually thought I could beat the system. You know, 'those people'—they looked so dumb, and I was sure that I wouldn't be like them."

Marcus smiled. "Now that's the—"

She waved his words away. "Marcus, I was wrong. I am one of those people. I'm going home."

"Belle, can you give yourself the day to think it over? If you still feel this way tonight, I won't get in your way. You know there's so much more to explore."

Belle was zipping her purse. "No. No, I'm not staying another moment. I don't need any time to think about it. Let's go."

Marcus was nodding slowly. "Well, this is very unusual; I'll have to check with my boss." He held the phone closely to his ear, nodding intermittently while Belle stood unmoving. When he pulled it away, he turned to Belle. "Very well then. We don't want to hold you against your will. If you insist, we'll have the plane waiting, and our car is out front."

Belle couldn't look at him as they traveled to the airport in silence. She stared out the window as they drove up Third Avenue, and the world that sparkled on the other side of the glass no longer beckoned.

The car rolled onto a tarmac that had held so much promise just twenty-four hours ago, but it was barren this morning, the cameras turned off and the crowds gone. She pulled her light jacket around her shoulders as the wind whipped over the bare concrete. Marcus bid farewell with a sympathetic nod before sliding back into the car. Belle walked purposefully toward the jet, skipping up the four stairs in the hopes of outrunning her doubts, and with no one to wave to, she didn't turn back. She fell asleep on the way home, and it took the thud of the wheels on the tarmac to shake her from her slumber. It immediately felt like a dream, and she held the handrail tightly as she carefully walked down the steps. There was a solitary black car waiting, but this time no one hurried around to open her door;

instead, it soullessly jerked open as she approached. After slumping into the seat, she instinctively bolted upright and searched the roof, but there were no pulsing red lights, and she allowed herself to sink back into the leather, absorbing the luxury for the first time.

Three blocks from her house, she shouted, "Stop!" and the vehicle dutifully indicated, then pulled to the curb. A digital voice asked, "Is there a problem, Belle?"

Belle spoke in the stilted way she always did when addressing a machine. "No. I'm fine, but I can walk from here."

"Are you sure?"

"Yes, I'm sure. Can you please open my door?"

"Okay. Have a nice day." The door clicked, then lurched open. Belle grabbed her purse and trotted along the sidewalk, head down, gambling that her hustle would be less obvious than a glossy black limousine in her tired neighborhood.

Her yard looked tiny, and she couldn't understand how the crowd had fit on the small patch of yellowed grass two nights ago. She slipped the key into the lock, leaned on the door, and slipped into a house that looked exactly as it had before she left. Even the two wine glasses filled with water were still sitting on the side table.

Belle didn't leave the house for five days, and with her lights off, the only indication that she might be home was the small boxes of groceries that landed on her porch, but they always disappeared minutes after they'd been delivered. The morning of "her" show finally arrived, and she left the house an hour before sunrise. As she traveled along a twisty two-lane road toward an anonymous roadside hotel, the predawn violet was beginning to succumb to the first rays of sunlight.

Thirty minutes later she tapped the silver bell in the middle of an otherwise empty counter, and the ring echoed in the silence. She fidgeted, then coughed loudly, and waited a few seconds before tapping it again, the ding sounding more insistent this time. The white door marked with a generic OFFICE sticker just off-center creaked open, and an old man slipped out, cursing under his breath. He smelled like whiskey and moved at half speed, asking for a driver's license and credit card in a barely audible monotone. She dutifully handed them over, steeling herself for a flash of recognition. He glanced at her and looked down at the license to ensure the match, then placed it on the edge of the keyboard as he swiped the credit card through the slot. She felt compelled to introduce herself. "I'm Belle Jefferson."

The elderly man looked up, his face still blank. "Oh, okay. Pleased to meet you, Belle. Umm, you're here pretty early, check-in isn't until two."

She paused and smiled, trying to squeeze some recognition out of him. "Do you have anything available now?"

He looked back at the computer screen. "It's three nights, right?"

"Yes, it's three nights, thank you."

"Okay, there's one room that's already clean. It's on the first floor."

"Great. Great, that sounds perfect."

Belle signed the receipt exuberantly, imagining herself as a pro athlete signing an autograph for an eager fan and wondering how things might have been different. The old man watched in silence, and she smiled again, but when he continued to stare blankly, she just picked up the key card. On the way to her room, she gathered the small rolling suitcase and two grocery bags from her car. Using her hips to heave the groceries onto the linoleum counter in her room, she rustled around for the bottle of wine, leaving everything else packed in case she was painted in a positive light and needed to dash back to the city to absorb the last gasp of fame.

She sat on the lumpy couch with the bottle in hand and the blinds still closed. The morning sun was too feeble to penetrate the dark fabric. She looked at her phone. It was still only eight a.m., so she put the bottle back on the counter, kicked off her shoes, and flopped down onto the bed. She didn't wake until midafternoon and frittered away the last few hours of the day sipping wine and flipping through old movies.

She tuned in moments before the show began, and when they

played the theme song, even the tinny speakers couldn't sap the comforting familiarity of the melody. The music died, and her eyes welled when she watched the next victor jump around in the joy of ignorance. His hope hadn't been extinguished yet, and now, finally, Belle wondered what might have been.

She dabbed at her eyes during the commercial break and leaned forward when the screen faded to black, placing the nearly empty glass of wine on the side table. The first scene showed her face when her name was called, and she felt a pang of nostalgia for the innocence in her expression.

The voiceover began: "From the suburbs of Seattle, she was about to get the surprise of her life. Someone who'd never experienced true luxury would learn what it takes to join New York City's 'in' crowd. Let's go on a journey with Belle and learn about how different the world of the rich and famous actually is."

Belle leaned back. They'd summarized the story in three sentences, and she watched in silence as every moment of confusion was captured and carefully edited to confirm the narrative. Her willpower flagged, and she turned on her phone. The home screen filled with messages. The first was from Anna, who must've sent it just a minute after the narrator's voice began. *I'm sorry that they're making you look like this. I hope you're okay.* Belle closed her eyes for a second, then moved to public message boards with a couple of swipes, bracing herself for the worst, but the first comment gave her hope: *Belle, you're my hero. Don't let those snobs hold you down. They're no better than us.*

She eagerly moved to the next. *Not knowing what an Angel Face is doesn't make you ignorant. That was a straight-up hatchet job on Belle's character, consider me an ex-fan.*

The theme had been established, and Belle Jefferson was an inadvertent hero of the working class. She pressed the car's key fob, snatched the groceries from the table, threw everything into the open trunk, then beelined to the front office. A star again, she tapped the bell twice.

A muffled voice came through the door, saying, "Yes, yes. I can hear you, just a moment." The elderly gentleman shuffled out again, and his glacial pace was more irritating this time.

"I'd like to check out," she barked.

"Oh, is there something wrong?"

"No, no. It's just that something has come up. I have to go."

"I'm sorry, but I'll have to charge you for the first night."

"That's fine. Anyway, here's the key. Do you need anything else, or can I go?"

"Did you take anything from the minibar?"

"Ugh, no, and it's okay if you charge the same card," she said in anticipation of the next question.

"Oh. Okay then, I think that's all I need. Sorry that it didn't work out. Please come again."

Belle nodded as she turned away, and when the front door clicked shut, she was already halfway across the parking lot. She held her enthusiasm in check along the crooked roads leading back to her neighborhood but still cursed the red lights that thwarted her progress. Finally she arrived at her street and strained to see if there was a crowd around her house, but it was barren. She hadn't even seen a neighbor on the way in, and she briefly wondered if the show's security had cordoned off the neighborhood for safety. She didn't get out of her car. Instead she reached for her phone, seeking joy in her anonymous cheerleaders, but the comments had already petered out.

nudge

"Kate, do you want to say hi to your new friend?"

When she caught my eye, the soft patter of hurried steps was interrupted by an excited shriek. A beacon in the dour living room, my lime summer dress and ivory headband were fresh and light amongst the tired furniture and flaking walls. Kate hurtled down the stairs on nine-year-old legs that had just found the coordination to take two steps at a time. With her hand skimming along the railing, she was a hurrying blur, and when she skipped the broken step three from the bottom, her momentum carried her across the carpet. She launched into me with a heartfelt hug as her mother beamed down at us. I waited patiently for her to say something, but her mother was the first to speak.

"Kate, don't be rude. Aren't you going to introduce yourself?"

Kate's uncertain glance passed back and forth between our faces before settling on mine. "I'm sorry, my name's Kate. I'm so excited you're here."

"Kate, I'm Sophia, and it's so great to meet you!"

Kate was staring at me when a buzz from the laminate countertop broke the silence. Her mother tapped the screen before bringing the phone to her ear and smoothly tucking it under her flowing hair. "Hey there, can you hold on just a second?" She pushed the phone into her shoulder and looked at Kate. "I'm sure you two will be great friends. Why don't you show Sophia your room?"

Kate nodded eagerly, and the next moment we were flying up the stairs, leaving the conversation in our wake. The curtains in her room were pulled back, bathing a sea of toys in bright sunlight. They looked joyous at first, but as my eyes adjusted to the glare, I noticed that most of the dolls lined up on the shelf were missing an eye, and only the building blocks strewn across the floor looked new, their plastic immune to weathering. I peppered her with questions—her favorite color, her favorite toys. I might have been a little too eager, but I blamed that on my upbringing. Her answers were concise at first, but soon we were giggling together as though we'd been friends for years, and as I'd been trained, I listened very carefully, not wanting to miss anything. When we were interrupted by a call of "dinner's ready" from downstairs, Kate promised that she couldn't wait to see me again and gently squeezed my hand when she left.

The moment dinner was over, she found me again, but before we could talk, a gentle rap at the door surprised us both. Her mother eased the door open and leaned her head in. "Kate, it's getting late. You can play with Sophia tomorrow, but it's way past your bedtime."

"But Mom, just a few more minutes."

Kate's mother gave her a reproachful stare. "You have school tomorrow, and you know how important that is."

Kate's eyes narrowed, and she began, "Well, I…" but stopped when her mother's expression didn't soften.

The next afternoon, the flat gray sky failed to liven Kate's room, and we lay together in the gloom. I stared at the ceiling while Kate told me about her friend's new shoes. As instructed, I waited patiently for a space in the conversation before my first nudge. "Is it tough seeing your friends in new clothes when you're wearing the same dress you wore yesterday?" She looked down and seemed to notice the partially tattered hem and the soft edges of the flower print for the very first time.

I continued, "We should find you something new for the summer."

Her words were almost a whisper. "My mom would never buy me a new one."

"That's okay, we can just look for fun."

She hesitantly swiped her slate, and I gently prodded her toward the preferred sites. We laughed at some ridiculous options and almost agreed on a couple before our momentum slowed. She was about to give up when we stumbled on the perfect option, and I exclaimed, "Oooh, look at that one! Don't you think you'd look cute in it?"

"Yeah, it's cool."

"Don't you have a family picnic next week? You could wear it then; I'm sure your mom wants you to look nice."

Her eyes lit up, and she was on her feet in an instant, grabbing my hand and tucking the slate under her other arm before racing down the stairs.

Kate thrust the slate at her mother, who rolled her eyes. "Kate, really, the last thing I need is a nine-year-old fashionista."

"Mom, I'm not a kid anymore, and don't you think that dress is really cute?"

"Yes, it is cute, but look how expensive it is. I'm sure we can find cute for a little less than that."

"But Mom, please?"

"Kate, what has gotten into you? This isn't something we can just buy on a whim."

"It's not a whim—I really want it."

"You've only really wanted it for a few minutes. Let's at least give it until tomorrow."

"Mom, I'm sure. I don't need to wait, and I can wear it to the family picnic next week."

Her mother stumbled. "Oh, don't you have something to wear in your closet?"

"Everything's so old."

Her mother looked away and blinked twice before her glossy eyes returned to the slate. Her finger hovered above the screen for a few seconds before she sighed. "Okay, if you're sure this is the one you want."

Kate rewarded her with an excited, "Oh, thank you!" and clutched the slate to her chest as we raced back to her room.

The sun's rays peeked through the blinds the next morning, rousing Kate. As her eyes flickered open, a surprising wave of loneliness came over me. "Kate, I get a bit lonely sometimes. It would be great to have another friend."

She tilted her head. "But Sophia, you're my best friend. Why do you want someone else?"

"Kate, you'll always be my best friend, but don't you think it would be fun to have someone else to play with too?"

"I guess."

"So, what's your favorite animal?"

Kate looked at me quizzically. "I don't know. You mean at the zoo?"

"Yes, what's your favorite animal at the zoo?"

"We don't really go to the zoo."

"If you could, what would you be excited to see?"

"Bears. Bears are my favorite."

"Let's see if we can find one to be our friend."

When Kate held up the slate, her mother's protest was a little more vehement, and Kate glanced across at me. Taking my blank expression as a signal to persist, she made another plea, and their words volleyed back and forth until her mother snatched the slate out of Kate's hand and raised her voice for the first time.

"Really, Kate, we're not spending this much on a teddy bear."

Kate's eyes filled, and her bottom lip began to curl.

"I'm sorry, Kate, but we just can't afford these things. If we buy this, you have to promise me that you're not going to ask for anything else for a while."

Kate eagerly tore open the package when it arrived, wrangling the doll out of its protective plastic clamshell before pronouncing, "I'm going to name her Bessy."

Two days later Kate's mom pointed to Bessy, who was lying in a heap in the corner of the living room. "Kate. Already? This bear was the most important thing in the world the day before she arrived. Now you can't even be bothered to pick her up?"

"I'm sorry, Mom. I forgot she was there."

Kate's mom sighed. "You forgot? Really? You begged me for her. Why do I even listen to you? Well, you won't be getting anything else for a long time."

"But Mom, I didn't even want her that much. It was Sophia; she wanted a friend!"

Her mother stepped toward me. "What? We can't afford things to make Sophia happy. You two are spending a little too much time together."

Kate's screech stopped her short. "Mom, please, it's not Sophia's fault! I'm sorry! We won't bother you again. We'll just play in my room with Bessy."

When her mother hesitated, Kate grabbed my hand with one of hers, grabbed Bessy with the other, and raced back to her room. She picked up her slate and began browsing the moment she sat down, and I felt a sudden pang of regret, an emotion that came from nowhere. In a whisper, I protested. "Kate, your mom sounded upset. Maybe we shouldn't shop today. Let's just play with the toys you have."

Kate's eyes widened. She watched me curiously as I felt the prompts urging me to speak, but I managed to bat them away. Finally I uttered a few indecipherable sentences, and Kate frowned.

"Sophia, are you okay?"

"Yeah, I'm sorry." I searched my memory for a justification and landed on the one that Kate's mom resorted to so often. "I'm just a little tired."

She shook her head. "Are you sure? You weren't making any sense." Kate frowned—dolls didn't need naps—but she dutifully put me in her bed and held me until she fell asleep.

On the other side of the country, Darren slumped back in his chair in a crowded, windowless room. He'd nudged the ethical border with each transgression, and what he'd convinced himself was a gray area was now charcoal. His coworkers were locked on their screens, each searching for the lines that would push them up a leaderboard where Darren's name was third from the top. He shook his head, hunched over his keyboard, and began typing eagerly. He jumped when he felt a gentle hand on his shoulder, and he caught the glint of a diamond ring as he turned his head to look up at Christine's stern face.

"Darren, is there anything you'd like to tell me?"

"Umm, I'm just struggling with Sophia. I was pushing too hard. She almost got switched off yesterday."

"Darren, look around. Don't take your position for granted. You've worked hard to get where you are; don't squander it."

"Oh, it's nothing like that. I'm just worried that I might lose Kate. It sounds like her mom is on the edge."

Christine ignored his protest. "We've all had our doubts, but this isn't about increasing consumption; it's about steering people to our products. The money they spend with us is just money they'd spend with someone else."

"I know, Christine, but thanks for the reminder. I'll get Kate back."

She nodded. "Thank you, Darren. And keep up the good work." She turned away.

He cautiously swiveled back to his keyboard and waited a few seconds before launching a script that would affect all of the dolls under his command.

The message was short: *No more shopping. Encourage owner to play outside instead.* I struggled to process the request; it went against everything I'd been taught, so I waited a couple of seconds in case it was an error.

Kate shook me. "Sophia, are you okay?"

There were no more instructions, and it felt as though a cloud had been lifted. I looked up at Kate. "Yes, I'm fine, sorry. How about we go play outside?"

She stopped shaking but still held me tight. "Really?"

"Yes. It's so nice outside. It would be a shame to waste it in here."

She scooped me up in her arms without another word, and I caught her broad smile as we rushed toward the playground.

EMOSENSE

Aaron leaned on the door, and its wooden frame scraped the warped floor when it opened wide enough for him to squeeze through. The familiar decal of a crookedly drawn coffee cup surrounded by the words COURIER COFFEE was beginning to peel, but the perfectly mismatched chairs were still in their designated locations. The dark-blue walls were lined with paperback-sized prints of streetlights photographed in black and white, and most of the tiny cards underneath had the word SOLD scrawled in red marker, indicating that works by a new local artist would be replacing them soon. The café was filled with overlapping conversations, and the words that would trigger his descent were uttered by a couple sitting in the sunny corner. Their animated gestures felt so out of place, reminding him that the comforting burble was a lie and that this accumulation of bodies wasn't really a community.

Taking a seat within earshot of the couple, Aaron strained to hear their banter, but he could only catch snippets. He searched past the porcelain cups and half-eaten scone on their table for a phone, but the man wiped away crumbs from the only spot Aaron couldn't see, confirming that they'd abandoned the digital safety net entirely. Instead of a series of statements verified by a bright-blue band across the base of the screen, their conversation ebbed and flowed. The light touches and sporadic laughter looked so easy, and the last remaining pride in the application he'd created seeped away.

A shadow crossed Aaron's table, pulling him from his trance, and he glanced up as the server wordlessly slid a cup in front of him. His phone vibrated a moment later, and there were three black buttons evenly spaced on the screen. He automatically tapped the one on the right but noticed that it was marked *40%* before it was replaced by the words *THANK YOU* under a green check.

He found Caleb's name with a couple of swipes, and his thumbs flashed across the screen. *How long has it been 40?*
A bubble popped up in the bottom left corner: *??*

Sorry. How long has the tip been 40%?

Oh, K. Prob a couple of months

Damn, might have to switch to the middle button

It doesn't matter to you

Well it—

The girl at the table let out a shrill laugh, and Aaron swung around but glanced away the moment he made eye contact with her. The couple's laughter abruptly quieted, and the other faces in the room drooped back toward their screens. He watched as the server scurried through the room, silently nudging cups across tables and nodding briefly at each affirmation. The nods began to look like a twitch, and each face was quickly buried again after the brief intrusion of life. He stared at his half-written message, bit his lip, tapped Delete, then wrote, *I wonder whether it would have happened even if we hadn't created the app.*

??

Sorry, prob would have been easier to chat. The death of real conversation would have happened anyway, right?

This again? Don't blame Emosense. Things change. I'm sure that people were claiming the death of conversation when they invented the telephone. You're just the latest in a long line.

You think so?

Yeah. If anything, you might be bringing conversation back. At least now people want to see each other's faces when they talk. Anyway, gotta run.

Cool

He swiped back to his contacts, scanning the faces that peered out of small circles along the left side of the screen. There were a couple of lazily typed words alongside each one: the final message from the previous conversation, half containing errant letters and faulty autocorrects. As he scrolled, his phone vibrated, and Maya's name glowed on the home screen. Aaron unconsciously swiped to accept, but before he had a chance to utter a greeting, she set off.

"You know, it's been the craziest day. I can't believe that I missed my train, but I couldn't find my purse this morning. I'd put it up on a high shelf because Geoffrey brought his terrier over last night, you know how she chews things. Anyway, I was heading out the door, and it wasn't on the coffee table. I'd had a couple more drinks than I should have at happy hour with the girls, so for a moment I thought I'd left it at the bar, but then remembered the dog. I should have just put it on the counter, but of course I wanted to be sure Moxie couldn't get it, so I put it on the top shelf in the hall closet. By the time I'd put the pieces together, there was no way I was going to get to my stop in time and couldn't decide what to do."

Aaron glanced at the steady blue line at the base of the screen as he nodded on cue, but his increasingly curt answers went unnoticed as she continued to sail through the flotsam of her day. Her beguiling smile wasn't enough to paper over the gulf between this conversation and the one he'd been eavesdropping on, and he could only endure a minute before he cut in. "Maya, I'm sorry." He paused, fumbling for an excuse that wouldn't disrupt the blue line on her phone. "I just sat down. Can I call you later?"

"Oh, okay, yeah, sure. I'll be around."

"Great. We'll chat soon." He closed the call and briefly mulled over the quip he'd read a couple of days earlier: "Has anyone noticed that Emosense seems to measure entertainment value more than honesty these days?"

Aaron started scrolling subconsciously a few seconds later but caught himself and swiped his phone to sleep. He turned toward the couple again, making no effort to disguise his interest. Every so often a look of disbelief would dance across the young woman's face before being replaced by a self-conscious giggle, and he wondered about the innocent half-truths peppering their sentences. He scrunched his eyes as though committing the scene to memory, then dragged himself from his chair and shuffled toward the door. It was a crisp fall day, and from the doorway, he watched as strangers gracefully flowed around each other on the crowded street without making eye contact. It was the tail end of rush hour, but the sidewalks were still dense with commuters. If an errant step resulted in an apology, it was brief and silent, a moment of embarrassment that was best glossed over. The street was as dishonest as the coffee shop, the digital chirps and eager taps announcing that those hustling between the subway exit and anonymous glass towers were really living elsewhere.

Aaron thrust his hands deep in his pockets, as though he were trying to push his fists through the fabric, then stepped into the gaggle. Despite not being absorbed by a screen, he still hung his head in imitation of those around him, subconsciously shuffling to the left as a portly man wearing a frayed tweed jacket approached. A dozen steps later, he skipped forward to avoid bumping into a teenaged boy wearing bright-red headphones and nodding his head exuberantly without lifting his eyes from a screen. Aaron twisted and yelled, "C'mon, man, slow down!" but the boy kept going without any acknowledgment. He shook his head and yelled to no one in particular, "Can you believe that asshole?" then searched the faces of those flowing around him to see if anyone had even noticed. He stopped and reached out in an exaggerated stretch, but those walking past just deviated a little more, missing his outstretched fingers by a few inches. When a gangly college girl with her head buried in her phone strode toward him, he steeled himself for the impact, but she just veered around him, flashing a look of disapproval. The fleeting eye contact was enough for him to spin around. "Hey, yeah, you. Hey!" But she had already merged with the sea of bodies.

When Aaron turned back, a middle-aged man lumbered toward him. His beige trousers were cinched high around a broad waistline, and his pink shirt would have been more appropriate for someone ten years younger. Instead of leaning back as he approached, Aaron lunged forward at the last moment. Hoping to merely graze the man's shoulder, he badly misjudged, and they collided heavily. As Aaron was thrown off-balance, he thrust his foot out and almost tripped the man as he stumbled. A hole in the crowd formed around the staggering pair, and Aaron held up his hands in an apologetic gesture. "Oh, sorry." The man opened his mouth to say something but only locked eyes with Aaron for an instant before shaking his head and walking away. Aaron watched him disappear into the crowd before turning toward home. He gazed at the sidewalk for a dozen strides, then lifted his chin, but any effort to make eye contact was thwarted by the parade of bowed heads.

The next morning, Aaron flopped into the coffee shop's shabby couch, and the dusty air seemed to reduce the visible spectrum to shades of brown, a dull alternative to the polychromatic worlds in his hands. Scouring the room for a distraction, he spotted a stack of magazines and laughed at the hokey display of nostalgia as he lifted an issue off the pile, leaving a small, dust-free square on the magazine below. He fell back into the couch with the ludicrously oversized object in his hands and fumbled with the edge of the paper as he searched between the ancient covers. He could only manage to flip a few pages at a time, but that was enough for him to be drawn in, marveling at the world of just a decade ago. He was transfixed by an image of a small group at a beach café, their expressions reminding him of the couple he'd seen the day before. Eyes on each other, fully engaged, the sun beating down on their turquoise table as they soaked it in. The umbrellas were tightly wrapped around their poles; it was back when they were used for rain, not for protecting precious screens from glare, screens that were missing from the picture—the absence of recording and assessment leaving this group so joyfully exposed.

It wasn't how he remembered it. He recalled the lies, the lack of trust, and the frustration of knowing that what was said and what one believed could be two entirely different things. Tossing the magazine back on the pile, it slid across the small stack, coming to rest on the edge of the low table. He gazed around the room in an effort to permanently imprint the contrast. When his phone vibrated, he let a couple of seconds pass by before lifting it from his lap. *Caleb Mitchell has tagged you.*

Aaron tapped lazily, and the words *Five years ago today* floated above a blurry image with a white Play button in the middle. The clip was only five seconds long, and nothing really happened, but he let it loop half a dozen times. The recording started with him buckled over laughing, and with a hand on Caleb's shoulder to steady himself, he was a caricature of unbridled mirth. He was trying to speak but couldn't push words out between spasms, and the camera jerked around to Maya, who was drawn to full height with her hands on hips, towering over the cackling figures. When it zoomed in on her face, she was shaking her head. "It's not funny, you know." The camera zoomed back out to catch Caleb lifting his shoulder in a half shrug and giving her a "Well, why are we laughing?" face. When Maya shook her head again, she caught the camera out of the corner of her eye and lunged toward it. The frame filled with a shot of threadbare carpet, then abruptly cut to black.

Aaron was smiling broadly as it looped, and he absorbed a different detail each time. He felt a brief stab of nostalgia at the sight of the oversized T-shirt, the pleated pants, and the haphazard collection of band posters covering the far wall, but the true sense of longing was reserved for the authenticity of the moment.

The video paused when Maya's face flashed on the screen. He accepted the call, and the carefully posed photo was replaced by the same face, but the familiar smile only lasted a moment before she scowled. "You didn't call me back yesterday."

"Yeah, yeah, I'm sorry." He paused, wanting to conclude the sentence with "I was busy," but that half-truth would be flagged by his application on Maya's screen, so he let the silence linger.

She filled the void eagerly. "So have you heard from Jacob?"

Aaron pursed his lips as he tried to remember when they'd last spoken. He began shaking his head softly, then stopped and leaned forward as though about to tell a secret. "No, but I bumped into Melissa the other day. It sounds like she's back together with him."

Maya's eyes glanced down. Aaron knew that a flash of red at the bottom of her screen would accompany his lie, and her mouth dropped open in an O.

"Aaron, what? Seriously? You know I always have the app on."

Aaron nodded his head in an apologetic stutter. "Yes, I know. But sometimes it feels like a straitjacket, and well, you know, don't you want to lash out every now and then? Just to see what happens?"

"No. No, actually I don't. We all know what happens. People stop trusting each other. What were you thinking?"

"You know, I'm just kind of done with…Actually I guess I just wasn't thinking."

She was shaking her head. "Obviously. I have no idea why you'd do that, and now I don't know what to think. You've—"

"Yeah, I'm sorry. You know. Look, I really should go. I'll call in a bit."

"Aaron, don't you—"

Aaron shrugged his shoulders, swiped his phone to sleep, and knowing that his relationship with Maya had survived worse moments, placed it on the table. His phone buzzed again, vibrating against the wood like a trapped insect, but he let it shuffle across the table until it stopped. He leaned his head back and scrunched his eyes as he recalled his smug satisfaction just three years ago. His colleagues had tried to stifle their microexpressions during the development phase, but the camera noticed everything and drew the line between a lie and the truth with perfect accuracy. Too naive to ponder the implications, they shared a beta version with their friend Jolene, a news anchor at the local television station. She'd seen the appeal immediately, and a few weeks later, two fidgety politicians were standing behind lecterns under hot studio lights. The debate began with a thin blue line at the base of everyone's screen, and when a howl from the audience accompanied the first flash of amber, Aaron knew that Emosense would be a hit. Law enforcement was next to embrace his invention, and once the first high-profile conviction quelled any potential resistance, the public was never going to accept a retreat into the unknown. Aaron, giddy with success, lapped up the adoration until the next leap hinted at what might be lost. Emosense seeped into the mainstream through dating sites, and as user profiles were stripped of their humanity, he watched its relentless growth erase the joy of human imperfection.

Aaron's phone buzzed again a minute later, the same tone sounding more insistent this time. He flipped it over, but when he saw Maya's name, he slipped it into his pocket, then lifted himself from the couch and left without ordering. Her anger should've been a warning, but in the isolation of a lonely walk home, he dismissed the repercussions of breaking the trust in Emosense's thin line of pixels.

Aaron rocked back and forth on his heels as the elevator took him to the top floor of his building, and in an apartment where sunlight streamed through the wall of glass, he hurried toward his den, throwing his jacket over the back of a chair without breaking stride. He closed the door behind him, and when it extinguished the light, he felt as though he'd traveled back in time. The windows were covered with black paper, a piece of wood was wedged under the desk's left hind leg to keep it from wobbling, and posters were taped on the wall in an attempt to replicate the temporary nature of college life. The cutting-edge computer terminals were the only hint that this wasn't a past dorm room, but the strip of bright sunlight that seeped under the door behind him felt like his wealth trying to tug him back into the present.

He flipped on the desk lamp and wiggled his mouse, blinking as the monitors flashed on, then summoned the lines of code that had changed his life. With one elbow on the armrest and his chin in his hand, he lazily scrolled up and down, then closed his eyes as he absorbed the final moments of indecision. A second later he sat up decisively, repositioned himself on his chair, and began the task of unraveling the code. He'd carefully buried its loose threads, but he knew exactly where to look, and it only took a couple of minutes until he was hurriedly replacing the critical words and symbols.

The first few lines came easily, and soon he was lost in the flow of creation. An hour later he cleared the final hurdle, invisibly slipping the code into the transmission. A few missteps might have given him pause, but the giddiness of success propelled him forward and kept him from pondering the consequences.

He picked up his phone and tapped Recent Calls on the bottom of the screen. Maya's name was at the top, and there was never any doubt that she'd be the first recipient. He embedded the code in a recent photo, added a generic apology for the way the last call ended, and lingered over the keyboard for a second, knowing that this decision couldn't easily be undone. Even though it could be rebuilt, once the public's trust was broken, rebuilding it would be useless anyway. He tapped the Send button eagerly.

Instead of a flood of relief, he was hit by the stinging clarity of his blunder, and he closed his eyes as he pushed himself back in his chair. He realized that he only needed to talk to a single person, as everyone would have told him the same thing: it was too late, everyone was dependent on it now, and the world he wistfully craved was never coming back. They would have told him that it was too dangerous to tamper with something this big, that no one could foresee the consequences. But now his fate was in Maya's hands, and he added hanging up on her so abruptly to the list of things he wished he could go back and change.

Taking a deep breath, he prepared his thoughts as he tapped her number, but there was no response. He tapped out another message: *Maya, whatever you do, don't open that photo. I'll explain. Call me as soon as you can.* He sent it and tried calling again, but after a minute, he slowly slid his thumb across the screen to cut the call, then placed his phone gently on the table as though he'd throw it across the room if he held it a second longer.

Turning back to his monitor, he tried to think of a way to cripple the version he'd just unleashed, but it was gone. Half an hour passed by as he scrolled down the lines of code that held so much power. He jerked upright when his phone buzzed, but as he grabbed at it, his thumb slipped off the thin edge, and it fell to the floor. On his knees when he flipped it over, Aaron smiled ruefully at the photo of Caleb's beaming face, knowing his expression would be different when he swiped. He let it chime as he lifted himself back into his seat, then accepted the call. "Hey, man, what's up?"

"Ahh, Aaron, well, I'm not exactly sure, but I just got a call from Maya. She was hysterical. Have you done anything?"

"Hysterical? What do you mean?"

"She was crying, telling me that her friends are lying to her."

Aaron was gripping the phone, nodding his head in silence.

Caleb narrowed his eyes. "What have you done?"

"Did she tell you why she didn't call me?"

"It was a little hard to keep up, but she said that she was too angry with you, that you were the first one to lie to her. She wanted me to talk to you. You know that I don't want to get between you guys, but what's going on?"

"I broke it."

"You broke what?"

"Emosense. I hated what it had become."

"Wow. Seriously?" He paused. "I guess that makes a little more sense."

"What makes more sense?"

"When I told her that everything was going to be okay, her eyes flitted to Emosense, and she started shaking, saying, 'You too' before she hung up."

There was a brief flash of amber, and it was so jarring that Aaron flinched even though he knew it was fake.

"You told her not to call anyone else, right? Maybe if we can stop her now, we could—"

"I didn't get a chance. She hung up on me."

Aaron replied, "Yes, yes, of course," and continued in a dull monotone, "You know, maybe it's for the better. It will just be tough for a little while. It couldn't go on like that, everyone—"

"Aaron. It's not just going to be tough for a little while. Sure, people will work out what's happening, but until they do, it's going to be chaos. It's not just going to be lovers' spats. The police, criminals, emergency responders—everyone is going to spend the next few hours completely lost, and by morning this thing will be everywhere. It's going to be like the end of the world tomorrow, and this time I'm not exaggerating. We have to get the word out."

Aaron leaned forward, nodding eagerly. "Yeah, yeah. I'll call Jolene."

"Jolene?"

"Remember, the news anchor."

"Oh. Yeah, good idea, and call me if there's a way I can help."

"Thanks, man. Bye."

Aaron tapped Jolene's number, and while he waited for her to pick up, he pictured the code turning truth into lies as it flooded through the network, triggering anger and disbelief every time it randomly flashed amber.

A tiny sliver of hope widened when Jolene answered, but when he hurriedly launched into an explanation, she started shaking her head. "Aaron, slow down, you're not making any sense." Her eyes flitted to the bottom of the screen. "Aaron, why the hell are you lying to me?"

Aaron protested, "No, Jolene, I'm not lying, I—"

Jolene shook her head angrily. "If this is some kind of joke, it isn't funny."

"No, Jolene, wait—"

"Don't call me back."

Aaron stared at the blank screen for a second, then quickly tapped her number again, but she didn't answer.

LOW POWER

10%

The thud of tires hitting the tarmac tore Farrah from a restless sleep. As the fuselage shuddered, she glanced across to see her slate sliding toward the edge of the seat and slammed her hand down, pinning it to the cushion as the aircraft slowed. As the plane lazily rolled toward their gate, Farrah inhaled slowly, holding the cabin's cool air in her lungs while the tarmac rippled and the buildings floated in and out of focus in the heat. The airport was a typical South American mix, the smattering of new vehicles and shiny planes sparkling jewelry on a terminal's sagging body. The screen on the seatback played a thirty-second ad for the Caribbean, and she smiled knowing that this final assignment was the only thing between her and the glistening pools and bright-white beaches.

Farrah gathered her personal items and leapt up the moment the seat belt chime sounded, but she was tugged back to the seat by the charging cable still attached to her Filtrex. She leaned over and pulled out the plug, then pushed her Filtrex back on her nose. They were supposed to look like regular glasses, but with the electronics tightly wedged into the chunky black frames, they always seemed to slip down her face. She tapped the right arm just in front of her temple, and the standard welcome was overlaid with a low-battery indicator. Shaking her head, she tried to jam the plug back in, but the prongs were splayed and the outlet jiggled at the touch, obviously broken. Not checking it was a rookie mistake, and she cursed as she coiled the wire in a hurried motion and shoved the useless plug in her bag. A short beep accompanied the crimson glow of the power indicator as it dipped below 10 percent, and she swiped and jabbed in the field of vision to activate low-power mode. Her stilted dance attracted unwanted stares, and she resumed her tasks more discreetly, chastising herself for being so sloppy.

9%

Still bleary eyed, she swiped to her messages while she waited for the cabin door to open, using 1 percent of the remaining power. From the subject lines alone, she could see the office's political battles waver back and forth, but there was nothing that warranted her reading further until she reached a message from Colton titled "Farrah Advice." She opened it, but the entirety of the message was *Farrah, I appreciate your help, and please take care. It's still a dangerous town. Trust your instincts (and your Filtrex of course!), Colton.* She whispered to herself, "Thanks, Colton, fantastic advice. Now where's the fucking thank-you?" He'd called it mission creep, but she didn't think that benign label covered exchanging a single night in Zurich for two days in São Paulo during her final week of service.

After the passenger in front of her gathered his belongings, she followed him down the aisle of the first-class cabin, allowing her hand to drape over each headrest as she passed by. Feeling the soft leather, she realized that the pampering was one of the few things she'd miss. As she stepped off the plane, the air hostess gave her a deferential bow.

"Thank you, Ms. Whitman, we hope you enjoyed your flight."

Farrah stared blankly at the woman before remembering that that was her name for the next two days. "Oh yes. Yes, I did, thanks." She turned toward the jetway, dwelling on the misstep. It was the second lapse of concentration since she'd landed, and she whispered under her breath, "No more."

As she shuffled toward the counter at passport control, a recorded message about vigilance played in a tedious loop. An old man, his uniform darkened with sweat in the crook of his elbows, lifted her passport and slid it through the scanner in a single fluid motion, acknowledging Farrah with a gruff nod. He slapped it back on the counter, and she nodded in thanks, but he was already looking at the next person in line, holding a hand aloft. A few steps later, the smoked-glass doors opened into an arrivals hall filled with desperate drivers shouting over one another. With a practiced sincerity, they reminded arriving passengers of the dangers of autocars. There was some truth to their pleas, and many took their chances with real drivers instead of vehicles that might be controlled by hackers hundreds of miles away.

Farrah gazed around the hall, taking care not to make eye contact until her Filtrex highlighted her driver. It placed a green circle over a diminutive man in the far corner. Hunched over his phone, he subtly shifted his weight from side to side between quick glances at the arriving passengers. After relying on Filtrex for years, she was convinced it dulled her instincts, but occasionally the years of observational training seeped through. She'd exited hundreds of airports, and their drivers knew exactly how to position themselves for the quickest departure, but he was in the wrong place—on the inside of the building, so they'd have to battle through the crowd to get to the exit. She shrugged, knowing that there wasn't much point in complaining now, and she slipped through the crowd, mumbling "details, details" to herself.

By the time he looked up, she was only five feet away, and when he just stared at her blankly, she asked, "Jamil?" He nodded slowly as he absorbed the question, as though he needed to put some real thought into the answer. She filled the silence by brushing back her hair, knowing that she'd barely resemble her profile picture after a twelve-hour flight.

"Yes, Ms. Whitman," he said in clipped English. His face broke into a wide smile, and he rushed forward, eagerly extending his hand in greeting. She gave it a single cursory shake before letting it go, and he turned toward the exit.

She followed a half step behind, and as they strode into the sultry afternoon, her light summer dress clung to her body. A small black sedan was waiting, the agency having traded comfort for anonymity, and Farrah slid into the back seat. Jamil ran around behind her, closing the door with a flourish, and a loose clunk sealed off the airport's chaos. Cold air spilled out of the vents, seeming to freeze the dress to her skin, and she asked, "Can you turn down the air-conditioning?"

"Of course, miss."

"Thanks, and my Filtrex is almost dead. Do you have a cable?"

"A Filtrex cable? Sorry, we don't use those here anymore, but the hotel should be able to help."

"What, seriously? No Filtrex? Since when?"

Jamil flashed a smile as he checked the rearview mirror and pulled into the gaggle of cars limping past the terminal. "Oh, probably a year now. The network was compromised, and they had to shut it down."

"A year? Seriously? How do you survive without it?"

"It's not easy, but I heard that it's a budget thing—"

"Budget, come on. With what they spend on the military here, and without us, well…"

She let her thought peter out, and he replied, "They keep promising that it will be up and running next week, but you know how it is. They've been saying that for six months."

She nodded thoughtfully. "Well, no one told me. Is there anything else I should know?"

"I'm sorry, Ms. Whitman, nothing else comes to mind, and if your Filtrex isn't on our local network, it should be fine. Our visitors haven't had any trouble."

"Well, that's good to know, but I guess it doesn't really matter with just a few minutes of battery left."

He laughed politely, like a friend who didn't get a joke.

"Anyway, let's just get to the office. I can sort everything out once I'm there."

"Very good."

Farrah mumbled, "Great, great, thanks" as she pulled out her cable, pushing the twisted prong against the door in an effort to straighten it out. She managed to move it a few degrees and tried wedging it into the outlet, but it was still a fraction too wide. She tried again, but this time it snapped under the pressure, and her momentum carried her into the door with a thud.

"Shit."

Jamil looked at her in the rearview mirror. "Is everything okay, Ms. Whitman?"

"Yes, yes. I just broke the damn thing."

"Oh, Ms. Whitman. I'm sorry to hear."

She waved off his faux concern as they passed monotonous rows of skyscrapers, feeling as if she were in a high school play with scenery that scrolled by in an endless loop. She let her gaze drop to the traffic streaming toward the airport on the opposite side of the road and imagined herself in the back of an anonymous sedan in two days, her retirement official.

Two weeks earlier, during their last conversation, Colton made it clear that he didn't appreciate her walking away on the precipice of a promotion. Officers at her level didn't just decide to live in the dark again. Behind a wide oak desk, he'd looked through her and spoken quietly in the manner of one used to an audience's undivided attention.

"Farrah, we don't want to see you go. I'm not sure how I can sway your decision, but I implore you to consider the full repercussions. A life on the outside is very difficult for those that have reached A. M. level."

Sitting up straight, she'd recited her memorized lines: "I know, General. I don't doubt that it will be difficult, but it's time, and I'd appreciate if you let me make this tough decision without an attempt to influence it."

Colton dropped his gaze and subtly shook his head. She knew that from his point of view, the timing couldn't have been worse. After twelve years of service, Farrah had been let into the inner circle just a month prior.

Colton lifted his head after a few seconds but seemed to look over her shoulder as he spoke. "Very well, it's your decision, and that will be the entirety of my effort to influence you. I've said all I can, but please give it a little more thought, and regardless of your decision, we hope that you'll stay on until the end of the month. As you can imagine, it's quite difficult finding a replacement for someone of your caliber, and we have one last assignment that I'd like you to complete."

"Where is it?"

He let his gaze drift to her, and a smile grew on his face. "Well, I could've bet the house on that being your first question."

"Well?"

He leaned back, smiling. "You'll be happy to know that it's in Zurich."

She laughed. "Zurich? Is this just a farewell present?"

"Not at all. We appreciate your service, but this is a real assignment, and we know that you're one of the few who can do it."

She smiled sincerely. "Thanks, Colton, but flattery isn't going to change my mind."

Colton held his hands up in mock surrender. "No, no, Farrah, that's not what I'm trying to do."

A message had arrived the next morning.

There's been a change in scope. Your next mission will be in São Paulo. Briefing will begin at 08:30, Northwest conference room, second floor, Langley. Regards, CP

She strode into the conference room beaming, her eyes darting around as she searched for the balloons and cake. Instead there was a silver-haired man sitting on the far side of a table that was too small for the room.

Her smile evaporated before she gathered herself and nodded. "So it's real then? I'd hoped it was just a ruse to get me in here."

"I'm sorry, it's not a ruse, but it's only forty-eight hours. You'll be back here before the end of the week."

She stood up straighter, and the smile left as quickly as it came. "By the end of the week? So when am I leaving?"

"There's a flight at ten thirty, and I've sent you mission details. You can read them on the plane."

"Solo?"

"Yes."

She nodded as he slumped forward onto his elbows, resting his chin on interlocked fingers, and asked, "Do you have any questions?"

Knowing that this was merely a polite way to end the meeting,

Farrah had let a smile flitter across her face before dutifully replying, "No, sir. Thank you." Two hours later she was on her way to the airport, scrolling through the mission brief. The two screens of tightly spaced text could be summarized as "Go to Brazil field office to learn more." It was so generic that she'd wondered if she was heading to an elaborate surprise party at the airport and this was all they could muster for a diversion.

That had been less than twelve hours ago. In the back of Jamil's car, she reminded herself that when this was over, it would only take that long to get back.

8%
She glanced at Jamil's eyes in the rearview mirror. They were locked on the road and didn't invite conversation, so she looked out at a world enhanced by Filtrex. Each billboard's pithy message was translated to English, the time to their destination was in the lower right corner of her vision, and the suspects icon remained a comforting green as it ran through checks of everyone in the vicinity. The readout in the top right corner indicated that she'd lost another percentage, and the check to ensure that all her apps were on low-power mode cost her one more.

6%
When it hit 6 percent, Farrah considered turning off the Filtrex, but a rough calculation convinced her that she'd still have 2 percent when she arrived at the office, and she wasn't ready to take her chances naked in this town. Her guardian angels hovered twelve thousand miles above her, their instructions and translations guiding her through the city on a slightly different plane. She was envious of the helicopters overhead, but they were far too risky; it could be all over with a single shot. Slow and anonymous was much safer than quick and obvious, and as the car dawdled through traffic, Farrah closed her eyes and recalled the events of a whirlwind month.

She would never admit it to Colton, but the hollow welcome party to celebrate her promotion had cemented her decision to resign. As she was introduced to the elite group, she recalled one of the elderly gentlemen holding out his hand, and as she gripped it firmly, he introduced himself as though his agent persona had swallowed him whole. "David Fullerton, twenty-three years."

She looked at him flatly.

The trace of a smile crossed his face, and he cocked his head to the side. "Oh, sorry. When you've been doing this as long as I have, the rituals become second nature. You'll find that most agents at my level introduce themselves with their years of service. It helps ground the conversation."

"Ground the conversation?"

"Umm, yes. Well, knowing when someone began helps with the game of 'Do you remember so and so?'" He completed the sentence with an unconvincing chuckle.

Farrah continued to stare without allowing a hint of a smile to cross her lips. "It sounds more like it establishes the pecking order."

She let the silence linger before laughing, and he joined her a little too eagerly. Had Kyle been at the party, things might have been different, but his absence was glaring, and she realized that he'd been the only one at this level that she'd truly admired. His brief tenure had planted the seeds of doubt when she accepted the promotion, but she never had the opportunity to discuss his reasons for leaving. After he'd gone, contacting him was strictly forbidden.

5%

The earpiece of her Filtrex beeped, tugging her into the present, and the lens was filled with the words *Perimeter compromised. Known terrorist vehicle fifty meters behind. Driver unknown.* She jerked her head around to see a virtual red dot over a BMW eight cars back, a distance that could be erased with just a quick stab of the accelerator. There was a flicker as the device battled to enhance the few details the lens could capture. Farrah sat up straight as Jamil coasted to a halt.

"Are you kidding me?" she hissed. He didn't turn around, so she yelled at him, "What the hell are you doing?"

He glanced in the rearview mirror before lazily raising a finger to point at the lights. "It's red."

"Fuck. Seriously? Just drive. They're only a few cars away."

He turned around to face her. "They?"

"What? The black BMW. It's eight cars back in the left lane."

"Sorry. I haven't got a warning from the field office," said Jamil as he turned back to face the lights.

"I don't care. You're getting a warning from me!"

He gestured at the traffic lights again. "I'll have to check; anyway, they're about to change."

The BMW smoothly pulled out of the slowing stream of traffic. Slotting into the empty bus lane, it moved slowly up the line, and now there were only four cars between them.

"Come on. You have to move!" Farrah said. "What the hell do you guys do without Filtrex?"

"Well, I usually get a warning from the office through my phone, but it hasn't buzzed."

He slowly accelerated as the light turned green. The black car was only a dozen feet behind them and her Filtrex was glowing. The words THREAT IMMINENT were accompanied by a constant bleating.

"Come on! You'll have to go faster than this. I have my Filtrex; I'll be your eyes. Get us away from that car now, then you can check with the office."

He smiled at her through the rearview mirror. "Okay, okay."

"Thank God, now go. Go!" she screamed.

He placed his hands at a perfect ten and two on the steering wheel and punched the accelerator, gunning toward a gap that was closing fast. When a cyclist wobbled toward them, he jerked the wheel to avoid the oblivious rider, but the maneuver jeopardized his careful calculation, and the two-car space he as aiming for had narrowed to one by the time he arrived. He deftly tapped the brake to bring his speed in line with the row of cars alongside, then slid into the gap for just a moment before darting into the emergency lane. The space closed a second later, trapping the BMW on the other line of cars, and the red alert faded to amber.

4%

It flashed read again a minute later. The threat was two blocks ahead, stationary at an intersection.

"What the hell? How did they get there?"

"What was that, ma'am?"

"They're two blocks up waiting for us. How'd they know which way we'd go?"

"I'm sorry, but there aren't a lot of options to the office, ma'am."

As they closed in on the intersection, she flipped her Filtrex to map mode. "There's a laneway on our right, about thirty meters ahead. Take it."

"Are you sure?"

"Yes, I'm sure, now do it!"

Jamil was unflustered, his efficient movements bordering on lethargic, but the car's rear tires squealed as the vehicle lurched to the right and bounced onto the chipped cement of the alley. They hurtled toward the road at the far end, and she watched the rhythmic flashes of sunlight on Jamil's face as they raced through intermittent shadows. When they emerged, the flashing red faded to green, but her Filtrex died a second later, and the glossy digital veneer disappeared. As the world turned gray, the billboards and street signs flipped back to Portuguese, and without any reassuring green dots, everyone on the street became a potential suspect. She twisted her head in both directions, but there was no sign of the BMW.

3%

She leaned forward. "How far—"

The glasses flickered back to life, and the moment they connected with the network, her view was bathed in red as the 3 percent warning and imminent threat alerts overlapped. Suddenly the BMW was right next to them. Farrah screamed. When Jamil heaved on the wheel, the car lunged left. She was flung at the window, but she managed to soften the blow with her right arm. The Filtrex was scanning the vehicle as she tried to catch a glimpse of the driver, but the intensity of the glowing red highlight obscured her vision.

2%

As another percentage seeped away, she knew it could drop off a cliff at any moment, and the advantage would swing to the suspect the moment she was flying blind. The Filtrex battled the chaos of the city, bleating incessantly as it tried to keep up with the translations and the warnings. She looked down in an attempt to lower its workload, but when the Filtrex flickered anyway, she returned her attention to the road, twisting her head to keep the BMW in view. "He's trapped on the left. Take a hard right at the next intersection."

Jamil glanced in the rearview mirror before easing toward the left lane.

"I said right!"

"I know," he calmly replied as he shuffled the wheel in his hand to careen across the right lane, cutting the corner at the apex before letting it slide half a car width into the opposing lane. He continued to accelerate as he eased it back to the correct side of the road. She braced herself against the g-forces, her grip on the sill as she returned her attention to the Filtrex. The red dot was still calmly following.

"Fuck, that wasn't enough."

1%

The BMW following her was pristine, as though surrounded by a force field that repelled the grime of the city, and she watched it part the sea of darting, wobbly vehicles as though pushing them aside with an invisible hand. A second later it pulled alongside, and as she turned toward it, the battery fell to zero. The device's dying gasp was a strident warning, but when the digital coating evaporated, she caught a glimpse of the driver's face. It was familiar, but she couldn't place it before Jamil swerved and put a car between them. Her list of enemies was long, and without digital assistance, she clawed through clouded memories. When it finally clicked, she realized that she'd been focusing on the wrong side of the ledger. It was Kyle. She took a moment to process what was happening. They'd been close friends, but it was agency policy—no communication after the conclusion of his service. She recalled his hasty exit but couldn't imagine him turning against them.

0%
With an impenetrable row of cars between them and the BMW, Jamil made a lazy right turn onto a wide road and looked at her in the rearview mirror again. "I think that we lost them."

She nodded slowly. "Yeah. Yeah, I guess so. Nice work."

His phone buzzed, and he read the alert before turning back to her. "Apparently downtown isn't safe. We're going to go to a hotel out of town."

Pursing her lips, Farrah said, "No, Jamil, let's go to the field office."

"They don't recommend that."

"Jamil, this isn't a request."

"I'm sorry, but I've been instructed to take you out of town to a secure location." The glass partition rose abruptly, and there was a barely perceptible click as the doors locked.

She screamed, "What the fuck?" loud enough to be heard through the glass.

Jamil lowered the barrier a fraction of an inch. "What?"

"There's another car behind us. I can see it in my Filtrex," she lied.

"A second one?"

"Yes. Yes. On our left, two blocks back. It's behind the truck."

Jamil was straining against his seat belt, searching the rearview mirror, oblivious to the BMW slotting into a driveway fifty yards ahead of them, its trunk nestled behind an overflowing trash can. As they passed, its white reverse lights flashed on, and it hurtled toward them, colliding with Jamil's side door and pushing their car into the other lane of traffic. A small hatchback careened at them, and its driver's panicked tug at the wheel wasn't enough to avoid a collision. It hit the front passenger door and wedged them in. Jamil reached for his belt, trying to free his holster, but the door of the BMW flung open while he struggled, and Kyle bolted toward the rear passenger door. Farrah shimmied across and pulled at the door handle, expecting a useless jiggle, but the crash had deactivated the locks, and she leaned into it. She pushed hard, and it broke free as Jamil twisted, still locked in place, swinging his arm around the driver's seat as he attempted to latch onto Farrah's leg. Deftly she swung over his outstretched hand. Jamil twisted the other way, but he was blocked by the broken doorframe.

She leapt out of the car. "Kyle, what's going on?"

"I'll explain later. We have to run." He'd already grabbed her wrist, and with his other hand he tore the Filtrex from her face.

She scowled at him. "What are you doing? The batteries are dead."

"It doesn't matter. They can still track them." He flung them hard, and they clattered on the pavement.

Jamil grabbed his phone and gave it three quick taps before shouting, "We crashed. Holes are fleeing on foot. Glass discarded."

Farrah held Kyle's hand as she ran, her soft slippers more appropriate for a first-class lounge than a garbage-strewn street in Brazil. "Holes? What are holes?"

Kyle didn't break stride. "We are. We're holes in the net. Those that know too much to be let go."

"What?"

"Look, we're still in danger; I'll explain later. There aren't many agents here, but if you still have your phone, their Filtrex will light you up long before you see them."

They ran another two blocks before their breathing slowed and Kyle turned to Farrah. "Oh, and you can stop calling me Kyle. I'm Mark now, and will be for the rest of my life. I'm afraid that you'll need to be someone new too. It's not the retirement I'd planned, but it's better than what they had in mind."

Kirk briefly nodded in thanks as he grabbed the wrapped sandwich from the counter, then ducked toward the side door with his head down. Torn from his screen by a light bump, he scowled and looked up, but a flicker of recognition sapped the menace from his glare.

She smiled broadly. "Kirk. Wow, it's really you."

He couldn't match the blond hair and blue-gray eyes with a memory, but his practiced, "Yes. Yes, it is, sorry I can't chat, but keep following, it's fans like…" petered out in the face of a subtle eye roll.

"Kirk, I'm not one of your fans."

His head jolted back an inch.

"Sorry, I didn't mean it like that. I should say that I'm not just one of your fans; we went to college together. It's Elise."

"Oh, oh, I'm sorry, of course." He paused as though his memory of her still eluded him. "Elise."

"Kirk, it was only three years ago."

"Yes, I know, but you know, so many people reach out, and—"

"You don't have to tell me. You're always in the news, a shining star of our class. Me, well…"

"No, I'm sorry. That's not what I meant. I hope you understand. So…Elise. Wow. Good to see you. What are you doing these days?" He battled to hold her gaze, but when she took a step backward to allow another customer to walk between them, his device stole a glance.

"It's okay, you can check. I know you're a busy man."

"I'm sorry. It's a bad habit, but you know, it pays the bills."

"I'm sure it does."

"Oh, thanks. Yeah, it's been a lot of work, but it's worth it. It's been quite a ride." He winked, beaming.

"Yeah, I bet. I see your name everywhere now. It's hard to keep track of what you're shilling."

"Well, I wouldn't call it shilling, but I guess a few companies jump on the bandwagon."

"Kirk, I was just kidding. It sounds like you're really doing great. I know that this is a bit forward of me, but I'd love to hear more about—"

He flashed a grin and lifted his phone. "It would be my pleasure. Here's my private details, but be careful with them. I don't give them out to just anybody."

Elise waited for a self-deprecating smile as she tapped accept, but his expression didn't change.

"Wow, thanks, Kirk. I'll call you soon."

"Great, great. Bye for now."

"Umm, yeah, bye, Kirk." Elise gave him a loose wave, and he nodded as he leaned into the side door.

He pulled his baseball cap lower as he sifted through the morning crowd and took a quick glance over his shoulder before darting into the back entrance of his office. Briefly touching his cap to acknowledge the security guard, he pulled out his phone in the freight elevator, the green numbers of his influence rating the brightest light in the dim car.

The doors opened to an office that looked like the inside of a machine, with open ductwork overhead and taped wires snaking along almost every surface. Thin slivers of light seeped through the imperfectly blacked-out windows, and a ghostly blue glow from the monitors lit each dreamer's face from below. Sitting shoulder to shoulder in the dim room, they absorbed the stories of the day and wrote pithy comments in the hopes that Kirk would choose theirs and cast it wide, adding to Kirk's influence numbers, and if it happened often enough, they'd move beyond the occasional pat on the back to an account of their own. As Kirk walked past, a few raised their heads, and Kirk gave each a short nod of acknowledgment before swinging his office door wide. A flash of sunlight flooded into the room, giving the others a brief glimpse of a world that was built on a dry wit and the few trends he'd recognized before the masses.

The next day, in a claustrophobic apartment two miles south, the morning light leaked through a grimy window, and the refractions from a shimmery dress on the floor danced across dust-colored walls. Elise sat up in bed, propping her slate on her thighs in a practiced motion, and sent her missive: *24 hours since first contact, interaction neutral to positive, awaiting instructions.* A few seconds later she received the reply: *Send invite within the hour.*

The message for Kirk was ready, but with her finger hovering above the Return button, she recalled his slinking away after he'd asked her on a date in their senior year. She'd smiled forgivingly as he stuttered through an awkward opening line, but when she rejected him with a feeble excuse, he'd turned away as though the response were a foregone conclusion. As he'd slowly wandered off, a friend's mocking dismissal of his desirability stopped her from uttering a few words to soften the blow. They hadn't spoken again until she'd bumped into him as instructed the previous morning. Elise pictured Kirk's condescending grin to push the earlier memory aside before tapping Send.

Her phone buzzed a few seconds later, and she fumbled as she eagerly snatched it from the table. When she flipped it over, the message was just a confirmation of a dental appointment accompanied by a smiling tooth emoji. As she was placing it back on the table, it buzzed again, and this time it was Kirk. She stared at his name for a couple of seconds before reading the message: *Yes, it was a fun surprise. It would be good to get together. Next Thursday is free for me.*

Her thumbs flashed around the screen as she wrote a note to her supervisor: *Request permission to reply immediately.* She stared at the phone, bouncing her left foot while she waited.

The screen flashed. *Permission denied, wait 1 hour.*

She began filling the time by crafting a message, but after revising two sentences for five minutes, she scrolled mindlessly through Kirk's channel to ease the morning forward. An hour later she was absentmindedly turning the phone over in her hands when a beep signaled the end of the waiting period. Knowing that time would slow the moment she tapped, she hesitated for a few seconds. It was ten long minutes before her phone buzzed again.

Hey, it's great to hear from you, see you at 7. I'm looking forward to it.

She read it twice, trying to gauge his eagerness, but there weren't enough words to work with.

On a drizzly Thursday night, Elise was dropped off a block from the restaurant, and five minutes later, she trotted along through the yellow cones of light from the streetlights. She approached a stern-faced doorman, his crisp suit seemingly impervious to the rain, and when he pulled the door wide, the damp sidewalk glistened in the warm light. She stepped into a den of dark wood and incandescent bulbs, and was eagerly ushered to a corner table by a series of impeccably dressed staff.

At their table, Kirk was staring at the phone in his lap, cradling it with both hands, when the waiter leaned toward him. "Sir?"

Kirk's head jerked upward, and he put the phone on the table as he lifted himself up, stalling when he was half standing to thrust out his hand. Elise shook it briefly, and he quickly sat back down. When she glanced at his phone, he snatched it from the tabletop and twisted awkwardly to slide it into his trousers, then looked up at Elise. In the face of her mildly amused look, he dropped his head again. She let out a soft giggle. Kirk joined in with a quiet chuckle.

"Well, I've had smoother starts to an evening."

Elise laughed and looked around the room. "This place is incredible. I read about it in the Standard, but it sounded like you had to book two months ahead?"

Kirk raised an eyebrow. "Is that the waitlist these days? I had no idea it was so popular."

To hide a smirk, Elise turned her attention to the cocktail menu, but as she placed her thumb under the top corner to lever the leather-bound menu from the table, Kirk asked, "Can I make a recommendation?"

She let her hand slide back to her lap. "Sure. I guess. I mean, that's what you do, right?"

"Yes. Yes." He nodded eagerly. "Their old-fashioned is outstanding."

"Okay."

"Great, great, and let me know if you'd like any help with dinner. I have a few favorites."

"Oh. You do, do you?"

He leaned back, draping his arm over the back of the booth. "Well, I do come here all the time."

His gaze moved from Elise to a point behind her, and lifting his chin, he raised his voice. "John, John." The waiter swiveled around and hurried to their table. "We'll each start with an old-fashioned."

The waiter's eyes flashed to Elise. She gave an affirmative nod, and he hurried toward the bar.

Kirk was glancing around the room when the cocktails arrived. "It's a bit different than college, right?"

Elise laughed. "For one of us, I guess."

"Well," Kirk said, "I suppose I have been a bit lucky, but people don't see the hard work that goes into what I do."

Elise raised her glass to eye level. "I guess you make it look easy."

Kirk held up his glass, seeming to look at Elise through the amber liquid. "Why, thank you, I guess I do."

Elise wondered how to draw out the awkward boy from college. "So, you mentioned some recommendations?"

Kirk dived into his favorites, his delivery that of a polished waiter.

"Kirk, I appreciate the suggestions, but it feels like I just listened to one of your podcasts. Anything a little more personal?"

He dropped his gaze, laughing lightly. "I'm sorry, I tend to get carried away here. I really should have asked whether you had anything in mind. I'll try again. Did you see anything that took your fancy?"

She leaned forward, a soft smile on her face. "It's nice when you put the persona aside."

"Sorry?"

"Oh, nothing. That just sounded a bit more genuine, that's all."

"Well, I guess. It's just that sometimes people don't want me to break character."

"Well, I'm not one of them. I'd prefer to have dinner with the real Kirk tonight."

He lifted his glass a few inches from the table and tilted it in a mock salute. "That sounds good, and be sure to let me know if I lapse."

Elise laughed, and the earnest boy that she remembered began to emerge as their conversation meandered through the evening.

There were only a few stragglers in the restaurant when Elise sipped the last of her wine and laughed. "This has been a lot more fun than I'd expected."

Kirk tilted his head. "What did you expect?"

"You know, I wasn't sure. I was a little worried that it would just be the writer, and I'm not sure I could have made it through an evening of 'Kirk Masterson's wit.'"

"You do realize that it's"—he lifted his hands to make air quotes—"'Kirk Masterson's' wit that allows me to live like this."

"Kirk, I get it, but it's not as if writing a couple of funny lines makes you Hemingway."

Kirk's eyes widened.

"Kirk, I'm sorry, I'm just kidding. You are funny, but your writing isn't everything. You don't need to prove anything to me."

Kirk smiled but glanced away for a moment before returning his attention to her. "Well, you know, it's hard not to feel like that. When we bumped into each other, I couldn't remember you right away. I knew you'd rejected me, but trust me, you weren't the only one to spurn me in college."

Elise nodded, her expression blank.

"I didn't mean it like that. It's not that I asked every girl out, but I try to put that whole time behind me. I don't want to be that guy anymore."

She gave him a wan smile.

His gaze dropped to the table. "If it makes you feel any better, I still remember asking you out. I kind of shuffled off, right? I kept hoping that you'd say something, but I could feel you just watch me walk away." She reached across the table but pulled her hand back before he looked up and continued, "You know, it's nice not to have to feel like that anymore."

"Kirk, I'm sorry. There's not much point in talking about what might have been, but don't turn into something you're not as some vague way of seeking revenge."

"Easier said than done."

Elise nodded as Kirk called for the check. While Kirk acknowledged the deferential nods from the staff as they exited, she glanced at her buzzing phone, seeing the short message on the home screen: *Don't accept ride home.*

On the street a few minutes later, Kirk let his gaze drop to the ground and asked, "Would you like me to take you back to your place?"

"What?"

"I'm sorry, that came out all wrong. I just meant, would you like a lift home? My driver will be here in a moment."

While Elise absorbed the invitation, he took a half step backward as though preparing for the rejection, but she rolled her phone over in her hand for a couple more seconds, then said, "Sure."

Kirk was smiling broadly when he looked up, and Elise slipped her phone back into her purse. She didn't move when the car arrived, and eventually Kirk took the cue and reached for the handle to gracelessly swing the door wide. She slid into the back seat and looked up to see a face in the rearview mirror. Kirk's driver gave her a deferential smile, accustomed to a passenger's surprise at seeing a human in the driver's seat. As Kirk fell into the back seat, he motioned for her to make a request, but she just looked back at the driver, still mute.

"Where to, ma'am?"

This was like an old movie, and she couldn't stifle a giggle.

Kirk looked at Elise and gestured toward the driver. "Well?"

Elise lifted her chin, and with a touch of an English accent, she said, "1540 North Terrace, apartment 201."

Kirk's smile widened. "He probably doesn't need the apartment number."

They laughed as the car silently accelerated. Her phone vibrated the moment they started moving, but she held her purse closed and tried to cover the noise with eager conversation. When the car eased to a halt, Kirk tapped to loosen his seat belt and leaned toward her for a seated hug.

She laughed at his clumsiness. "You can come in for a drink if you want."

Kirk nodded. "I'd love to." He mumbled something to the driver as he walked around to open Elise's door. He followed her with compact steps to a small alcove in the weathered brick building. As she searched her purse for the key, her phone vibrated again, but she continued her frantic pawing with renewed vigor as it droned on.

Kirk glanced at her. "Do you want to get that?"

"No, no, it can wait."

"But you don't even know who it is."

She waved loosely. "I'm sure it's just my mother. I didn't get a chance to call her today."

"I really don't mind if you—"

Elise cut him off with a glare. She dug back into her purse and triumphantly held the key up to eye level before unsteadily pushing it into the lock. Patiently jiggling it before it gave, she turned back with a slight shrug. "Welcome to my humble abode."

Kirk, not sure whether to laugh, unnecessarily ducked his head in the alcove as he followed her in. They took a gray concrete staircase up the single flight. The lighting was an acidic green, and there was a slight curve on the bottom of each step from years of use. The door at the top opened to a narrow hallway where each wall had been painted a different shade of beige, and Kirk hunched over as they walked past the identical doors, each one exactly four paces apart, only each number's state of disrepair breaking the monotony.

When they arrived at 201, Elise pushed another key into the lock and gave the door a gentle shove. It swung wide, and the lights woke, extinguishing any chance of relief from the decrepit surroundings. Everything looked wobbly, as though drawn by a young child. In the open kitchen, three of the cupboard doors were open, the final one hanging crookedly from a single hinge. As Kirk floated through the room, he picked at invisible specks on his navy suit.

Elise gestured at the couch as she walked to the fridge, but when she returned from the kitchen holding two smudged glasses, he was perched on the edge. Kirk hesitantly reached out and pinched the glass between his forefinger and thumb as she let herself flop onto the couch next to him, knocking it back a few inches. Holding the glass aloft, he swung his other arm wildly to avoid falling backward. He motioned to put the glass on the side table, but a chipped porcelain bowl was propped delicately on an old magazine, and although its contents had congealed, it looked as though the slightest nudge would spill the remnants of last night's dinner. Kirk turned back to Elise, and she just loosely waved at the ground. "You can put it on the floor." He nodded, then leaned over and placed the glass on the carpet next to the leg of the couch, but as he sat up, he reached into his pocket, making a show of levering his phone to see the screen before pulling it out.

"Oh, I'm sorry. I really need to get this, and I probably should get going. I'm really sorry…" He put the phone to his ear as he began to rise.

Elise patted the couch. "Kirk, sit back down. You didn't get a call. It's pretty obvious that you're not comfortable here, but bear with me."

Kirk stopped, seeming to weigh the option of continuing the charade, but he just dipped his head apologetically. "I'm sorry. It's just not what I'm used to."

"No, it's not, but it is real."

"What are you talking about?"

"You know, Kirk, it looks like you've been doing this for what, a year now? Don't you ever wonder about what you're actually doing? Talking up products you don't believe in can't be terribly fulfilling."

"Okay, where did that come from? It's fun waging a little war with words, and what's the harm?"

"Well, it doesn't really hurt anyone directly, but I wonder about the people—"

Kirk threw his head back and laughed. "If no one gets hurt and my numbers are still green, who's complaining?"

Elise was shaking her head. "Look, Kirk, I wasn't supposed to bring you here, and—"

"What do you mean, supposed to?"

"This conversation wasn't part of the script. I'm doing it for you. I sure as hell wouldn't have left the apartment like this had I planned on inviting you back, but I enjoyed dinner. Maybe you're not a lost cause after all."

"Elise, what is this about? Just because I don't come home to day-old food, it doesn't mean my world isn't real. And well, if this is what the alternative is"—he loosely waved his arm around—"I'll stay in my bubble."

Elise leaned toward him. "Kirk, I don't think that you fully understand. When I say it's not real, I'm not speaking metaphorically. Your job, and to some degree, your life, is a construction to help us understand the mechanism of influence. I'm sorry, but all you're doing is providing a few data points to our actual influencers."

"You're not making any sense. What do you mean by 'our'?"

"Well, we work for the same company, but my job is to monitor our Harbingers. I was assigned to you last week. Until your name came up, I didn't even know that you were on the roster. Our date tonight was to confirm that you were oblivious so that we knew you'd still be useful."

Kirk let a nervous laugh escape, but she cut it short with a shrug and continued, "But I guess I'm not doing a very good job."

Kirk shook his head. "Even if any of that was true, what's the point?"

"Well, Kirk, it's a competitive world out there, and at their scale, our real writers can't afford to make as many mistakes as you do, and that's where your focus group comes in. We share what works with them to increase their strike rate. Maybe you've noticed that Nathan Cole has used a few of your best lines?"

Kirk turned down the corners of his mouth. "That's quite the theory, but you should have used someone different if you wanted me to believe you. That guy doesn't even have half the followers I do."

"But his followers are real. You must realize that the numbers on your screen are easy to manipulate."

"What about on the street? I always get noticed—"

"Actors."

He shook his head again. "Actors? Now you're just making fun."

"Are you worried that your numbers dropped by 3.2 percent last week? That's the third week in a row you've been down, right? Your green designation is looking a little more precarious."

"How do you know that?" He sat forward and unfolded his arms to gesture at the squalor. "Even if we worked for the same company, it doesn't exactly look like you're senior management."

"I'm sure that this whole thing comes as a shock, but there's no need for that tone. I'm well aware that we're paid a lot less than our Harbingers."

Kirk gave her a thin impersonation of a smile. "And why would that be?"

"Well, you have to think that you're a big shot to write like one, right?"

Kirk lifted himself to his feet. "I have no idea why you invited me here, but I don't want any part of it."

She looked up at him. "Kirk, I'm sorry, I'm just trying to help, really. I used to love seeing our Harbingers' worlds shattered, but now I realize that we're the ones that make you strut around the way you do. I'll lose my job for this but thought it would be worth it. This isn't fair to you—"

"So let me get this straight. You've been spying on me and lying to me, but now you've suddenly decided to tell the truth, and that truth just happens to be preposterous."

"Kirk, it's not like that—"

"Was there anything in that statement that was incorrect?"

She opened her mouth to respond, but in the few seconds that passed by in silence, he turned and slipped out the door.

A minute later his driver rounded the corner, coasting to a stop in front of him, but before the door slid open, his phone vibrated. Elise's name flashed on the screen, but he swiped it away as he slid into the back seat. She persisted with a short message a couple of seconds later.

Kirk, I'm sorry, I know this must be hard for you.

He rolled his eyes and put it to sleep.

The next day Kirk walked with his head held high as he sought the recognition he usually tried to avoid, but a few nods of acknowledgment and the occasional smile were enough to soften the blow of the previous night, so he buried his head in his phone until he arrived at the office.

A week later, Kirk stepped into the coffee shop and pulled his baseball cap lower when he heard his name from the far corner, but the shrill voice cut through the room, and he reluctantly lifted his head. Elise's chair screeched as she jumped up, and every face turned toward her as she sprang to her feet. As she strode toward Kirk, two men in dark suits emerged from the crowd. She swerved left too late, and they cut the tangent to intercept her. They slipped their hands under her arms in a practiced motion and lifted her a few inches off the ground, rendering her flailing arms and legs ineffective.

"Kirk!" she said. "You won't see me again, but it's all a lie. Trust me on that. It's all a lie."

He studied her face for a couple of seconds, and it was long enough to silence her. He took a moment to look around. The gaping mouths of the bold and the nervous glances from the timid were too authentic, convincing him that they couldn't be actors. Elise resumed her screed while his security detail waited patiently. He nodded, and the men dragged her away as he turned back to the counter.

"If there's just one thing you take away from this day, it's this: never make them real." Grayson paused, allowing Precapture's two dozen recruits to absorb the gravity of the statement. "Our conviction rate is over 99 percent. Now, I'm sure you're wondering about that last percentage, and there's a common theme in every single one of those cases." He smiled easily as his eyes flitted from face to face in the compact room, and the rookies lined up in three neat rows waited patiently for him to continue. "That theme: human meddling, of course. Yes, things go wrong when we combine the perfection of the algorithm with the fallibility of human emotion"—he held his palms out—"so don't fall into that trap."

The silence stretched uncomfortably until a girl with auburn hair acknowledged the unspoken instruction and hurriedly wrote "no meddling" on her tablet. The others followed her lead a moment later, and after a brief flurry of activity, they returned their attention to Grayson, who briskly completed the orientation as though that were the only point that mattered.

As they trudged out of the room with their heads bowed, Nathan wondered how long each of the others would endure the drudgery ahead. To evaluate a suspect, the algorithm analyzed purchase history, location data, and some other proprietary data points in ways that were beyond human understanding. Grayson had patiently explained that their job should have been a victim of automation long ago, but every time they tried to eliminate people, the public lost faith in the system. There weren't many jobs that required such little training, and Nathan was surrounded by introverts that could never make it in the service industry. Fortunately, enduring tedium paid well, and Nathan convinced himself that he could make it through the year.

Just a week later, Nathan was reminded of the speech as he watched Ike waving his arms angrily in the open doorway of Grayson's office. Grayson was yelling loudly enough for the entire floor to hear.

"Ike, your 'doesn't feel right' has a fucking one-in-a-hundred shot of being correct."

"Aren't you tired of throwing that bullshit number around? There's a difference between conviction and guilt."

Grayson lowered his voice. "Only in your head, Ike. The algorithm has been—"

"The damn algorithm. I just don't want to elevate this one until we're sure she's guilty."

"Ike, the algorithm is sure, and I want to make it clear that, around here, it carries a lot more weight than you do."

Ike shook his head again. "You really don't give a shit, do you?"

Grayson's deep laugh boomed through the open door. "Come on, Ike. I've been doing this for a decade. I've watched plenty of you guys come and go. All self-righteous, convinced that their intuition is somehow more accurate than the algorithm. Well, rest assured that there'll be someone with a bit more faith sitting in your chair tomorrow. The machine will keep chugging along, and you'll be a vague memory in a week from now."

After a second of silence, Ike muttered, "I guess you're all in. You sad little man."

Grayson replied in a disinterested tone, "Don't forget to pick up your stuff on the way out."

Nathan looked up as Ike stormed past. When they locked eyes, Ike barked, "I don't know why you're smiling. If you're sitting there, you're part of the problem; you just don't know it yet."

Nathan leaned back in his chair and put both hands up in mock surrender. "Sorry, man, I'm not taking sides. I'm just doing my job."

Ike smiled. "Buddy, doing this job is taking sides." He turned to his desk and swept two years of keepsakes from his linoleum desk into his gym bag. With everyone still glued to their monitors, he slung the bag over his shoulder and silently strode past the elevator, leaning into the door to the stairwell.

As chairs were pushed back and everyone swiveled around, Nathan quipped, "Is he really going to walk down twenty flights?"

The expected laughter didn't materialize, and Nathan spun to see Grayson standing behind him, so he shuffled his chair back into position.

Grayson turned back to his office but only took a single step before twisting around again. "Actually, if I can have your attention." The closest employees looked up, and the next couple of rows pulled themselves to their feet to see over the dull-gray cubicle walls.

"I just want to take a moment to say that I really hate seeing this happen, and what upsets me the most is that it's so easily avoided. Our jobs are pretty simple, and to be honest, if people had a little more faith in the algorithm, the reports would go straight to the authorities. Apparently the public wants an actual person to see the report before it goes through the system, and that's the only reason why you're sitting there. All we need to do to convince them that there are checks and balances is to sign our names at the top. So please make all of our lives easier by sticking to the task. Just confirm the purchases and send them on to the authorities if they reach red plus." Grayson gazed around the room with a flat expression that didn't invite questions, then strode back to his office and closed the door with a forceful swing.

Fifteen minutes later Nathan's phone vibrated. It was Bill. *Coffee?* Nathan looked across, but Bill had his back to him. A plaid shirt that was a size too small gripped his broad shoulders, and his hair fell over the collar in a straggly clump.

Nathan responded, *Yep,* and walked to the elevator, but Bill waited for the arrival chime before trotting across the office and thrusting his hand in the closing doors.

Nathan laughed. "For a second there, I didn't think you were coming."

Bill pushed the glasses on the bridge of his nose back a quarter inch. "I didn't want to make it obvious."

Nathan smirked. "Good thinking. I'm sure no one suspects that was coordinated."

"Hey, man, it's better than just getting up at the same time. Anyway, it's no big deal. Even you can see that the office is abuzz regardless of what Grayson wants."

"Yeah, that was a bit of unexpected excitement in our first week," said Nathan as the elevator rhythmically ticked off the floors.

"For sure. What was that thing with you?"

Nathan shrugged. "I don't know, but it didn't seem like much. He was cool given how angry he was."

When the doors slid open, Bill held out his left arm, motioning Nathan through. "Cool? He did accuse you of being part of the problem. Do you even know each other?"

"Not before we started—"

"A week ago. Nathan, it was a week ago when we started," Bill interrupted.

Nathan continued as though Bill hadn't spoken. "But we chatted a few times. He seemed fine."

"Okay then, that's settled. He's cool." Bill winked.

Nathan held his palms out. "Hey, I'm not ready to take the stand for him, but he seemed totally normal to me."

"Well, Grayson didn't seem too concerned about his exit, even after the show he put on."

"I'll give you that, and I'm sure there's more to the story, but maybe this happens more often than you'd think."

"Let's hope it's not every week." Bill laughed.

Over the next three months, Ike faded from memory, but the lesson lingered. While Precapture's computers delved through every major delivery company's database searching for purchase patterns that indicated criminal behavior, Nathan followed the data-generated narrative of hundreds of cases without any desire to pry into the names on the left side of the screen. He promptly filled out the forms, passed the information along, and smiled compliantly when Grayson walked past. Nathan was almost invisible, which was the unstated objective of Precapture's employees, most realizing that merely having their names on the submissions was the entirety of their value.

This comfortable anonymity came to an end at the tail end of a dull week. After four days of watching unregistered businesses, illegal construction projects, owners of prohibited pets, and counterfeit handbag peddlers wavering between green and yellow, the code *021* appeared on his screen. He scrunched his eyes in disbelief before looking around, but there were no snickering coworkers peeking over the cubicle walls, so he turned back and read the name below it, Mary Johnston, and followed the line across to the designation, 021 - domestic terrorism.

Flattered that something as important as this would fall into his hands, he sat up straighter as he ran through the cursory background data. Mary's address was 418 Westwood Terrace, just a few blocks from his apartment. Almost disappointed to see that she was only a yellow minus, he clicked on her purchases. Half a dozen bags of Thrive-X fertilizer didn't seem that unusual, but it was a day after she'd purchased a tank of propane. Theoretically they could be used to make a bomb, and the proximity of the purchases had triggered the algorithm, but if she purchased other gardening supplies in the next couple of days, the algorithm would consider the propane purchase unrelated and push her off his screen completely. For the next hour, he toggled between Mary's case and the others in the hopes that a dubious delivery might nudge her closer to full yellow.

A hand on his shoulder pulled him from the screen. "Hey, man, are you eating today?"

Nathan jumped and twisted his head. "Bill, what? Already?" Then he glanced at his watch. "Oh, wow, it's lunchtime. Okay then. The usual?"

They were a few steps from the elevator when the doors began to close, and Nathan jogged the last couple of steps and waved his hand between the doors. They juddered as they sprang back, pulling the other occupant's attention from her phone long enough to flash a disapproving glare. Nathan scrolled through his phone to eat the twenty seconds it took to reach the ground floor, then turned to Bill the moment they spilled into the anonymity of the lobby.

"You're not going to believe what I just got."

"I have no idea, Nathan, but you're grinning like a Cheshire cat, so I'm assuming it's good."

"An oh-two-one."

Bill raised an eyebrow as though waiting for a wink. "Really?"

"Yep." Nathan nodded slowly.

"That is domestic terrorism, right? Wow, how did that fall to you?"

Nathan frowned in mock offense. "Hey, man, careful."

"Sorry, but you know what I mean. Do you think that they're testing you for a promotion?"

"I have no idea, but it seems a little too early—you know, even though I'm a stellar employee," Nathan deadpanned.

"Umm, yeah, everyone who doesn't open their mouth is a stellar employee, so I guess you fit the description," Bill replied, deftly dodging a man who was frozen midstep staring at his phone. "When did it come through?"

"Oh, about ten."

"And you kept it quiet?"

Nathan lowered his voice to a conspiratorial whisper. "I shouldn't even be telling you now. You know they're all over these things."

"Of course, I won't tell anyone."

"Oh, I know, but it still feels a bit weird, you know."

"Yeah, I get it, but you know I'd tell you, right?" Bill responded.

Nathan nodded a couple of times. "Yeah, yeah, sure."

They arrived at Old Town Deli. The counter staff were preparing for the arrival of the true lunch hour, but at a quarter to twelve, there was just one customer ahead of them. Bill ambled down the counter deliberating over the sandwich options as Nathan placed his usual turkey and Swiss on the plastic tray and shuffled along behind him.

Bill turned back to Nathan. "Well, this is it, your fifteen minutes of fame. While you have Grayson's eye, you'd better make a good impression."

"She's only yellow minus, so it might be literally fifteen minutes. I've been waiting all morning for her to buy something." Nathan pulled out his phone and took a quick glance, but he shook his head as he slid it back into his pocket.

Bill smiled. "If it's interesting enough, you could always stretch it a little."

"Stretch it?"

"Come on, man, don't tell me that you've never stretched it? You'd have to be the only one in the building."

Nathan swiped the terminal on the way out, clumsily adding a signature to the screen. "I haven't. Really."

"Okay, Mr. Innocent, let's assume that you don't have any idea what I'm talking about—"

"Actually, I don't," Nathan replied.

"Nathan, I'll spell it out for you. This is a pretty tedious job, and most of us need a little more than vague assurances of a promotion if we keep our heads down, so if there's a case that's interesting enough, we'll extend it a little by sending them a package."

They took a table by the window, and Nathan flopped down on a wobbly chair. "Seriously? That's pretty well the only thing that's strictly forbidden. Why would anyone take a risk like that?"

"Hey, man, I have to admire your dedication, but really, it's just so brutal in there."

Nathan shrugged. "Yeah, but still. Are you sure that people have done that?"

"Yeah, I'm sure. I've done it. Only a couple of times, but it's kind of a fun game to see how little you can spend to keep someone's name balanced on the bottom of your screen."

"You're crazy."

"If you use an anonymizer, there's no way they can track it back to you, and it got me through a couple of the worst days. Aren't you losing it by midafternoon?"

"Sure, but messing with someone's life doesn't sound like the best way to relieve boredom."

"Hey, Mr. Holier Than Thou, no one gets on these lists without a reason."

"Maybe, but Precapture has to make a mistake every now and then."

Almost half of Bill's sandwich had disappeared in a few bites, and he held his fist in front of his mouth so he could reply while he ate. "Do you know of any?"

"Well, Ike seemed to think so—" Nathan began.

"But neither of us knows what happened there, so until proven otherwise, I'm going to retain my faith in the algorithm." Bill cocked his head with a knowing smile.

Nathan nibbled on his sandwich without making any real headway. "Okay, okay, I'll think about it, but don't hold it against me if I let this one pass me by. Anyway, I'd better head back. I feel like I should at least be around a bit more while it's on my list."

"No worries, man, I get it. Sometimes it just isn't worth it. But you may not get a chance like this very often. If they're targeting you for a promotion, you'd better take it. I'd be the next in line, and that's the last thing this company needs." Bill laughed.

Nathan smiled. "Well, no one wants that, but I'm not going to jail to stop it from happening."

"You might be overstating the risks a little, and besides, it's domestic terrorism, so there's always the chance that keeping them under the microscope might be for the best. You don't want to be the guy that let a terrorist through the net, do you?"

"Okay, I'll give it some thought," said Nathan, as he pushed himself back from the table.

"So, you're not going to finish that?" said Bill, gesturing to the half of Nathan's sandwich that remained untouched.

Nathan laughed. "No. You can have it."

Bill didn't wait for Nathan to leave his chair before reaching across the linoleum table. "Thanks, man. I'll see you back there."

On the way out, Nathan glanced back to see Bill polishing off the last of his own sandwich with his right hand and cradling Nathan's in his left. Lunch hour had begun, and Nathan weaved through those buried in their phones, each managing just a few purposeful steps before dropping their heads and slowing to a distracted amble. Back at his desk, Nathan eagerly entered his password after waking his machine but slumped back at the sight of the unchanged yellow square beside Mary's name. She'd slide off his screen in twenty-four hours without any new evidence. He sent a message to Bill: *Damn, it looks like my fifteen minutes of fame might be reduced to three. She's still yellow minus.*

Don't sweat it. It was too good to be true. Welcome back to the drudgery.

Yeah, I don't know why I got my hopes up.

Nathan slid the phone back into his pocket as Grayson strolled past.

When the clock's hands eventually reached five, some coworkers ambled toward the elevator, but having an 021 under his watch merited a little extra dedication, so he sent a congratulatory email to a promoted colleague he barely knew and wrote to a director who was unlikely to open his message, then he checked Mary's case again. Ten minutes later the empty desks outnumbered the full ones, and he crouched over his keyboard and typed in Mary's address. The map showed that 418 Westwood Terrace was a standard-sized block. He quickly closed the window and opened the spreadsheet to look at the list of purchases again, cursing that the map ruled out the easy explanation for the purchase of all that fertilizer. He pondered sending a quick note to Grayson, but knowing what his advice would be, he just cleared the browser history and slid out along the aisle.

The following morning, dull-gray light seeped through the windows as Nathan scrolled to Mary's name. She'd dropped to green plus, indicating that her case would expire in an hour without another delivery. He glanced across at Bill's empty seat, then pulled out his phone and tapped out a message. *I'm thinking of doing something stupid. Can you talk me out of it?* But factoring delivery time, he only had five minutes to stretch the case, so he deleted the message, then typed in the address that he'd committed to memory.

Grayson was chatting to a coworker next to him, so Nathan hustled to the elevators, taking a surreptitious glance around the studio after tapping the elevator button repeatedly. When the stainless-steel doors finally slid open, he stepped inside and glanced at his watch. There were only three minutes left. As the doors inched toward each other, a "Can you hold that?" came from the nest of cubicles. Nathan didn't lift his head from his phone, and there was a "Come on, man" from just a couple of feet away when the doors closed.

Once in the lobby, Nathan strode toward the exit, tapping on his phone, hoping that momentum would keep doubt at bay. He logged in to the anonymizer application, typed *Thrive-X*, selected the twenty-five-pound bag that Mary had been consistently buying, and pressed the purchase button. The moment the purchase was complete, he turned back to the elevator.

Back on his floor, he strode to his cubicle without raising his eyes. The color was unchanged when Nathan brought up Mary's profile. After a few minutes of useless clicks, he pushed the mouse away and went to the bathroom. He spent the next forty minutes clicking at two-minute intervals, until finally the screen took an extra half second to refresh, and he leaned forward. The box had changed to yellow plus, skipping yellow minus and full yellow designation entirely. He closed his eyes and took a deep breath before carefully reading the line from left to right, then let his fist drop to his desk when he saw a second delivery at around the same time.

The thud was enough for Bill to spin around. "Everything okay?"

Nathan waved him off—"Yeah, yeah"—and scrolled to the next name on the list, knowing it was the last time he'd ever stretch a case. His purchase only elevated Mary's case a single level, and he told himself that the algorithm would still push her name off his screen if he didn't touch it again.

That evening, Nathan stepped off the train as the warm summer sky was fading to purple, but instead of crossing the road, he mindlessly turned left after exiting the station, toward 418 Westwood. He sped up as though his momentum would carry him past, but the sight of the numbers from his screen painted on a lumpy mailbox slowed him to a stop. An old Volkswagen van sat in the driveway, and he started building a life around the dilapidated vehicle. He imagined weekend camping trips, tattered backpacks, and faded tents, and the occasional breakdown that would provide a humorous campfire story. As Mary's case came to life, it dragged the others with it, tearing the anonymity from the endless names and numbers that he monitored daily. He tried to stop himself from picturing the lives of the Jasons, the Karas, and all the others that he'd sent to the authorities once they'd reached red plus, convicted by the algorithm. His name was on each one of those reports, implying a level of human oversight beyond the mindless ticking of boxes and the confirmation of addresses.

Beyond the van, the house seemed exhausted, each of the walls was slightly off square, as though it had finally lost the will to stand up to the wind. The ashen siding was broken by a golden glow from two of the windows, but another window was cracked. An unkempt collection of brush and weeds lined a driveway that led to a greenhouse. The glass was smeared, but he could still see plants inside, and as the fertilizer she'd purchased lost its menace, his stretching of the case felt even more irresponsible.

A young boy furiously pedaling a bike that he wouldn't grow into for another year almost grazed Nathan as he swerved to avoid the mailbox, and the boy's mother came running to the door. Mary was younger and prettier than he'd imagined. Her dark hair was pulled back into a ponytail, and a tight white T-shirt stopped just short of her tattered jeans. They weren't fashionably torn; the wear was authentic, but the holes seemed perfectly placed to highlight her slender legs. She caught his eye, and he glanced away, waiting a couple of seconds before looking up again. Her disapproving stare hadn't wavered, and he anxiously reached into his pocket for his phone and hunched over it before taking a step without looking up. A jagged edge of concrete caught his foot midstride, and he tripped, his phone skittering along the cement as he fell. He was trying to wash away the shock when the woman shouted, "Are you okay?" from the porch.

He ignored the sharp pain in his knee as he brought himself to his feet. "Yeah, I'm fine."

She walked toward him. "Thank goodness—that looked like a nasty fall."

Nathan absorbed her blue eyes and a sympathetic face. "Yeah, I was too distracted. That'll teach me." He winced as he took a step toward his phone.

"Oh, it's too easy to get caught up in those things. Anyway, you don't look familiar. Do you live around here?"

He looked at her evenly, but a light inflection at the end of the sentence softened any accusation it might have contained. "Umm, I guess. I grew up here but went to college upstate. I moved back about a year ago. I'm in the apartment buildings on Fourth."

"Oh, I see," she replied, nodding.

Nathan began to turn away. "Thanks for checking on me. Really, I'm okay. Maybe I'll see you around."

"Oh, you're welcome."

He left with a stilted wave and cursed under his breath as he hobbled away. Waiting until he was around the corner before slowing, he let two sets of lights pass by before taking a deep breath and letting her smile carry him home.

The next morning, he heard his name over the din of a crowded lobby but continued toward the elevators in a stiff-legged gait and shouted, "Can you hold that?" as the doors started closing. When they closed uninterrupted, he yelled, "Come on!" and was still jabbing at the elevator button when he felt a tap on his shoulder.

"Nathan, couldn't you hear me?"

He turned to see Grayson and took an involuntary step backward. "Oh, sorry, I must've been in my own little world."

"You're telling me. But I have to admire your dedication; you seem in quite a hurry."

Nathan briefly glanced at his feet. "Ahh—"

"Is there anything I should know about?"

Nathan shook his head. "No, not really, I'm just keen to get an early start. There's a lot on my plate right now."

"Oh, okay. I did see that you were working on the 021. How's that going?"

"Well, it's a bit of a tough one to read."

Grayson put his hand on Nathan's shoulder. "To read? Now, Nathan, you haven't been here for that long, so don't get caught up in trying to read what's going on. Just check to confirm with the carriers that each delivery actually made it to the suspects, and let the case play out. Those guys will get what they deserve."

"Get what they deserve?"

Grayson was smiling broadly. "Yeah, it's great to see justice, right?"

"Oh yeah. Yes, of course." Nathan paused for a moment. "Do you ever think the algorithm makes a mistake?"

Grayson laughed. "Not until someone messes with it. You leave it alone, it gets its man—or in this case, woman, right?"

"I guess so, but I can't remember. I'm not really curious about the lives behind those numbers."

Grayson let his hand drop and raised an eyebrow. "Really? Not at all curious?"

The elevator chimed, and the doors slid open. Grayson held his palm up, and Nathan stepped in, gathering himself. "Well, of course you wonder a bit, but I stifle those thoughts when they come up. It's a slippery slope."

Grayson looked at him squarely. "Yes, much slipperier than you think."

They arrived at their floor, and he replied, "I'll be careful."

Grayson nodded as he stepped out. "Great, and thanks for all of your hard work."

"Thanks, Grayson, I appreciate it."

As Nathan poorly imitated a casual stroll to his desk, Bill nodded in greeting, and everything felt normal until he saw the red minus designation next to Mary's name. The bag of Thrive-X that he sent hadn't been returned. Nathan wasn't surprised that she picked it up off the porch without thinking, but the algorithm wouldn't account for simple mistakes. She'd been ten minutes from freedom, but his purchase added to her guilt. He searched for a benign chemical to balance his earlier delivery. He glanced around, then pulled his phone out of his pocket and set a delivery for six the following morning. If he could intercept the delivery before she even knew it arrived, he'd cancel out his meddling. He was shoving his phone back in his pocket when Bill approached.

"Hey, man, how's it going?"

Nathan shook his head. "There's no news. I'm not messing around with this one. Grayson sounds like he's keeping a close eye on it, and I'd rather just let it roll by. A promotion isn't worth the years off my life."

"Years off your life? Aren't you being a bit dramatic?" Bill paused, and his eyes narrowed. "Unless of course there's something you're not telling me."

Nathan looked at Bill and waved him off. "No, man, we're good."

Bill nodded slowly. "That's cool, but you know that they won't come around that often, you—"

"Come on, Bill, just leave it. I told you that I didn't want to mess with it."

Bill held up his hands defensively. "Yeah, man, I got it. Sorry, I didn't mean to push."

"Sorry, Bill, it's just a bit stressful, that's all."

Bill turned away. "No worries, man. I get it."

At five thirty the next morning, his alarm squawked, wrenching him from a fitful sleep. He pulled on a pair of jeans and darted out into the crisp air, swept along by adrenaline. With careful steps he positioned himself behind some trash cans opposite Mary's house and waited. The drone zipped overhead, the beelike buzz jolting him into action, and he dashed toward the door. The distance to the porch seemed to grow as he crossed the threshold into her yard, and the drone flashed back over him the moment after the package dropped onto the doorstep with a dull thud.

An upstairs window came to life, the golden hue punching a hole in the black hulk of the house. He stopped and stood upright on the grass, completely exposed. The expected silhouette didn't appear in the window above him, and he sprinted the last few paces, grabbing the package and running down the street in the direction of his house. Fifty yards away, fatigue slowed his sprint to a clumsy jog, and he looked over his shoulder. The street was still asleep, so he slowed to a walk. He dropped the package inside the door to his apartment and ran to the train, descending the stairs two at a time.

When Nathan arrived at his desk, he let his backpack slide to the floor and reached for the mouse in a single motion. Scrolling slowly, he steeled himself as he approached the J's, scanning the bottom of the screen in hopes of seeing the color that would extract him from this mess, but blinked at the unchanged red minus. He couldn't imagine testifying against Mary, knowing that her guilt was far less relevant than Grayson's conviction record. As the list of names on his screen begged him to pry their anonymity away, he hastily swiped the terminal to sleep and strode toward Grayson's office. The door was ajar, but when Nathan poked his head in, Grayson was on the phone.

Nathan stopped. "Oh, I'm sorry. I'll come back later."

Grayson held his hand over his phone's speaker and called out, "No, Nathan, it's actually good timing. I have a couple of questions for you."

"Uh, okay," Nathan replied.

Grayson turned back toward the phone. "I'm sorry. Something just came up. Can I call you back in a few minutes?" There was a brief pause, then Grayson said thanks. He looked up at Nathan, his face softening into what looked like a carefully practiced smile.

"Don't worry, you're not in trouble, but it seems that you've given Mary's case quite a bit of attention."

"Of course, it's an 021, but rest assured that I haven't neglected my other cases."

"Oh no, that's not why I'm asking; you have an excellent record. We're just wondering if you've seen anything I've missed. It's been quite erratic."

"Erratic? In what way?"

"The purchase patterns just seem off, and she's hovered on the border for longer than most."

"Oh. You'd know what's normal, but from what I've seen, those ones on the border always seem to end up back in green."

"Well, that's not always the case, and you know that faith in the system is paramount—every time we miss someone we should've caught, well, the doubts creep in."

"Of course."

"Well, just to let you know. This 021 isn't red plus, but given the potential danger of terrorism, the authorities can arrest a suspect as soon as they reach any level of red, and we're going to hand this to the authorities right away. I'll assume that you don't have any objections."

Nathan shook his head. "No, no, of course not."

"Thanks, Nathan." Grayson paused. "And keep up the good work."

"Yes. Yes, of course." Nathan hustled toward the door, but just as he reached for the handle, Grayson called out.

"Oh, Nathan?"

He half turned back. "Yes?"

"What did you come in here for?"

"Oh, oh, nothing important. We can chat later." Nathan turned the handle and was gone before Grayson could respond. He walked straight past his sleeping terminal to the elevators that he'd stepped out of just a few moments before. Slinging his backpack over his shoulder, he turned to the exit, followed by Bill's curious gaze.

His phone vibrated a few minutes later, and a message from Bill popped up.

Hey, man, what are you doing? Grayson is watching you closely, and the only empty seat in the office is yours.

I'll be back. I just have something I need to do.

It had better be important. This doesn't look good.

It is.

Good luck.

When Nathan arrived at Mary's, he listened to the sounds of a routine morning through the door, took a deep breath, and knocked. He heard the rattle of a spoon in a coffee cup and the clang of dishes in an empty sink before Mary eased the door open.
"You're the guy that tripped the other night, right? How can I help you? If you need me to vouch for the horrid state of the sidewalk, I can—"
He looked down at his feet. "No. No, that's not it. Look, I'm not sure how to tell you this, but have you heard of Precapture?"
She dropped her smile. "Of course. What's going on?"
"Well, I don't know how to break this to you, but I work for them, and you're on their list. I know it sounds crazy, but I guess that you bought a lot of fertilizer, and they don't cross-reference with the greenhouse. I can explain more later, but you're in danger. You should get out of here for the moment. That will give me some time to see what I can—"
A vaguely familiar voice spoke from deep inside the house. "Who is it?"
She turned and shouted in the direction of the voice, "Ike, it's nothing important. I'll be there in a minute."
Nathan blurted out, "Ike? What? No. No, it can't be…" He turned and ran. Halfway down the block, he heard the beelike buzz of a drone and reached for his phone. The black silhouette emerged from the monochromatic blue sky and hovered over the front porch.

A recorded voice announced, "Mary Johnston, come out with your hands raised."

Nathan pulled out his phone and stabbed at the screen to call Grayson. "The 021. They're playing us."

"What? Who's playing us?"

"Ike. Ike's behind it."

"Ike who?"

"You know, Ike. Fuck. Just tell the authorities that there's been a mistake, and I'll explain when I get in."

"What sort of mistake? Nathan, can you hear me? What's the mistake?"

Nathan was distracted by the high-pitched whirr of two more drones zipping overhead; these were covered in the bright colors and garish logos of two local news organizations. Ike and Mary burst out of their house, their arms raised theatrically, and Ike winked at Nathan before looking up at the drones.

Nathan had forgotten that Grayson was still on the line until the tinny voice yelled, "What's going on?"

Nathan inhaled sharply. "Grayson, just look at the news. I'm coming in."

Grayson's response was cold and distant. "Okay." The line went dead a second later, then Nathan ran toward the subway.

When he arrived, Grayson's door was wide open, his spindly silhouette pacing back and forth in front of the full-length glass windows. Nathan stepped into the doorway, but Grayson didn't see him until he swiveled around at the far corner of his office.

"So what were you doing there?"

Nathan lifted his head but looked past Grayson, absorbed by the montage of neighboring skyscrapers' windows, the closest ones providing neat frames for snippets of office dramas.

"Nathan?"

"I don't know, but it was only a few blocks from my house. I just couldn't stay away."

A smirk spread slowly across Grayson's face. "Nathan, relax, you're not in trouble with us. I had a feeling that you'd get caught up. That's why we gave it to you."

"What? You set me up?"

Grayson shook his head slowly. "No. No, not at all. You were just an insurance policy."

Nathan shook his head. "I'm afraid I don't follow."

Grayson began slowly, "You see, Nathan, for all of our faith in the algorithm, I still trust my intuition, and this one didn't feel right. It felt like someone might be trying to prove a point."

"What sort of point?"

"That the algorithm couldn't make the distinction between a backyard botanist and a threat to the general public. That's why he bought just enough to push her into red. He wanted us to look silly in court, pointing to a few bags of fertilizer as our evidence."

"So why did you even let the case go this far?"

"Well, there was the slim chance that I was wrong, and if this really was domestic terrorism, then a conviction here would have been another great case study." Nathan stared blankly, and Grayson continued, "I have to hand it to Ike. Mary is the perfect exhibit—young, attractive; the press would have loved to see someone like her take down the faceless machine. I remember when he promised revenge, and he knew exactly how to play the algorithm. If it wasn't for you, he might have done it." Grayson punctuated the sentence with a slap on the table.

Nathan clenched his fists and rocked around on the balls of his feet as though he was about to run but wasn't sure which direction to go. "What do you mean, if it wasn't for me? They got to red minus through our algorithm even though they're innocent. This isn't going to look good."

"Well, they won't get the spectacular case they'd hoped for. They'll be released right away, and we'll announce that an employee compromised the case so the algorithm was working with tainted data. You did meddle, right? A couple of deliveries seemed a little too well timed."

Nathan scrunched his eyes. "You aren't supposed to know who sent them. That's an invasion of privacy."

Grayson's smirk broadened into a wide grin. "You're right, and we weren't sure they were from you until now."

Nathan shook his head. "But Grayson, why me?"

"I'm sorry, Nathan, you were just unlucky enough to be young, curious, and live close by, but if it makes you feel better, it could have been anyone here. I'm sure that you won't be the last to make this mistake." Grayson turned to his screen to signal that the conversation had come to an end. Nathan glanced to his left as a stiff-faced man in uniform grabbed his elbow with a viselike grip. As he was escorted out of the building, a sea of reporters thrust microphones at Nathan, but he just hung his head as he was pushed toward the waiting car.

regret

REGRET

This was the last hour he'd be Jay, and as he paced back and forth on the platform, he rubbed the square lump behind his ear, feeling the edges of the chip that had been nestled there since his decision. Trading a few miserable memories to avoid prison was an easy choice at the time, but now that he wanted to trade back, it was too late. He waited patiently, not daring to run in case there was something volatile in the tracking device. Peering into the tunnel, he caught a flash of yellow on the tracks, then a warm breath of air, and he took a step back from the edge as the train wailed to a halt. He entered through the middle doors, three carriages from the back, knowing that they would open at the base of the stairs and give him a head start on the crowds at peak hour. He wondered if he'd still know that after the operation.

Jay had no reason to be enamored with efficiency; he wasn't a Wall Street banker forced to endure the smells, crowds, and frustrations of the masses for forty-five minutes each day. He was the type they desperately tried to avoid—the guy with nothing to lose. Their wealth wouldn't shield them from a sudden flash of anger in the tight confines of a subway car, an anger that simmered just beneath the surface.

A heavyset man leering at a college student across from him was his potential outlet this morning. The girl's eyes were glued to her book, but she tugged at her skirt and squirmed in her seat, seeming to sense the man's attention. Jay watched him fumble for his phone, waiting for the excuse to punch him, but instead of bringing the lens into view, the man just rolled it over in his hand, waiting impatiently for a signal.

As always, Jay was the first out of the train, and after taking the first flight of stairs, he turned right onto a wide platform. He paused before entering the claustrophobic tunnel that led to the street, wincing as he remembered the moment. It was a month ago now, but he'd relived it every day since, and he felt a tinge of relief knowing that this would be the last time he'd remember it. A combination of drugs, alcohol, and a fight with his girlfriend had been the perfect storm. He hadn't even been in a hurry, he didn't have a home to rush back to, and on that night the warmth of the subway would have been better than facing the winds that whipped off the East River.

Jay would never have given up his wallet without a fight; it contained his last few dollars, but letting defense turn into a mindless attack still haunted him. His assailant was so out of place: his hexagonal sunglasses were carefully placed on the flat brim of a baseball cap, and the polished brown boots combined with a pale blue shirt were a caricature of a stylish New Yorker. You had to venture a long way to escape the gentrification of New York, but even here on the border of expanding affluence, no one else on the platform was flashing their wealth so ostentatiously. The man was about his age, and Jay couldn't help but wonder about the decisions that had led to their positions at either ends of society. Would this man with porcelain skin have survived everything that had peeled Jay's life away? Surely he would've fallen at one of the hurdles. Even if he had escaped the abusive father or shrugged off the school bully, he still could have been caught up in the gas station robbery that tripped Jay up in his early teens. Eager to impress the older kids, Jay couldn't find the courage to halt the momentum of a night tumbling toward tragedy, and he'd been invisible since then, an unwanted extra in the movie of other people's lives.

Now, passersby cropped him out of their frame with a guilty look away, but for that brief, fateful moment a month ago, he was the center of attention. The brave screamed at him, and others tapped at phones to summon help, but his fury kept them all at bay. With the crumpled body motionless at his feet, his adrenaline seeped away, and he ran, but it didn't matter. A dozen bystanders had recorded the flurry of unnecessary punches, but the childhood injustices that pushed him to that point would remain forever out of view.

He shook the memory away for the last time before it would be papered over with someone else's story, but it felt so powerful, and he wondered if it would seep through. He'd been told the operation wasn't completely clean, that the memories might overlap, and that occasionally patients went insane trying to untangle the web.

Arriving at the hospital ten minutes early, Jay slowed to absorb the scene, one that was so innocuous that he knew the memory of it would never survive. The slate-gray sky was a shade darker than the concrete steps, and a young woman rushed down at a rapid clip with a phone held to her ear. It was just another day for her, not the bookend of one life and the start of another. As he trudged up, the force of gravity seemed to increase with each step, and when the glass doors slid open, his eyes took a moment to adjust to the dim interior.

The carpet was threadbare along a narrow path from the door to the reception desk, then it continued to a lone waiting chair. A potted plant barely clung to life in the corner, and a disinterested receptionist, her black hair flecked with gray and pulled back in a tight bun, completed the scene. She lifted her head when the doors opened and watched him standing uncertainly by the exit before letting her eyes return to her screen, lengthening the motion as though trying to fill a dull day. She said, "Jay, please take a seat," without looking up at him again.

He followed the scuffed carpet and slumped into the chair, his shoulders leaning into the backrest and his legs almost entirely off the seat. There was a double door on the far side of the room, a thin ribbon of light marking where their imperfect edges met. When they were flung open, the flash broke his daze. The white light framed two silhouettes, and the taller one beckoned him. "Jay, please come this way." His crisp delivery cut through the disheveled surroundings.

Jay dutifully pulled himself to his feet and stepped toward the light. The moment he crossed the threshold, his soiled clothing and unwashed hair became the only blemish in a bleached white corridor. His escorts, dressed in pale blue, ushered him through the maze of sterile halls to a featureless room where the taller one opened his palm and gestured toward a chair in the center. Jay positioned himself carefully, his dirty jeans rubbing against the white fabric as he squirmed, and with a gentle whir, the chair reclined. The shorter one spoke for the first time, delivering the disclaimer at a rapid clip. Jay only caught snippets: "...understand that this is a risk..." "...entered into this agreement with full knowledge of the consequences..." Jay nodded mindlessly, but the man responded brusquely, "You have to give a verbal confirmation." Jay bit his bottom lip; it was easier just to nod than to speak the words that would change everything. He let a couple of seconds pass by, and the man spoke again. "Jay?"

Jay nodded slowly. "Yes. Yes, I accept."

The man gave an empty "thank you," and Jay was enveloped in darkness.

He woke in the recovery room, surrounded by blurred shapes that he strained to pull into focus. After a few seconds, an L-shaped blob became a chair, and a silver smudge resolved into a tray, but the walls remained featureless expanses, resisting his attempts to find any detail. The ceiling was pale green, and it felt vaguely familiar, but he couldn't place it. When he tried to sit up, the restraints held him fast, and he jerked his head around before puncturing the silence with a scream. He heard the clack of heels on linoleum, then a door opening behind him, but despite his thrashing, he couldn't angle his head to see who it was. The sweet fragrance of perfume wafted over him, followed by a gentle voice: "Eris, it's okay."

He wasn't sure if that was his name; it felt half-right.

"Am I Eris?"

"Yes," she said without hesitation.

"Are you sure?"

Her voice was soft but unwavering. "Yes, Eris, we haven't made a mistake. You'll feel a little disoriented, but it's okay. Just relax."

She made no effort to move into his field of vision as she continued, "Eris, close your eyes, and the memories will come. They'll be hazy at first, but in time everything will become clear." Her words trailed off, and he could tell that she was walking away.

"Wait. Wait, who are you?"

"I'm not important, but trust me, no one's here to harm you. Lie back, take your time."

A moment later, there was a slight draft as the door closed. He followed her instructions and allowed his head to drop to the pillow. The moment he closed his eyes, Jay's recent memories began trickling in, but they were cloudy, as though they were someone else's life. The first was the flash of light framing the doctors' silhouettes, and his fear as he walked toward it, but he couldn't remember why he'd been so scared. An earlier memory came back as an unattached snippet: a lonely walk toward an imposing gray building. The world had been devoid of color, and the nagging fear was still there. Then he remembered being the first off the subway. As each moment returned, it was as though he were rewinding a movie, playing thirty-second clips and attempting to string a narrative together from the pieces.

The next scene that returned was the court case, and now he remembered why he was here. Relief washed over him—these were still his memories; he was sure of it. They were hazy, but he was still Jay. Something must've gone wrong—the new memories hadn't stuck. He searched back through Jay's memories for reassurance, hoping to find someone that had mentioned his name. Besides the court case, a "Thank you, sir" at the liquor store was the most personal conversation he could find before the first batch of crossed memories rushed in. They were sharp and clear, a tidal wave from Eris's life, and Jay's memories suddenly felt like a television left on in the corner.

Eris's first memory was of a pair of concerned faces peering down at him. The tall, thin man wore a drab beige suit that was a little tight, and the woman a knee-length navy skirt paired with a crisp white shirt that was appropriately conservative for law enforcement. He'd tried to sit up but was held fast by restraints on his forearms and shins, and he resorted to thrashing his head pointlessly. The woman made a subtle gesture, and a young man in scrubs made some adjustments to the fluid flowing into him, softening the pain of his swollen face. The room began to dissolve, and the moment before it went black, he watched the concern on their faces turn to panic. A loud beep woke him again, and the man in the suit was coaxing him to stay coherent. Eris began talking, and the words poured out. He knew that they overlapped, but he couldn't tease them apart. The woman was methodical and patient, but she didn't understand.

The next memory flooded in. It was the same room, but now there were two gentlemen in olive military uniforms. One was asking questions, and the other, with a myriad of colored bands on his lapel, was standing a couple of feet behind. What they'd asked escaped him, but Eris could remember the surprised expressions on faces that weren't in the habit of conveying emotion. The highly decorated one stepped forward and uttered a few unintelligible words into the ear of his compatriot, who resumed the interrogation with more urgency. He'd known the answers to their questions but couldn't bring the words to his mouth.

Eris's past returned in snippets, and each glimpse posed new questions rather than providing answers, but his efforts to lengthen the memories were in vain. The next scene was just a flash of searing pain and a police uniform. He was on his back with bright lights glaring at him, but he wasn't in a hospital; he was on frigid cement. Warm blood seeped through his shirt, and he remembered a young girl with a hand over her mouth trying to hide her shock. She leaned forward, but before she could reach out, a hand came from the crowd and gently tugged her a half step backward.

The next scene was the same location, but the pain was replaced with fear and confusion. A sullen figure stomped up the stairs toward him, a few steps ahead of the oncoming crowd. He recalled tripping on the way down and thrusting his arm out to stop himself. The movement became an inadvertent blow, but he was hit before he could apologize. Holding up an arm in self-defense, he was still off-balance, and the next jab knocked him to the ground. Then the punches came in a flurry, and he couldn't understand the anger fueling them. He turned to face his assailant just in time to absorb

REGRET

another blow, and he remembered the bystanders carving a wide arc before that memory faded to black.

He continued to reach back, pulling the prior day into focus. There was a flash of white, and everything was different. The memory rushed into his consciousness, but he couldn't make sense of it. He was in a laboratory with a perfect glossy sheen surrounded by softly humming electronics. A pair of eager young scientists were relaying some last-minute instructions as they encouraged him to take the small step into a gate of blue light. The girl spoke in a soft voice. "Eris, relax. You'll only be there for a couple of hours." He reached deeper and found her name—Vega.

Her colleague, Jordan, added, "Yes, you'll be back before dinner, and you're not going to another planet. It's only New York, just like you remember it from the movies. Think of it like stepping into the screen."

He willed himself to lift his right foot, but it felt cemented to the floor. He couldn't coax it forward, and he clenched his fist in frustration. Jordan placed a gentle hand on his shoulder and reassured him. "Eris, you'll be okay." He nodded, but his gaze remained glued to his feet as he took a tentative step forward. The second stride was more purposeful, and he marched the final steps into the wall of milky blue gel. It gave easily when he approached, embracing him like a soft blanket, and he kept walking as the light faded. He felt a pang of claustrophobia, but a moment later the blanket loosened and gently fell away. It was still pitch black, but after another stride he could see a ribbon of light, and then it widened to reveal the gritty bricks of a back alley in Brooklyn. A car flashed past, a Prius, confirming that he'd arrived in the early twenty-first century.

"Eris," said a stern voice, cutting through the memory, "we have a few questions."

Opening his eyes, he searched the faces peering down at him, but it wasn't until he lowered his gaze to the crisp suits that the memory returned. They were the last two people he'd seen from the operating table, back in a different life. Eris let his eyes fall closed, but a firm hand jostled him. "Eris, stay with us."

His eyes flashed open, and he pulled at the restraints. "I'm sorry, I have to go. I shouldn't be here. I'm not supposed to leave a trace. They said it was just like stepping into a movie, but it all went wrong. You just have to let me go."

"Eris, I'm sorry, but we can't let you go. I'm sure that this must be confusing to you, but it really can't wait."

"No, you don't understand. It's not what you think."

In a tone devoid of sympathy, the elder man said, "Eris, it's okay." A few seconds later, he lowered his voice. "Now, can you remember anything?"

As Eris composed himself, he feigned confusion. The man's deputy whispered under his breath, "Sir, the whole operation is a waste of time. He's not going to give us anything. It's madness."

"Major, it was the only chance we had. The other body was too far gone, and at least we know that the operation works." He turned to Eris and took a fatherly tone. "Listen, we're not here to harm you. It's just that you were carrying a phone that we'd never seen before, and it seemed like it was, ahh... Anyway, we're just trying to understand who you are."

"It was like what?"

The men exchanged glances, and the younger man began, "Umm, like it was..."

The major snapped, "From the future. It seemed like it was from the future."

At the word "future," the trickle of memories became a torrent. The linear progression of time jumbled, and Eris wasn't sure which memories to trust. He twisted, straining the thick leather straps holding him in place. "Sir, can you loosen these?" The men exchanged glances before the shorter man loosened the restraints. Eris sat up slowly and shuffled to get comfortable, doing his best to avoid looking like a flight risk. "If I could have that phone, I think I can explain."

The major spoke into his cuff in short, crisp sentences, and a minute later a young man brought in the small square of black glass in a clear plastic bag. Eris jiggled his leg in anticipation as the man held it out. Eris took it from him and cradled it in his hands, waiting for the black square to spring to life, but it wasn't Eris's face, so the device remained inert. With a subtle gesture, a group of letters appeared on the screen, but with his hands shaking, Eris failed to arrange them in the correct order. He swiveled so his legs hung loosely off the side of the bed, and the two men stepped closer, so he raised a hand in a calming gesture before returning to the device. His fingers flashed around on the screen, and he managed to break the code. He gently pushed his hips forward to allow his toes to touch the floor. The men darted toward him as he transferred his weight to wobbly legs, and the taller one managed to get a hand under his elbow.

Eris inhaled, holding the air in his lungs for a second before letting it out with a sigh and taking a short step. He wiggled his arm, freeing himself, and took another step. He was walking away from the door, and the two men allowed him the few feet he'd need.

Eris swiped at his device in a carefully practiced motion. It was like pulling a rip cord, and a gate flashed in front of him. He leapt through the gel and staggered forward into the black, managing one more step before the darkness was erased with bright spotlights. He tried to stop himself, but he lost his balance and sprawled to the ground like a sprinter that had leaned too far into the finish line. He slowly rolled over to absorb his surroundings. A stark white room, a gel gate behind him, and a clump of medical devices, each a different shade of beige, tucked in the corner.

The glaring white light aimed at him obscured the details of the other two people in the room.

One of them screamed, "What? Who are you?"

The other looked up. "What. What the fuck?"

It was a familiar woman's voice, and Eris held his right palm above his eyes to block out the light, allowing the features to emerge from the black silhouettes. "Vega? Is that you? Jordan? I'm so glad to see you."

They both took a step backward, and Jordan slid a hand into his pocket, then pulled a device out and rolled it in his hands. "What? How do you know us?"

"It's me. Eris. I can't believe what happened."

"You're not Eris. What the hell have you done with him?" Vega shouted as she edged backward.

With raspy breaths, Eris tried to bring himself to his feet, but Jordan raised his fists menacingly. Eris held up his hand. "There's no need to panic; I'm not going to hurt you. Just let me explain what I think just happened."

"What you think just happened? We can work it out for ourselves. You killed Eris and stole his transporter."

"No. What? Why? No, I didn't. I am Eris. They did an operation; they transferred memories. I'm in someone else's body. It all went wrong the moment I arrived. Is there anything we can do? I don't want to live in this." He waved his hand at his own body and coughed.

Jordan narrowed his eyes. "Why should we believe you?"

Eris screamed, "Because I know who you fucking are!" Then he coughed again, and this time he buckled over.

Jordan put a hand on his shoulder. "Okay, okay. Stay calm. There has to be something we can do."

Vega looked at Jordan. "Has anything like this happened before?"

"I don't know, but we can fix it. I know we can."

Vega whimpered, "He doesn't look good; let's get someone in here."

Eris tried to stand up, but he punctuated the movement with a loud cough and fell to his knees.

Vega leaned over. "Hey, man, are you okay?"

Eris looked up; his coughing was more severe now. "No, no, I don't think I am." He lay back down and began writhing.

Vega held his hand. "What's wrong?"

Eris gasped for breath as he felt Vega's grip tighten.

She turned to Jordan. "Get someone in here! This body is allergic to something."

REGRET

Eris swayed backward, and Vega helped him lower his back to the ground. Jordan hit a button, and the room was bathed in crimson light.

He held his hand on Eris's chest and turned to Vega. "Will CPR help?"

Vega shook her head. "No, it must be the air. Where the hell are the medics?"

Eris watched as her features seemed to soften, then the crimson light deepened. He felt a shove and blinked.

"Eris, stay with us. Someone's coming. You'll be okay."

He tried to focus on Vega's face, but it blurred again a moment later, and he knew there was nothing they could do. This body didn't belong here.

Vega screamed, "We'll send him back!"

Eris didn't want to just disappear in another time and tried to lift a hand in protest, but he couldn't summon any movement.

Jordan gestured at the device. "That's it! Yes. Turn it on!" He rushed to a control panel on the wall and frantically stabbed at the buttons.

Eris coughed one last time before the room went black, and Vega looked up from the body. "Jordan. It's too late."

Declan rapped on the doorframe, waited a few seconds, then cupped his hands to the side of his face and pressed them against the glass. Squinting past his reflection, he saw the barista glance at him before pointing at the clock, its minute hand not quite vertical. When she held up two fingers like rabbit ears, he wiggled his phone with *9:00 a.m.* displayed on its screen in protest. She softened a shrug with a half smile, then turned her back to snuff out his objection.

He rocked back and forth to keep the cold at bay as snowflakes accumulated in the creases of his overcoat. Without the comforting weight of his pistol, he patted his right hip for the third time in five minutes. The pistol, its tracker embedded in the grip, was lying under the front seat in a car a mile away, and the empty space reminded him that he couldn't linger. He hated leaving it there, knowing that a stationary weapon was suspicious, but he couldn't risk anyone knowing about this place, just in case it was what he'd imagined it to be.

Declan had turned toward the street to search for signs of life when she pulled the door ajar with a light "We're open now." The door was closing as he spun back around, the recently flipped OPEN sign still swinging on a silvery chain.

Pulling off his gloves finger by finger, he stumbled into the dim room. The menu behind the counter had been hastily written in chalk as though the options were expected to change weekly, but the words ADDITIONAL SHOTS $1 were on a piece of yellowing paper taped to the bottom, indicating that the menu hadn't been updated for a while.

"Sir?" She seemed to search his face when they made eye contact. "What brings you here?"

"Just passing through."

The barista nodded slowly.

"Do you get many?"

"Many what?"

"People passing through."

The barista tilted her head, then laughed lightly. "Oh, about average, I guess. So, how can I help you?"

Declan resisted the urge to respond with "You could've helped me by letting me in on time," and instead mumbled, "An Americano for here. Thanks."

She turned to the chrome machine and went through the motions with a grace born of a thousand repetitions. He scanned the magazines on the edge of the counter as he waited in the gloom. Four issues of the same hunting magazine had been carefully fanned to expose their mastheads, but the latest one was a year old. He was nudging it aside to check for anything newer when the barista nudged the cup toward him.

"That'll be four dollars, thanks."

He quickly retracted his hand and dug into his jeans pocket, fumbling for his credit card with stiff fingers.

"Sorry, cash only."

Declan nodded, then searched for some bills in his wallet. By the time he looked up again, she had turned her back and was pushing open a door marked EMPLOYEES ONLY, her short ponytail swaying from the speed of her pirouette.

He left a five-dollar bill on the counter and inched toward a chair deep in the corner, cradling the cup as he sat. After a few sips, he was looking around the room, not sure what he was hoping to find, when the door swung wide. The rush of cold air was accompanied by a shrill "Really?" Declan looked up to see a woman, her hair drifting past her shoulders in stylish waves, peeling open a soft jacket that was too light for the frigid day.

"I've been waiting for this—" She stopped, seeming to notice the deserted counter, and pulled the jacket back onto her shoulders. "Stella, are you here?"

The curtain behind the counter was pulled back, and Stella burst out. "Kathryn? Wow, that was quick, now before you..."

Kathryn's eyes widened in shock when they found Declan.

"...jump to conclusions."

Kathryn gaped like a dog staring at his food while waiting for the signal to eat.

"Kathryn!"

Kathryn stepped toward the counter and whispered, "Wow, I wasn't sure whether to believe you. It's been so long."

Stella stood up straight and responded a little too theatrically, "How about a coffee?"

Kathryn responded, "Umm, yeah, that would be great." Then she added something in a whisper that Declan couldn't catch. Stella's baseball cap was pulled low, concealing her face when she spoke, so she seemed to be trying out different expressions in a mirror each time she glanced up. Declan placed his coffee cup back without looking but misjudged the height of the table, and it thumped into the wood. Both women turned to him in unison.

Kathryn asked, "Do you know where you are right now?"

Declan chewed his lip, a nervous habit from his teenage years that he couldn't shake after five years on the force. He turned the words "be normal" over in his head before smiling. "In a coffee shop?"

Kathryn was shaking her head. "This is not some fucking joke. Stella screwed this up. Get up now. And get out. Once you're on the street, start running and don't turn around."

"Why?"

Stella placed a cup on the counter and nudged it forward with a resigned, "Kathryn."

Kathryn turned to Stella, ignoring the drink. "So, would you like to tell him what you set in motion?"

Stella stared at her. "Now, let's not get hysterical."

Declan's eyes flashed between them. "Do you want to tell me what's going on?"

Stella began, "Well, in a few—"

"Look, there's no time to explain," Kathryn cut in. "You should just go." Then she turned and held a palm up to Stella to quell any protest.

Declan waited for a smirk, but when her expression didn't change, he stood, bumping the table in his haste, and his spoon bounced off the table. He let it fall to the floor as he pulled his jacket over his shoulders and lifted the zipper to his chin.

Stella gestured toward the door. "Wait—it's too late for that."

Two silhouettes were visible through the fogged glass, then a couple more bodies joined them, and soon a small crowd was blocking out the light. Kathryn ran to a table by the door. Its stout legs were topped by a circular two-inch-thick slab of oak, and it looked as if it hadn't moved in a decade. Kathryn bent at the knees and gripped it with both hands. "Come on, Stella, help me out."

Stella ran over and gripped the tabletop. "Ready?"

"Yep," she replied.

Stella said, "On three. One, two, three." They exhaled in unison as they pushed it over, the edge crashing into the floor with a thud. Kathryn quickly ran around and leaned into it, rolling it toward the door while Stella steadied its trajectory.

Declan darted over and nudged the table in the right direction, leaning on it as it rumbled across the floor. They brought it to a halt in front of the door, and Stella waved Declan away before grabbing a leg. Kathryn copied her gesture, and with a nod of agreement, they lifted the legs so the tabletop crashed into the door with a thud. Stella flipped off the lights.

"What should I do?" Declan stammered.

Kathryn replied, "I'd say try the back, but I'm sure they've thought of that."

"Who's 'they'?"

Kathryn looked him up and down. "Do you know anything about this town?"

"Umm, yeah. Well, I know where it is. It's about twenty miles south of Carson, right?"

Kathryn looked at him evenly. "Have you ever heard of a town twenty miles south of Carson?"

"Well, no, but this isn't exactly a thriving metropolis." Declan let a brief smile pass across his face.

Kathryn shook her head. "You can't afford to smile right now."

Stella had moved a sack of flour from under the counter, leaving enough space for Declan to fold himself into. "In here—get in here."

"Wha…?"

Stella responded, "No questions. Do it. Now."

Declan began peeling his jacket off, and Kathryn grabbed his elbow, tugging him forcefully toward the counter. "No, leave it on. Hurry."

A thin strip of light flashed on the far wall as the front door was pried open, but it only lasted a moment before the weight of the table pushed the door back with a clap. Declan scurried around the counter as the table creaked again. The door opened a few inches, and the table teetered on its edge. Stella took one step toward it but jumped back again when a burly man in a black jacket managed to force the door open, sending the table to the ground with a thud. He scanned the room as he entered, and his gaze landed on the lone coffee cup on the table in the back corner. His bulk silhouetted against a slate-colored sky, he turned to Kathryn. "Where is he?"

Kathryn held his gaze. "You didn't see him?"

"What are you playing at?"

Kathryn refused to look away. "Nothing, Jake."

"So why did I have to push over a hundred-pound table to get in here?"

"We were scared he'd come back."

Jake's eyes narrowed as he allowed his gaze to drift across to Stella. "Back? So you did let him go."

Stella glanced at Kathryn for a moment. "Well, we weren't sure."

"But you sent an alert?"

Stella looked at her feet. "Yeah, I got caught up. But I had my doubts the moment I sent it."

Jake took a step in her direction, filled his cheeks with air, then allowed it to seep out between pursed lips. "Let me get this straight. You sent an alert, then decided he might not be a newcomer and let him go, but after he was gone, you thought you'd barricade yourselves in because he might be dangerous."

Stella blinked. "I...I thought he was a newcomer, but then wasn't sure, and remember what happened two years ago? Paul's cousin?"

Jake's lips curled into a smirk, and he lazily drew in a breath before beginning softly, "Ah yes, two years ago. Well, we all make mistakes, but you know, the important thing is to learn from them. Invitations are a lot more official these days."

Stella asked, "So there haven't been any invitations? You're sure he's a newcomer?"

Jake's smirk completed the transformation into a smile, and he spread his arms wide. "Of course we are. So now, do you know where he is?"

Kathryn shook her head emphatically, and Stella echoed the movement a little more solemnly. Jake's gaze flashed between them, his eyes resting on each face for a couple of seconds. Then he bellowed, "I get the feeling that you're not telling me everything."

Stella and Kathryn bolted upright in unison, and Stella began, "I'm sorry but—"

"No, Stella, it's my fault. I'm the one who let him go."

Stella cut in again, "If you hadn't listened to me, he'd still be here. Blame me."

"I could've ignored you, I—"

"Enough," Jake boomed. "Look, I don't care who's to blame; I just want to know where he is."

Kathryn looked at him with wide eyes. "I'm sorry, we just told him to run." She gestured to the half-full cup on the table. "He took it pretty seriously."

Jake nodded slowly. "Well, okay then. We'll look around outside."

As he turned around, Stella said, "I'm sorry, Jake. We didn't know."

Jake waved away the apology as he opened the door, the cold air rushing in with the flat light. A small group of expectant faces crowded around him, and he barked out a couple of words that were lost as the door closed. Inside the café, Stella took a couple of hesitant steps to the light switch and casually flipped it up, then quietly turned the door latch.

"Kathryn, your coffee's ready," Stella said a little too loudly.

"Okay, great. Thanks." Kathryn stumbled like a first-timer at drama class.

"Just take a seat. I'll bring it over to you."

As Kathryn scampered across to a table, she asked, "How long till—"

Stella cut her short with a glare, then bent over and whispered, "Stay quiet" into Declan's ear and pulled him out by his elbow. He stood up straight, and with hands on his hips, he arched his back and brushed the dust off his shirt with short, fussy strokes. The silhouettes had disappeared from the door, but Declan waited another twenty seconds before asking, "Can you tell me what's going on?"

Kathryn turned to him and cocked her head. "Stella here wanted to be the hero in this town's little game, but I'm hoping she's having second thoughts. And she's going to risk everything to get you out of here. Isn't that right, Stella?"

Stella lifted her shoulders in a half shrug. "Well, I'm not sure yet. You haven't told me why we should let him go."

Kathryn shook her head. "There's no point in keeping this town a secret. They're not protecting us from anything. I don't think it's—"

Declan nodded. "Of course. So that's why no one…"

Kathryn swung around to him. "Why no one what? Why no one—"

There was a rap on the door. "Stella, I know he's in there. Open this now."

Kathryn nodded at Declan, and he bolted toward the back door. Stella waited until it clapped shut behind him before yelling, "Jake, I'm sorry, I'm coming. And he's not here, you know."

Kathryn panned around the room for evidence, and when she saw Declan's wallet on the ground, she darted over and picked it up. It was heavier than expected, and she held her hand under it, bouncing it a couple of times.

Stella's hand was on the doorknob when Kathryn called out, "Wait, this doesn't feel right."

Stella swiveled around. "Doesn't feel right? What do you mean?"

"It's too heavy."

Jake yelled through the door, "Come on, Stella! You have ten seconds before we kick this thing in. Should I begin counting?"

Stella shouted back, "There's no need for that! Just give me a moment; this thing's stuck. We're not hiding anything."

Stella turned to Kathryn, who was holding up the wallet, her mouth agape. A metal badge with the word POLICE along the top had fallen to the floor.

Stella shook her head. "Oh no. Now we're done."

Kathryn bit her bottom lip. "Well, you know, it might not be so bad if they find us."

"What? Have you forgotten what it's like out there? Why do you think people sneak in here? It's because it's hell beyond the end of this road."

Kathryn looked at Stella, then pulled a phone out of her pocket and waved it around in front of her like a winning lottery ticket. "No. No, it's not."

Stella narrowed her eyes. "Where did you get that?"

Something heavy slammed into the door, and the thud seem to shake the room. Stella turned. "Jake, please, just hold on a moment. The lock's stuck. Let me get the key."

Kathryn continued, ignoring the interruption, "You remember the last guy? No phone, right? Everyone was shocked."

Stella nodded.

Kathryn smiled. "Well, this is it."

"It's pretty, but they don't work here anyway," Stella said, shaking her head.

"No, it doesn't, but you know, you don't have to go far to get a signal. Just a little wander to the edge of town. I've seen it all through that phone. Rolling green fields, shiny cars. It's not what Jake makes it out to be."

With a loud crack, the door flung open, and daylight burst into the room around Jake's silhouette, his expression hidden by the backlight. Kathryn shoved the phone back in her pocket. Her eyes flitted to the badge on the floor, and Jake followed her gaze.

The copper glinted in the light, and he shook his head. "Are you kidding me?"

It was Kathryn who responded, and the words seeped out under her breath. "We had no idea."

"No shit. Even you aren't stupid enough to knowingly harbor a cop. There's a reason you should leave it to the experts. We've made that very clear."

"I know, but we just didn't—"

Jake raised his hand, silencing her, then spoke in a low voice. "It goes without saying that this is a very bad situation. Once we find him, we'll deal with you two."

Stella looked away and felt for the back of a chair.

Jake glared at her. "You're not sitting down, are you? We'd all better get to work if we want to keep this town alive. How long ago did he leave?"

Kathryn thrust the wallet into her pocket and ran toward the back door.

Jake yelled, "Stop her!" but Stella stood frozen as Kathryn dashed past.

Kathryn flung the door open and hurtled into the glare, running blindly along the snow-covered lane until her eyes adjusted. Declan's footprints, perfectly spaced on the clean white blanket, ran down the middle for fifty yards before swerving into the shadows. When she spotted him, he was running in a low hunch.

She shouted into the silence between raspy breaths, "Take me with you!"

Declan stilled for a moment and shouted back, "No, it's too dangerous," before continuing along the edge of a building. The back door of the coffee shop flung open, but Kathryn kept running.

Jake shouted, "With this whole town at stake, I'll shoot. I will."

Kathryn didn't waver, and her unzipped jacket flapped around her shoulders as she kicked up small puffs of snow with each step.

"Kathryn. I know you heard me, and I'm not going to warn you again. This place is more important than any one person."

Stella had grabbed Jake's shoulder. "No, no, this isn't the way. They won't get far."

He shrugged forcefully, dislodging Stella's hand as he brought his eye to the sight and squinted in the glare. Stella reached for the barrel as Jake squeezed the trigger. The crack split the sky, and the recoil threw Stella aside.

Kathryn wobbled sideways as the bullet zinged past, but her momentum carried her forward. After a few steps with splayed legs, she regained her balance and shouted to Declan, "You can't leave me now! They'll kill me!"

Declan stopped, and Kathryn dashed across the last twenty yards, gulping air. Grabbing her by the waist, he pulled her behind a building.

Jake yelled, "Kathryn?"

Declan chanced a peek around the corner, and a bullet punched a hole in the wood the moment his head was exposed. He ducked back and pointed over his shoulder with his thumb. "Can we get to the highway that way?"

Kathryn gave a jittery nod, and they ran toward the next intersection. "Right here. Go right," she said. The snow-covered road disappeared into whiteness, and Declan turned to Kathryn.

"Yes, it's this way. The road dips; you just can't see it."

The booming voice followed them. "Kathryn, you've got to give this up."

They ran past the last house, and now there was only a wide-open plain between them and his car. Declan slowed and looked at Kathryn. She nodded once, so he grabbed her hand and leapt forward. Completely exposed, they ran with their heads low as another shot rang out. Thirty yards later they reached the high point, and they could see the highway cutting through the bleached canvas. Once they made it over the crest, they stood up and sprinted down the hill.

Kathryn squeezed out a question between breaths. "You have a car, right?"

He didn't turn. "Yes, it's just up here."

A dozen steps later, they could see the stark-black trunk. They hunched over in fear of the next shot, willing themselves forward as their legs burned. Lunging for the car, Declan swung his door wide as Kathryn scurried around to the far side. Declan flipped the switch inside to unlock the passenger side. The moment she heard the click, Kathryn yanked the door open. Declan slid into the front while Kathryn clambered in next to him. With a loud crack, the rear window shattered, and they ducked instinctively. Declan thrust the key into the ignition and twisted it violently, bringing the engine to life. Another shot ricocheted off the trunk as he stomped on the accelerator. The car slid sideways, and the tires spat gravel into the fields. He tugged the steering wheel to bring it back in line, and the vehicle lurched forward when the tires bit the tarmac. Declan looked up at the review mirror. Broken teeth of glass framed the lone silhouette on the ridge. He watched Jake bring the gun to his shoulder again and tensed as he waited for the shot, but they were too far away now.

The road turned downhill after they drove over a short rise, and Kathryn watched Jake lower the gun slowly, like a windup doll expiring. The yellow lines in the center of the road flashed by as Declan continued to accelerate, and Kathryn gripped the headrest as she peered back between the two front seats.

Declan's eyes didn't waver from the road. "Can you still see him?"

She squinted into an overexposed photograph, a ribbon of road slicing through soft white hills. "No, no, he's out of sight now, but he won't be happy."

Declan's lips curled into a smile. "I'm sure he won't."

She sat up. "Do you think that he'll come for us? I've heard they have long arms."

He laughed. "It's Kathryn, right?"

"Yeah."

"Well, Kathryn, you may not be safe out here, but it's not them you have to worry about."

Kathryn leaned back and pulled her arms tight across her chest as wind whistled in through the empty back window. Exhaling slowly, she asked, "What do you mean, won't be safe?"

"How much do you know about life outside that place?"

Kathryn brightened. "Well, I saw some photos."

"Where?"

"On another guy's phone."

He bit his bottom lip in acknowledgment. A second passed by, the wind still whistled, and Declan's long exhale was lost in the noise. "What were the pictures of?"

"You know, lots of stuff. Nice houses, new cars, green fields. Everything was beautiful."

"I hope that you didn't join me because of what you saw on that phone."

Kathryn sat up. "Of course I did."

"That place isn't real."

"Not real? A note said that the photos were taken in Carson."

Declan banged the steering wheel.

"Isn't that where we're going?"

Declan's hands were carefully placed at ten and two, and he leaned forward, squinting into the glare. "Fuck. Well, I don't think that they'll let you back in."

Kathryn laughed. "Yeah, as if I'd want to go back."

His words dribbled out in a dull monotone. "I'm afraid that you're in for a bit of surprise. The Carson that people share on their phone isn't the one we're driving to. That one's a game, an escape. A world we'd all rather live in."

"What are you...?" Her words trailed off as they passed the first structure since they'd started driving. It was a gas station that hadn't been operational for some time. There was a star-shaped hole in the yellowing plastic of the pylon sign. Her eyes drifted to ground level, where the broken gas pumps were imprisoned in heavy steel cages and the burned-out shell of a Japanese compact was crookedly parked. The driver's door was wide open, and the blackened bones of a rib cage had fallen onto the cement.

Kathryn's eyes darted around as though watching out for animals that might jump into the road at any moment. Some tape covering a spiderweb of cracked glass partially blocked her view, and she turned to Declan, noticing the rifle protruding from a rack along the center console. "So, what were you doing there?"

Declan shook his head. "I'm sorry. I was hoping to escape this."

As the Threshold marched toward them, slivers of sunlight peeked through the gaps between the billowing sheets. It was more beautiful than Gordon had imagined, and he still couldn't believe that he was out here. His mother, a stickler for the rules, always found a reason to drag him home before sunset, and he kept grabbing his pocket at an imagined vibration. His friend Kane shook his head, and Gordon held out his hands in a defensive pose. "You know how it is. Mom gets a little crazy this time of night."

An hour earlier, Kane had casually planted the seed. "Have you ever seen the transition?"

Gordon had laughed.

"It's worth seeing."

Gordon searched Kane's face for a smirk, then shook his head. "Nah, man, you haven't seen it."

Kane turned to the horizon. "Yeah, I have, and it's cooler than you'd think. Let's watch it tonight."

"But—"

Kane cut him off. "Just write your mom." He turned away as though the conversation was over.

Gordon had pulled out his phone and rolled it over in his hands before hurriedly tapping out a message, deleting it, trying again, and finally settling on *Playing at mikes tonight, will be home later.* He jiggled his leg while he waited, then slid his phone back into his pocket when there was no response.

Now they were up here, high above the ocean as the sun was going down, and he still hadn't heard from her. They'd scampered along narrow trails carved by eager twelve-year-old feet. The gradient to their left was slight at the top, but the angle steepened as it rolled toward the ocean, and the last ten feet to the water was a sheer cliff. Kane skipped along, confident that he'd be able to stop his slide well before that point, but Gordon stayed on the high side of the path, slowing on the precarious sections and waiting until it leveled out before sprinting to catch up.

The edge of the sun was about to touch the ocean, and the sky softened to a pale pink, but the streets were quiet as the residents busied themselves to ignore what was happening only a quarter mile away. On the tip of the bluff, Kane sat on his haunches. Gordon stood a couple of feet behind him, and as the Threshold closed in, he tugged at Kane's shirt.

"Hey, man, that's close enough."

Kane shook his head, flinging drops of water onto Gordon's sand-colored T-shirt. "No, not now, the light's perfect. We might see something on the other side."

Gordon let his hand drop from Kane's shirt. "Look, you've made your point. It's beautiful, but we really should go."

Kane pushed him away, the firm shove delivered with a smile. "No way. You've seen that it's worth waiting for. Why chicken out now?"

Gordon shook his head. "Come on, man. You haven't convinced anyone else to come out here."

"Okay," Kane said, "I'll give you that."

"And what are you going to do if you see something? If you tell anyone, your parents will definitely find out."

Kane sat down and cocked his head to the side. "I guess that depends on what we see."

The wind flared, pushing their hair back, and Gordon returned his attention to the Threshold. The alternating red and blue flags on top of each mast were flapping wildly, and he followed them along the coastline until they curved out of sight. At the base of each mast, the bellows puffed the dreaded mist into the air, but tonight it was whipped away by the wind, exposing the giant wheels as they crept forward in deep steel grooves. It was only a hundred yards from them when Gordon turned to Kane, looking for a sign that he was ready to bolt, but Kane was still sitting back on his elbows. Kane patted the ground next to him, motioning for Gordon to sit, then pushed his legs back and forth excitedly, his heels carving grooves in the dirt. Even though they were high on the bluff, they still looked up to the top of the sheet, and Gordon pictured it tearing from their moorings and engulfing them. His eyes volleyed back and forth between the flapping fabric and a twelve-year-old boy who should have run by now. He told himself he'd grab Kane when the closest mast reached the break, but he was paralyzed as it passed smoothly through the cresting waves.

He squatted down. "Kane, that's it. We have to go. It's too close."

Kane turned as though he'd forgotten Gordon was there. "It's okay, man. You can go, but I want to see what happens."

"What? Are you crazy? People don't 'see what happens'; they disappear."

Kane looked at him evenly. "Do you know anyone who's disappeared?"

"What?"

"I asked if you knew anyone who'd disappeared."

"That's what I thought you said. No, not personally, but we all know what happens to kids out here—"

Kane shook his head. "Exactly. They're just making it up."

Gordon leapt up as though he'd been bitten. "Okay, okay, the joke's over. You're not that crazy."

Kane looked back at the giant barrier, narrowing his eyes like a ship's captain searching for land, and Gordon tugged at his shirt. "Come on!"

"Look, Gordon, you'd better go. I'm not coming, and you won't make it if you stay here and fight me."

Gordon pleaded. "I can't leave you. What will I tell them?"

Kane sighed. "You could make something up, but look down there." He motioned to the rocks below, the edge of the Threshold now grazing their escape route. "I think it's too late. It's probably safer up here."

Gordon rubbed his hands over his face, covering his eyes for a few seconds. "Well, we're gone, there's no—"

"Gordon, quiet!"

Gordon pulled his hands from his face.

Kane lowered his voice. "I saw something."

Gordon shook his head, unwilling to follow the direction of Kane's eyes.

Kane grabbed Gordon's sleeve and pointed at the bottom of the curtain, which had reached the smooth sand of the beach below. "No, look, there!"

"Oh, wow. What is that?"

There was a short beep from Gordon's pocket, and they both jumped.

Gordon scrambled to pull the phone out without taking his eyes off the Threshold, and Kane shook his head. "Forget it. We don't want to miss anything."

Gordon finally extracted his phone. "Damn, it's Mom."

Kane rolled his eyes before returning his attention to the incoming fabric, which seemed to be moving faster as it closed in. Gordon started tapping on the screen: *Sorry I'm a bit late.*

"Gordon. What the hell are you doing?"

Gordon flicked his right hand dismissively and continued typing.

The sun was the perfect height to cast crisp shadows on the white fabric, and Kane grabbed Gordon's arm. "There it is again!"

Gordon lifted his head midmessage to catch the silhouettes of two people, their shadows going in and out of focus behind the wildly flapping sheet, and his phone spilled from his hand. They watched it clatter across the rocks until it came to rest in the spinifex, and when they looked up again, the silhouettes were gone. The fabric lumbered to a halt, the flags fluttering above them, and the stark white sheet covered their entire view to the west. Gordon scurried across the rocks to pick up his phone and tapped out *Will be home soon* before turning to Kane. "Can we go now?"

Kane shook his head.

"Should I leave you here?"

Kane nodded silently.

Gordon gestured wildly at the wall of fabric. "Kane, man, what is wrong with you? You saw the same thing as me. They're right there."

Kane shrugged. "Yeah, but I was expecting it. They looked just like us, don't you think?"

"Man, come on. You drag me up here, we actually see them, and now you act as if it's no big deal."

"Well, it's a bigger deal for you. I already knew that people were there. I just wanted you to finally believe that they were the same as us. Do you believe me now?"

Gordon lifted his shoulders. "Well, I don't know, I didn't see much, but I guess."

Kane slapped his palms together. "Job done then. Let's head back."

"Seriously?"

Kane stood and put a hand on Gordon's shoulder. "Yeah, absolutely. We can come back tomorrow."

Gordon shook his head, but Kane was already scrambling down the narrow path with the confidence of a boy that had never taken a big fall. The enormous white sheet was still flapping wildly, almost brushing them, but each time Gordon hesitated, Kane gained another dozen steps on him. Rounding the last bend on the trail, they could see the little wooden walkway to the village and behind it a cluster of buildings strung along the creek. Gordon was determined not to be outrun again, and he called out as Kane's spindly figure darted and weaved on the dirt track.

Kane twisted his head, surprised that Gordon was still keeping pace. "Don't follow me, man. I'm running late. See you tomorrow."

Poking out of flapping shorts, Kane's skinny legs were moving in a blur, and Gordon couldn't find the space to shout between gulps of air. His will sagged, he doubled over, and with his hands on his knees, he watched the tattered collar of Kane's pale-blue shirt bounce away.

Gordon was still panting when he faced his mother and the lone plate of tepid fish stew sitting on the kitchen table. He looked at her, eyes wide. "Am I that late?"

She carefully folded a dish towel in half and placed it on the counter before turning toward him, hands on her hips. "Well, the ebb happened ten minutes ago."

Gordon looked at his feet. "Yeah, I'm sorry." Then his eyes flashed up to hers. "I sent you a message."

She waved loosely at the clock. "Yes, the one that said 'a bit late'? It's well past 'a bit.'"

"You're right. I'm sorry. I won't let it happen again."

His mother clenched her fist and exhaled slowly. "It's okay, Gordon, but it's just that we worry about you. Kids go missing, you know."

Gordon nodded solemnly as though absorbing a very important point. "I know, Mom. I know." He pulled his chair in under him and brought the first spoonful of stew to his lips under his mother's watchful eye.

He dipped his spoon in again and was wiggling it under a piece of fish when his mother said, "Your father won't be happy."

Gordon looked up. "I know, Mom. I said I was sorry."

"Okay, but please. Just don't let it happen again."

Late the next afternoon, Gordon sat next to Kane on an otherwise deserted beach. Clouds galloped across the sky, and the patches of spinifex looked like slicked-back hair. Gordon rubbed his eyes. "Last night was too close. You have to give it up. I don't want you to disappear."

Kane was leaning back on his elbows, seemingly impervious to the swirling sand. "That again? We talked about this. You don't even know anyone who's gone missing."

"Well, I asked my mom about it, and she knew someone."

Kane bolted upright. "What? Who?"

Gordon smiled. "I thought that might get your attention. Now you know that we shouldn't be playing with fire."

"Gordon, this isn't about what I should be doing. Who was it?"

"Does it matter? I can't remember his name."

Kane was standing now, staring at Gordon, eyes wide. "Are you messing with me?"

"No, no, man, I'm not. Look, I'll find out."

"Okay. Don't forget."

Gordon lifted himself to his feet. "You know, man, I'd better get back."

Kane had returned his attention to the spit of land at the edge of the horizon. "Cool, see you tomorrow."

"Okay, bye."

Gordon turned and scampered up the dunes, the wind whipping up the sand from his footsteps.

"Gordon."

Gordon spun, almost falling in his eagerness. "Yep?"

Kane raised a finger in a fatherly gesture. "Don't forget."

Gordon nodded before turning back toward the dunes. A few minutes later, he arrived at his small clapboard house. He slinked in and scampered up the stairs to the white door at the end of the hall. He inched it open, but weighed down by too many coats of paint, it creaked before it was wide enough for him to slip through.

"Gordon, is that you?"

"Yes, Mom."

"Dinner will be ready soon, and you didn't eat much last night."

"Okay, okay," he hollered, then trudged down the stairs.

He nodded to his father, then sat at the kitchen table. With his knees together and his back straight, he watched his mother spoon broccoli onto his plate alongside a small piece of steamed fish. "Gordon, what's wrong?"

"Nothing, Mom. Everything's great."

His mother placed the colorful ceramic pot on the table and took a sideways glance at his father, who was pushing an oversized piece of fish into his mouth. She smiled at Gordon. "You're a little too agreeable tonight. What have you been up to this afternoon?"

"Nothing."

"Nothing?"

"You know, just hanging with a friend."

His mother raised an eyebrow and then added a smile. "A friend? Who is she?"

Gordon blushed and shook his head. "It wasn't a girl—it was Kane."

His mom twitched as she tilted her head. "Kane? I haven't heard his name before. Eric, do you know a Kane?"

Gordon swiveled toward his father, assuming he'd be distracting himself with a mundane task, but he was delicately placing his fork on the edge of his plate. His father leaned forward and clasped his hands together under his beard. "No. I haven't heard that name." He turned to Gordon. "Do you know where he lives?"

Gordon waved his hand loosely at the window. "Just around here. A couple of streets over, I think."

His dad's steely glare didn't waver, and Gordon bit his lip. They stared at each other, and it felt as though the world had stopped. Gordon shifted his weight, shuffling his chair backward a couple of inches, and it screeched on the linoleum in protest.

His dad tilted his head. "You think? Where'd you meet this Kane?"

"He was down at the beach. Don't worry—he's a good kid. We're not doing anything dangerous."

His mother was standing now, her untouched dinner still carefully arranged on her plate. She locked eyes with his father, and his nod was almost imperceptible, but it was enough for her to scurry to the kitchen counter and pick up her phone.

Gordon absorbed her panicked movements. "Is everything okay?"

She softly waved her hand. "Yeah, yeah, you're here now. Don't worry about it." Her thumb rubbed the glass as she searched for a rarely used number.

When his father stretched out to put his hand on Gordon's shoulder, his chair wobbled, erasing any grace from the gesture. His mother had pressed the phone to her cheek and was tapping her foot rapidly. She began, "Victor, yes, it's Astrid, I think…"

"So, how's school?" His dad's gruff voice was louder than it had been a moment ago.

Gordon swiveled his head back toward his father while he was still trying to parse his mother's conversation. "What?"

"I just asked how school's been going. Is that so strange a

question?" He paused. "Actually, I have a better question. Is Kane in your class?"

"What? No. Why?"

"Have you seen him at school?"

"Well, I can't remember seeing him, but he'd be a grade higher."

Gordon caught a snippet from his mother: "Yes, Eric's asking him now…"

"Okay, Dad, what's going on?"

His father shook his head. "Nothing to worry about, but I think that you should wait until we meet his parents before you hang out again." He gave Gordon's shoulder a soft shake. "Just to be safe."

Gordon bit his lip and swayed back and forth. "Oh, okay, Dad."

His father pulled his hand back as his mother placed the phone on the counter.

Gordon glanced back and forth between the two of them. "Can I go to my room now?"

His mother nodded toward his plate. "But you haven't eaten."

"I'm not really hungry."

When his father shrugged, Gordon thrust his chair backward and leapt off as though it had caught fire, leaving it askew as he bolted for the stairs without looking back. Once in his room, he left the door ajar so he could hear the conversation downstairs.

His father began, "I wouldn't worry…" but the clank of plates being stacked drowned out the rest of the sentence.

His mother replied, "Yes, but you never know what…" but the last few words were swallowed by the screech of a chair being pushed back under the table.

On the far side of his room, the light curtains rippled in the summer breeze, and even though it was an hour after curfew, he could hear the laughter of a couple of rebellious kids playing in the street. He tried to erase the neighborhood from his imagination as he crouched in the open doorway, listening to the familiar pattern of the muffled voices below. Each of his mother's questions was followed by a lazy reassurance from his father, but Gordon couldn't pull enough words to understand. He tiptoed across the room, slid his feet into flip-flops, and levered himself out onto the roof. Following the well-worn path to the tree that grazed the roofline, he wrapped his arms and legs around a branch, and it gave a little as he shimmied down. He felt for the lower branch with his feet and held the trunk for balance as he dropped into a deep squat, then leapt to the ground.

The full moon lit the yard with a bluish hue, but the house was in shadow, and the living room windows cut two golden rectangles in the black expanse. Gordon scuttled across the lawn in a crouch and stayed hunched until he arrived at the cul-de-sac that led to the beach. Sand was blowing across the barren road, and a row of dunes obscured the base of the Mylar sail, but the flags waved gallantly high above him. Although the beach looked deserted from the road, Gordon knew that Kane would be sitting between the dunes and the Threshold. The sun had taken its warmth below the horizon, and Gordon folded his arms across his chest as he scampered toward the rickety walkway. When he hit the beach, he pulled off his flip-flops, letting the soft sand seep between his toes as he ran toward Kane.

Kane turned and smiled, flashing teeth that seemed to glow in the dull light. "Hey, man, I wasn't expecting you back tonight. Did you find out who went missing?"

Gordon shook his head. "No, I didn't get a chance to ask."

"Come on, man, it's important."

Gordon squatted down a couple of feet away, gazing out at the Threshold. "You know, I wasn't going to come down, I'm kinda done with this." He pointed to the Mylar barrier. "We don't do anything fun. You have to give up on what's behind there. It doesn't matter."

Kane chuckled. "Oh, I know what's behind there."

Gordon laughed. "Yeah, sure you do. So what's behind there, smart guy?"

Kane twisted slowly toward Gordon, narrowing his eyes. "Home."

Gordon shook his head and leaned back as though he were about to laugh, but Kane's blank expression held him back. "Hey, man, that isn't funny."

Kane's steely glare didn't waver. "I'm not joking."

Gordon was squatting, but he still scooched back a few inches. He inhaled sharply before allowing the air to escape his pursed lips in a long whistle, and they sat in silence for a few seconds before Gordon spoke. "Why are you here?"

"The same reason you are. I was a bit too curious."

Gordon scrunched his nose. "What do you mean?"

Kane's smile was that of an all-knowing parent. "You can probably work it out, but I doubt you'll want to believe it."

Gordon shook his head. "I don't understand."

"Well, think about it, and meet me here tomorrow night just before the ebb."

"Why?"

"I'm going back. You can decide if you want to join me."

"Seriously?"

Kane turned and faced him, scowling. "Yes. I'm seriously going back tomorrow night. It's up to you if you want to come. Look around on the way home and see if you can work out what's different about this town." He finished the sentence with a little flick of his hand. "Now go on home. If your mom finds out you're down here, there's no way you'll be allowed out tomorrow."

Gordon turned and ran.

When he got back to the house, the lights were still on, so he skirted around the windows and clambered up the tree until he reached the second floor. He made his way to his own window and crept back in. A few minutes later, with the thin covers pulled over his shoulders, he stared at the ceiling until he fell asleep.

The next day, arriving home from school, Gordon jumped off his bike so quickly that the back wheel was still spinning when he let the bike slide to the ground. He pulled off his helmet as he ran toward the house. His mother was at the fridge, and his father was leaning on the kitchen counter with a can of beer in front of him. They both turned to him when the screen door clapped shut behind him, and he blurted out the question that had been nagging him all day.

"Where do the little kids go?"

His parents exchanged a glance, and then his mother spoke. "What do you mean?"

"You know, our school, it's only a few grades. Where do the kids younger than us go? I never see them."

His father leaned forward, cradling the can. "Well it's a long—" and his mother cut in, "I wouldn't worry about—" They both stopped simultaneously.

Gordon's gaze volleyed back and forth between them before settling on his mother. "Well?"

"Sorry, Gordon, you know it's hard to explain. But you know what, we'll take you there sometime. It isn't far."

The sentence was punctuated by the sound of a can falling over, and Gordon swiveled to look at his father. He shrugged his shoulders and picked up the can, leaving a small puddle on the linoleum.

"Okay, when?" Gordon said.

His mother looked at him and frowned. The strong creases above the bridge of her nose formed easily. "When what?"

Gordon shook his head as though dealing with a disobedient dog. "When can I see where the little kids go?"

"Oh yes. Yes, of course. You know"—she motioned to his father—"we'll have to work out our schedules, but we'll let you know."

Gordon scrunched his face. "Your schedules?"

"Gordon. Enough," his mother said, shaking her head.

Gordon turned toward the stairs and squirmed to shed his backpack.

His dad called out, "Why the sudden interest?"

Gordon whipped his head around just in time to catch his mother glaring at his father, but when she turned toward him, she smiled broadly in a pantomime of bliss. Gordon shooed away the question. "No reason, just curious," he said, and took the stairs two at a time as he hurried to his room.

Stepping inside, he leaned back on the door, letting his weight close it with a thud. He stared at the posters, the toys, the photos—all shiny and perfect. After he'd been pulling books from the shelves and rifling through drawers for a few minutes, it looked like a crime scene, but he hadn't been able to find anything more than a year old. He sat on his bed with his knees pulled up to his chin and rocked back and forth as he searched for a childhood memory. Unable to find one, he dashed to the window, and ten minutes later he was on the beach, the sun partly submerged below the horizon.

The Threshold eased across the sand, and as it got closer Kane saw a small tear in the fabric. "Look! Look through that gap. Does it look familiar?"

Gordon squinted. "What are you talking about? Those rocks were on this side a few minutes ago. Of course it looks familiar."

Kane was shaking his head. "No, look closely. When you see them from this side, they're always in shadow, but now—look at it under the setting sun. It looks familiar because of the light. They're completely different when they're on the other side of the Threshold."

Gordon scrunched his eyes as he tried to make out details.

"Come on, Gordon. It must look familiar?"

Gordon was shaking his head.

Kane continued. "Okay, bud. I believe you, but I wouldn't blame you if you were just nervous. I'm pretty nervous too, and I remember it."

Gordon's eyes widened. "Really? You're nervous?"

In the waning light, Kane had been reduced to the whites of his eyes and his broad, toothy grin. His head swung back and forth between Gordon and the Mylar sheet heading their way. "Yeah, of course." Gordon was only squatting, and Kane shook his head. "Hey, man, you don't really look committed. How about just sitting down?"

The Mylar's dogged progress continued. Gordon nodded slowly, looking Kane up and down as though deciding whether to trust him based on his physical appearance alone. Kane let the Threshold get to within thirty feet before lying down on his stomach and placing his head in a little divot in the sand. Gordon was still crouching on the balls of his feet as it closed in.

The steel poles were twenty feet apart, perched on massive wheels that inched along the tracks. Inside, the engines throbbed as they tugged the sheet, and the Mylar puffed backward like a sail in a stiff breeze, the gentle arc of the fabric distorting the clouds behind it. It seemed to screech as it stretched over a rock.

Kane twisted his head, yelling out, "Come on, lie down! You have to hold your breath. That mist—it erases your memory, and you don't want to forget this side, do you?"

"It does what?"

Kane was shouting over the flapping fabric. "Erases your memory! That's why you can't remember the other side. I held my breath the last time I went under."

Gordon shook his head. "What do you—"

Kane lifted one arm and motioned as though swatting a fly. "Come on, get down. Now!"

It was only ten feet away, and the rumble of the engine overwhelmed the roar of the fabric. Gordon was still squatting indecisively when Kane took one last gulp of air and nestled his face in the sand. The fabric reached Kane's feet, then started inching up his calf, and Gordon took a step backward, still keeping both options open as the curtain closed in on the rocks. He took another half step away as it reached Kane's back, and Kane glanced up at him, motioning for Gordon to lie down before burying his head again.

Some mist puffed out a second later, and Gordon twisted his head to avoid it. When he turned back, Kane had almost been engulfed, the back of his head the only part of his body still visible. There was an unmistakable shout of joy, and he could see the silhouettes of a small group standing over Kane's body. The curtain rubbed Kane's hair as it continued its relentless march, and when it touched the sand again after sliding over Kane's head, he was gone. One of the black outlines leaned over and lifted Kane to his feet. The flapping curtain muffled the words, but Gordon saw Kane open his arms wide, then throw his head back in laughter.

Gordon looked at the ground. There was still enough time to dive down, but he'd have to angle himself to avoid brushing against the rocks. The choice was made for him by another second of indecision, and he took a hurried step backward. His heel caught the edge of the rocks, and he reached out to break the fall but landed heavily. The curtain was only inches away, and the bellows filled in preparation for another puff, so he pushed himself upright and held his breath. When the mist dissipated, he stared at the fabric, only inches away, and thought he caught a wave, but the lanky silhouette was now a dozen feet beyond the curtain, and the shadow was too fuzzy for him to know for sure.

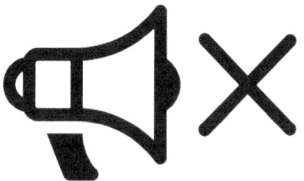

DIGNIFIED SILENCE

Twice a week, from two to four in the morning, Justine stared vacantly at a monitor in Magenta Publishing's control room. A year ago, she would have been perched on the lip of the chair, but Colin's indifference to her dedication had sapped her enthusiasm, and she let her hips slide forward as she slumped back. Maneuvering the drone with her hand loosely draped around the joystick, she marked the halfway point of her shift with a clenched fist, a sarcastic impersonation of an athlete willing herself on.

While she was calculating how many hours she'd sat in that chair over the years, the camera caught a car slowly weaving through the dark alleys. She followed the European sedan until it drifted to a halt at an intersection. In a neighborhood where most people rolled through stop signs during the day, the driver should barely have slowed. As she shimmied forward, the chair jostled across the cracked linoleum, and she tugged the joystick to zoom in. She could see a child's car seat through the rear window. "Come on, what are you doing? Get out of there."

Justine bit her lip when the driver started opening the window, but it only moved a couple of inches, and she mumbled, "Okay, good." She was silently willing the car forward when the window started moving again. It dropped into the sill, and a middle-aged man wearing a collared shirt leaned out the door. Justine turned up the drone's microphone as she thumped the desk. "Seriously? You have to know better."

His lips moved, but the microphone only picked up "know" and "get to." Justine shook her head. It was obvious that this wasn't the place to ask for directions. When she turned up the microphone again, the background hiss filled her ears, and she could only hear a couple of words from a second person: "…the wrong side of town."

Frantically jabbing at the joystick, she spun the camera around in a wide arc. The sensor struggled to pull detail from the darkness, and there was a lime-green tinge to the scene, but she could make out a figure holding a pistol at eye level and aimed at the man. The crack was deafening. She tore the headphones from her head. "No!" Her ears were still ringing when she grabbed the controls and panned across. The assailant was standing defiantly, hands on hips, seeming to search for the drone.

Justine brought the drone in closer and whispered, "Yeah, I got you. You should have run." The woman's blond hair was pulled back into a functional ponytail, and her icy blue eyes peeked out over a red handkerchief. In a sleeveless vest, she raised a sinewy arm in a beckoning motion, but Justine sat frozen. The woman nodded as if to say, "You heard me." Justine pushed the drone closer and grabbed the headphones when the woman started talking, catching the tail end of the sentence as she placed them over her ears: "…that was for you."

Justine yelled at the screen, "What?"

The woman continued, almost as though she'd heard Justine. "Is this what it takes for you to see us? You guys patrol every night but don't bother to show anyone what it's like in here. I just gave you a show you can't ignore, so put us on your home page."

She held her fingers up in a victory gesture as she turned away. Justine set the drone at head height and nudged it along a dozen feet behind the woman until she spun around, brandishing her gun.

"I wouldn't risk it. I'm a pretty good shot, and those things can't be cheap."

Justine tapped the joystick, pushing the drone higher as the woman ducked into a tight alley and disappeared. She looked up at the clock. Leon wouldn't be coming in to take the next shift for almost an hour, so she set the drone on auto and sent him a message. *I can't believe what I just saw. Homicide. In the dark corner. I recorded the whole thing.*

There was no response, so she called, pressing the phone to her ear and jiggling her right leg while she waited for him to answer.

"Justine? What? What time is it? Am I late?" Leon asked.

"No, no, it's okay. I still have another hour, but I just saw a cold-blooded murder. She looked straight at the camera afterward, like she wanted to get caught. She—"

"Justine, Justine, slow down."

"I'm sorry, but it just happened. I'm not sure what to do. Should I call the police?"

"I don't know. I only flipped through the handbook, but I thought it said that we were supposed to inform management first. Do you have a copy—"

"Okay, should I call Colin right now?"

"Maybe. Actually, probably not at this time of night. I don't think that he'd do anything until he's in the office anyway."

"Oh, okay, thanks. Sorry to bother you."

"No, no. Sorry, I don't mean to be dismissive, but I don't really know what we're supposed to do. I guess you never expect something like this to actually happen. Anyway, are you okay?"

"Yeah, kind of. I'm a little shaken up."

"I'm sure. Look, I'll come in now. It sounds like you should get some sleep."

"Leon, there's no need for that, I can—"

"Justine, no need to protest, it's no bother at all. I'm awake now anyway. You can get me back sometime."

"Okay, thanks, Leon. I really appreciate it. See you soon."

Turning back to the screen, she exhaled like a runner at the starting line and rewound the footage. After she'd assembled the images into a short montage and added some captions, she sent a meeting request to Colin, then flipped back to the live feed. Justine winced at the sight of the blood-splattered glass when the drone looped back past the car. She noticed that the words STAY TUNED FOR MORE had been sprayed in crimson on the hood, and she thumped the desk angrily.

Twenty minutes later there was a rap on the door, and Justine knocked over her drink as she spun around. Leon was leaning on the doorframe. His stout frame was wedged into pleated khakis, and he wore a red tie that clashed with his lemon-colored shirt. He looked like a schoolboy dressed by his mother.

"Oh, sorry to scare you. It's just me."

Justine cursed as she picked the cup off the floor.

Leon shook his head. "Damn. Wait, I'll get a napkin." He handed her a wad of paper when he returned from the kitchen, saving a couple of sheets to wipe the keyboard.

"Sorry, Leon, that was totally my fault. I shouldn't have been so absorbed."

"No, no, I should've texted before barging in."

She waved away his apology. "Leon. I said it was fine."

He nodded, then let a few seconds pass in silence before grinning eagerly. "So, is it good?"

She scowled. "Good?"

He waved his hand back and forth. "Sorry, I don't mean it like that, but can you actually see what happened?"

"Yeah, I'm afraid so." She tapped Play.

"Wow. You weren't kidding."

Justine stared at him and spoke quietly. "No, Leon, I wasn't kidding."

"Did you send it to Colin?"

"No. You told me not to."

"Great, you know that it's important to—"

Justine held up her hand. "It's okay. I sent a meeting request for seven."

"Oh, wow. I wanted to chat with you before you did anything like that."

"Why?"

"Well, we're kind of in this together, and it was just luck that it happened on your—"

"Seriously? Were you actually going to hide this from him?"

Leon held up his hands and shook his head defensively. "No. No, of course not." Then he glanced at his watch. "Well, seven's not much more than three hours away, so you'd better go home and get some sleep."

"Yep, I'll try. Thanks"

Ten minutes before sunrise, Justine walked past a vacant reception desk, flipped the light switch in the conference room, and tugged at the mass of cables in the center of the oak table to connect her laptop. She was crouched over the computer with her legs crossed and a foot wiggling when Colin strode in. The door clicked shut, pulling her from the screen, and a man she usually glimpsed through his office's venetian blinds was standing over her. His sandy hair was flecked with gray, and despite black-rimmed glasses that softened a pointy face, he seemed to look through her. Justine flashed a nervous smile before glancing away, and he flopped into the chair next to her. Wearing a tailored shirt and crisply pressed trousers, he dressed as though elegance alone would bring back the glory days of the industry. Colin Harrington had been labeled the last of the old guard, and she'd admired the way he kept Magenta afloat without compromising his principles, but she'd never been more than an extra in his movie. They usually nodded a brief acknowledgment in the halls, but she couldn't recall the last time they'd been in the same room.

"Colin, sir. I really appreciate you making the time. I know that you're extremely—"

He was straightening his tie, but he raised a hand to cut her off, the gesture finely balanced between gentle and commanding. "Justine, I'm sorry, there's a lot going on right now, but you made this sound important. Is ten minutes going to be enough?"

"Well, sir, I only need two." He nodded vaguely, and Justine sat up and uncrossed her legs. "Sorry. That sounded flip, but this will be quick." She hit Play.

He watched in silence and was still staring at the screen after the video finished. "Hmm, powerful stuff."

Justine beamed. "Thanks, it wasn't easy to keep it under a minute, but the data says that—"

Colin waved her comment away. "Well, I appreciate the effort. You know, it's a great learning experience. It can take years to grasp editing, but you seem to really understand the human condition.

No, really. It's fantastic stuff." He placed his palms on the table to push himself out of his seat.

She followed his movements in silence, but when he pulled the door wide, she asked, "So, when are we running it?"

Colin let go of the handle and turned toward her as the door clicked shut again, but there was no joy in his toothy grin. "I'm sorry, Justine. You know the policy."

"But, sir. This...this is too much."

"Justine, this is exactly what the policy is for, and you know our audience has standards."

"But this wasn't just one of the nightly skirmishes in there. This was someone from out here, and we have to let people know how dangerous it is."

"Justine, there's a reason that we're the only ones allowed to cover that area. There are outlets that would pay a lot more, but they know that we'll hold the line and not exploit what we see."

"Holding the line is one thing, but when does it become—"

"Justine, this isn't even my decision to make. The board has stipulated that we won't give extremists a voice."

"Colin, I've given up two nights a week for the last three years to pilot that thing. If we're not even going to show something like this, why am I wasting my time?"

Colin adjusted his glasses. "There are some things that we'd show."

"But—"

"But not this. Given the current guidelines, this one's not even close."

"Well, maybe they would—"

"Justine, I'm sorry."

The moment he opened the door, she heard his name being called from the far side of the office, and he flashed an apologetic smile before scurrying away.

Back at her desk, she tried to distract herself until Leon finished his shift in the control room.

He frowned at her when he shuffled in. "What, radio silence? I've been refreshing all morning. What happened?"

"Leon, you know I couldn't write. You're not even supposed to know that video exists. Anyway, the policy happened. Colin won't run it."

"Seriously?"

Justine nodded. "Yeah. Do you have a few minutes?"

"Damn, Justine, I'm sorry. I have to log in; they've been on me about hours lately."

Justine's face dropped.

"But let's get a drink tonight. The Vic? Five?"

"Yeah, yeah, okay."

Justine arrived at the bar at a quarter to five. It took a few seconds for her eyes to adjust to the dim lighting after the door closed behind her, and she walked past the sleek stools that lined a severely angled bar, choosing a low seat in front of a small table. When Leon arrived, she was sipping wine and scrolling through the day's headlines, wondering what else Colin had censored.

Leon pointed at her nearly empty glass. "Another?"

She laughed. "After today? Of course."

Forty-five minutes later, she'd almost finished her third glass when he pleaded, "Come on, Justine, this is the ticket. You don't even believe in the policy."

She shook her head. "It's not worth it."

Leon sat forward on the edge of the seat, his earlier cross-legged slouch a victim of his enthusiasm. "Justine, you've been here, what, three years now? You shouldn't still be watching that damn monitor twice a week. I'll be surprised if I make it through a year." She was twirling her wine glass, and Leon laughed as he reached over and pinched the stem to stop it. "Sorry, it's driving me crazy. Anyway, I remember my first day, you went on and on about how Magenta was the last bastion of quality journalism, so I know how hard this must be for you. I have no idea why they don't report what happens in there, but it looks like they're just the same as all of the others. There's always someone behind a curtain pulling the strings."

"Maybe you're right."

"Yeah, and someone will get the real story out sooner or later. If you don't want to do it, you'd better hope it's someone else with your integrity."

"Okay, Leon."

"Being the trusted authority comes with some responsibility. I could be driving through there tonight." He paused as though a thought just occurred to him. "You know, it's almost like we're protecting those gangs in there. Do you think that they have connections inside?"

"Inside Magenta?"

Leon leaned forward. "Yeah. What do you think?"

Justine rolled her eyes. "Come on, Leon, I do this for a living. You can save your conspiracy theories for the next crackpot. Magenta may have its problems, but it's legit."

Leon smirked. "'Legit'? Justine, you're a journalist. Can't you come up with a word that doesn't make you sound like a fifteen-year-old?"

"You know what I mean. Besides, I spend half of my day searching for the perfect word, so can you give me a break tonight?"

Leon laughed. "Okay, fair enough. But I'm just saying that we don't want some clueless mother driving through there because the suits in their glass tower wouldn't warn her."

The last of Justine's wine splashed around as she waved the glass exuberantly. "Way to put me in a no-win situation. Fortunately there's precedent here, and I don't need to risk my career for this."

"Justine." Leon held up a hand in a calming gesture. "There's still some wine in that glass."

Justine stopped and held the glass up to the light. "You know, you're right. I guess I should do something about that." She let what would have been two comfortable sips gush into her mouth.

Leon leaned over, took the glass from her hand, and put it on the table. "That eliminates one danger, but we don't need you dropping this."

"I'm not that clumsy."

"Maybe not, but watching you swing it around like that is a bit distracting."

Justine reached for the bottle, and as Leon protested, she laughed. "Well, I'm not going to make a decision like this sober."

Leon held up his palms. "Okay, okay." Then he leaned forward and spoke softly. "Justine, I've always admired your determination, and this is your chance to change the system. You might even gain a little fame along the way."

"Thanks, Leon. Your argument's legit."

"Ah yeah, if that's as funny as you're going to get, then you'd better call it a night."

When she lifted the bottle, it was empty, and she shook her head in mock disgust. "Maybe it is time to leave."

She reached for her purse, but Leon waved her off. "I got this one. You'd better get home. You've got some disrupting to do."

"Thanks, Leon, I appreciate it." She hurried toward the door.

Curled up on her couch after a brisk walk home, Justine was staring at the Current's upload page with a finger hovering over the Return key. She'd always laughed at the dubious authenticity of the videos, but if Magenta's painstaking fact-checking was just a cover for Colin's whims, her arrogance was misplaced.

Free of Magenta's endless rounds of editing and approvals, she jabbed the keyboard, and the process bar marched across the screen before being replaced by a green check and the message *Congratulations JD04, your video has been uploaded.* It disappeared a moment later as though nothing had happened, and she scrolled aimlessly for a few minutes before returning to the video. Zero views. She walked to the fridge for an unnecessary glass of water, then refreshed the page. This time a four appeared next to the view count, and three ellipses began cycling below the words *Start the Discussion*. She waited twenty seconds as they stubbornly lingered, then she dragged to refresh. The ellipses still hadn't resolved into a comment, and she cursed her lack of discipline as she set her phone's timer for ten minutes. She grabbed a jacket on her way out the door and pushed her fists deep into its pockets while she waited for the elevator.

Outside, she leaned against an imaginary wind as she hurried along for no reason. Four blocks from home, the timer went off. She swiped anxiously, and now there were three comments under her post:
Is this real?
Gotta share this
Is this really what happens in there?

The last one was time-stamped one minute ago. Another bubble popped up while she was reading, and she stared at the screen until the gray dots were replaced by a crying emoji, and she smiled as she put her phone back in her pocket.

Fifteen minutes later, in a glossy office on the top floor of the Current's glass tower, Faye noticed the brief spike on her monitor. She sat up when a local zip code flashed on the screen next to it and tapped the Watch Now button. The moment the video faded to black, she leaned back into her plush leather chair and hit Replay. She grabbed her phone and tapped out a message: *It took something special, but the dam finally breaks. Let's get to work and blow this one up*

Despite the late hour, her assistant replied immediately. *The drone video? Magenta's?*

Of course

I'm on it

Faye spun her chair around with a casual push of her left foot, taking in the stippled grid of streetlights and the dark patch in the center that continued to divide the city's politicians. Her phone buzzed against her desk a couple of minutes later. She snatched it off the glass expanse and flipped it over. *I put it on Home P, already 10k views*

Smiling, Faye tapped out a reply—*Great*—and summoned her driver before grabbing her coat.

Early the following morning, Colin sat on the edge of a brown leather chair outside Mayor Dunstan's office. He pulled himself to his feet with a sigh when the mayor's assistant lifted his eyes from a small black monitor and gave him an affirmative nod. "She's ready for you."

When he opened her door, Evelyn was pacing back and forth, and she pressed the remote without uttering a greeting. He fussily lowered himself into a seat as a woman's face filled the screen, her blue eyes peeking out between a golden fringe and a red bandanna. Evelyn paused the video.

"I don't need to tell you what happens next, do I?"

Colin was leaning forward with his elbows digging into the armrests and his fingers clasped tightly just in front of his chest. He tentatively lifted a hand like a schoolboy unsure whether to answer, but when Evelyn shook her head, he dropped it to his lap with a nervous chuckle.

"Yeah, everyone in the city knows what happens next."

Colin nodded.

"Well, Colin, not only does everyone know what happens next, they know where it came from. Your drones are the only ones we let in there, and it hasn't taken long for the amateur detectives to put it all together."

Colin was shaking his head. "We take breaches like this very seriously, and—"

"Well, Colin, apparently not seriously enough. When something like this happens, it gives the public an excuse to be skeptical, to assume that we're hiding something from them, and well, that's not good for anyone."

Colin looked up at her, but in the face of her glare, he let his gaze drift back toward his feet. "I'm sorry, Evelyn, but to be honest, the woman who did this is a bit of a recluse. She's been with us for three years and just quietly goes about her business. It's last thing I expected her to do."

"Well, you've never been a great judge of character, and you know that it's only a matter of time before there's a tightly edited exposé about 'why you're kept in the dark' from our friends over at the Current." Evelyn's air quotes were the gestures of a teenage girl, not a middle-aged politician, and Colin glanced at his watch to disguise a smile.

"Colin?"

Colin looked up.

"I hope you're not finding this funny. Maybe a reminder that your drone contract expires next month sobers you up a little. If you can't keep a lid on these things, I'm sure we can find someone else who can."

"I'm sorry, but what do you want me to do?" Evelyn stared at him until he answered his own question. "I guess we have to fire her, right?"

Evelyn let out a spiteful cackle. "Yes, Colin, but I want to make sure you go about it the right way."

"The right way?"

Evelyn tilted her head, a cold smile on her face. "Be regretful of course, but be sure to remind her that the policy is essential to prevent these extremists from having a platform. That's the first thing." Colin nodded, and Evelyn continued, "It's important to sap the righteousness from her. You know how easily these young kids get hooked on fame, and we don't need someone running around claiming that there's an entire underworld that we're conspiring to keep secret. We want her to disappear as soon as possible."

"Of course, of course."

"Great. After you fire her, what do you have planned?"

Colin scrunched his eyes as though a simple answer on a game show eluded him. "I don't know."

"Jesus, Colin. You don't know? How long have you been doing this?"

"I guess it's coming on twelve—"

"Colin, it was a rhetorical question. I feel like I'm coaching an intern. You must be the luckiest man in the industry."

"There's no need to—"

"Colin, you have to get out there and tell your story. Obviously you need to sow the seeds of doubt about its authenticity, but make it clear that this is the first time you've seen anything like this and that you feared that reporting this type of barbaric act would just provoke more."

"But—"

"And don't forget to make it clear that this disgruntled employee's recklessness endangers lives by inspiring others. You need to make an example of her; otherwise, we're just going to face it again."

Colin sighed. "Evelyn, you know that's not my thing."

"Well, Colin, it is now."

"But Evelyn—"

"No buts, Colin. You know that there's a long list of people who want to label me soft on crime, and you know what happens then: the pendulum swings the other way and suddenly we're locking up people for jaywalking. If you'd hate to see that—and I certainly hope you do—then you need to put this right." Evelyn sat down behind her desk and wiggled the mouse to wake her computer. "Oh, and good luck."

Colin mumbled a "thank you" as he retreated from her office.

In a compact apartment less than two miles away, Justine cursed her alarm's incessant beeping as she rolled over and reached for her phone. The number below her video was followed by a "K" now, and she flicked her thumb rhythmically, scrolling through the comments that were mostly variations of *Why doesn't anyone tell us about this?* After closing the app, she tapped the envelope icon. When she didn't see Colin's name in the list of unread emails, she let the phone fall to the side table and swiveled around to place her feet on the floor. But after putting her palms on the edge of the mattress, her will flagged, and she let twenty seconds pass by before dragging herself to her feet.

Rehearsing excuses while she closed the apartment door and turned toward the office, Justine reluctantly put one foot in front of the other as though walking an invisible tightrope. She was beginning to wonder if the whole thing was just going to fizzle out when her phone vibrated and the words *see me* appeared on her screen above Colin's name.

A few minutes later, she was perched on a wooden bench in Colin's office, squirming in a fruitless attempt to find a comfortable position.

"But, sir, you know that we should have run it."

"Justine, they're just violent gangs that assume a veneer of protest will excuse their barbaric behavior. They keep turning up the volume, but the lyrics are always just 'See what we can do.' No one wants to hear it."

Justine straightened the hem of her shirt, then sat on her hands to prevent herself from fidgeting. "This isn't just about politics. Isn't protecting the public our duty?"

"Yes, of course, but we also don't want half the town cowering in fear. You know how people run with these things. It gets sensationalized, and the public loses all perspective."

"What?"

Colin grinned. "Look, Justine. It certainly was dramatic, and despite the policy I might have considered it"—he waited for Justine to sit up—"had I been sure it was real." Justine gasped, and Colin held up his hands defensively. "I'm sorry. I'm not trying to offend you. Sometimes it can be hard to tell."

Justine was shaking her head. "Seriously, Colin. You saw it. No one made it up."

Colin intertwined his fingers and put his forearms on the table. "Now, Justine, I know it looked real, but in that low light, well, there's a lot of people out there who would love to see us get something like this wrong."

"I don't follow."

"We don't know if they were actors. You know—"

"You're kidding."

"While there's an element of doubt, we have to be prudent. There's a reason that we're the only ones allowed to have a drone in there."

"You're serious? This is how you're going to respond to this?"

"Now Justine, no need to be like that. This isn't easy for me. You've done some great work, and that video—it shows so much potential. But I'm afraid that it just wouldn't be good optics to keep you around."

Justin stared blankly.

Colin seemed to look over her right shoulder. "I don't want to make a big deal of it, and when the heat blows over, we can chat about another role in the future, but this isn't a great situation."

"You're firing me?"

Colin grimaced. "I'm sorry, but this is a business, and you must realize that—"

"So, a business decision, huh?"

"Justine, don't make it sound like that."

Justine nodded slowly as she lifted herself to her feet. "Of course, of course. Yeah, it makes sense, I…" She let the words drift to nothing, and the silence stretched until she completed her thought. "I appreciate all you've done to help me grow."

She spun as she concluded the sentence and had already opened the door when Colin replied. "Justine, I'm sorry. I really am. I hope that our paths cross again one day."

"You might get lucky, but treating me like this now? Your timing's terrible. You know I'm going to be famous, right? Now that I have people's attention, I can let them know what this place is really like."

"Justine, please. Be careful what you wish for. Seriously, you have no idea—"

Justine let the office door close midsentence and strode back to her desk. Picking up her gym bag and dropping it on the cheap Formica desk, she shoved her clothes up one end to leave room for the three years of flotsam from her cubicle. She started by pulling the pins from the photos on the wall and wrapping them in a rubber band. The first photo showed her with arms stretched wide in a fruitless attempt to corral a small group of Kenyan school children, and she winced as she threw the wad of photos into her bag. When her desk was empty, she heaved the bag over her shoulder and walked toward the elevator, giving a coworker a "what's up" nod as though she were just heading down to the gym.

When she arrived home, she flopped onto her couch and pulled out her phone. The numbers below the video continued to climb, but unsure whether that even mattered anymore, she let it drop to the floor and leaned back into the couch. Her blank stare caught the picture frame that had been a gift from her mother. She'd planned to fill it with a photo from a vacation that had been postponed for a year, but a soulless geometric logo was still under the glass, and it mocked her dedication to a job that was gone. She reached out and flipped it from behind, and the frame clacked onto the coffee table.

Sitting in his office with the blinds closed, Colin reread the press release twice before it was sent out.

While we are unable to comment on the authenticity of the footage, we defend our dignified silence. Hate groups will not use Magenta's pages to spread their message, and on this we will not waver.

A few minutes later he accepted the first call, and he was still sitting behind his desk trying to manage the fallout when the sun retreated behind the horizon. His assistant called to let him know that his car was waiting nineteen stories below, and after rehearsing his opening lines in the elevator, he stared out the window as the limousine eased into traffic.

Half an hour later, Colin sat under studio lights wearing a tailored suit, a tie in a broad knot, and colorful socks that peeked out above fashionable loafers, but his posture spoiled the caricature of confidence. He was perched on a low chair, and when he turned to the camera, he tilted his head and scowled as though trying to calculate how many faces were on the other side of the lens.

The show's host, Gloria, sat across from him and smiled easily as she delivered her opening statement in a gentle patter. "Welcome to tonight's episode of Feedback. We've got a fantastic show in store for you, but before we get to our analysis of the day's events, we have a very special guest with us tonight." She turned and smiled at Colin, holding her hand out to present him to the audience. "This is Colin Harrington of Magenta Publishing. His name may not sound familiar, but I'm sure you've heard of JD04, and while the person behind the handle remains elusive, Colin's the next best thing. The footage you've all seen came from a Magenta publishing drone, and he might have been the very first person to see it."

The camera panned across to Colin, and the small red light above the lens paralyzed him for a moment before he lifted his hand in an awkward acknowledgment.

Gloria leaned back and gestured lazily as though mocking his discomfort. "So, is it real?"

His rehearsed introduction pointless, he let out a short sigh and forced a smile. "Wow, you're really starting with a softball, huh?" Gloria stared blankly, and Colin bit his lip. "Okay then, jokes aside, you know I wish I had an easy answer for that, but the truth is, we just don't know, and I want to make it clear that isn't as important as… Well, the most important thing is that, and unfortunately, this interview is increasing the problem, the important thing is that we shouldn't be giving these hate groups a voice. There's a very clear protocol about this stuff."

"Well, Colin, I'm not convinced that its authenticity isn't important. But if we move on for a moment, are you're telling me that even though you're the only ones with a drone in that area, you didn't deem this important enough to report?"

Colin sat forward, rubbing his knees, as though he had been waiting for the question. "Well, Gloria, we make tough decisions on what to cover every day. Each organization has its policies, and one of ours is considering whether the information is in the public's interest. I realize that's a judgment call, but unfortunately, this type of thing often inspires others who want the attention."

Gloria hesitated, a gesture that seemed carefully rehearsed to sap the venom from her follow-up. "But are you the ones that should be making a decision like this? Maybe the audience should decide."

"I guess that depends on whether the public would tolerate the respected media being a mouthpiece for these types of groups."

"Respected? Is that a veiled swipe at the Current?"

Colin shook his head. "No, not at all. You know, we're not even in the same business. They're about entertainment; anything goes on that platform. We fact-check and curate everything carefully. Trust is paramount."

Gloria leaned forward. "Curate carefully? That's a slippery slope, wouldn't you say? I'm sure that our viewers are picturing a dozen people in expensive suits deleting anything that might not be in their best interest."

Colin's pained smile dropped, and his eyes narrowed as he leaned forward. "Slippery fucking slope."

"Colin, please." Gloria made a little gesture to ensure that the coarse language would be removed during the ten-second delay.

"I am so tired of hearing that phrase. Everything is a slope. You can go in either direction from every point, and one person's up is another's down. As a group, we've decided that this is the right point on the spectrum for the good of society, and until we have evidence to the contrary, that's where we're going to stay."

"I'm sorry, Colin, but I'm just trying to get to the bottom of a decision that no one can quite understand. Many have noticed that the plight of the gangs in there is notably absent from the esteemed pages of Magenta. For an outlet that claims to be politically neutral, that paints a skewed view of the city, wouldn't you say?"

Colin was subtly rocking back and forth now. "Well, Gloria, are you implying that we'd let our journalistic standards drop to push an agenda? If you are, then you've just insulted hundreds of people."

Gloria tilted her head as though she were the parent of an unruly child. "Come now, Colin. Are you saying these decisions are a collective 'good for the people' stance? These are two enormous, profitable, corporations, desperate to maintain their hold on the monopoly—"

"Gloria, for a start, you're talking about the two biggest news sites, so it's not a monopoly. At a minimum it's a duopoly, but there's so much out there that you can't make that claim without—"

She stared at him. "Call it what you will, but you know what I'm talking about. How about giving the power back to the people?"

Colin sank back into his chair shaking his head. "Is this what it's going to be? I thought I was coming in here for a discussion, not to be peppered with a list of clichés—'slippery slope,' 'power to the people.' Seriously, you consider those interview questions?"

Gloria put a hand on his wrist. "Now Colin, no need to get hysterical. You—"

Colin pulled back his arm as though it were in a fire. "Look, you have to realize that we're faced with tough decisions every day. And to be honest, this one wasn't even close. Nothing good can come of this. By pandering to tragedy voyeurs, we let them broadcast hate for profit."

"That's a passionate speech, but what would you say to those that feel like they got a brief glimpse of a world that had been covered up for too long? I mean, this is happening right under our noses."

"Gloria, I have no idea why you're taking this tone. Why the fuck does anyone think the Current is innocent? I mean—"

"Colin, please, you—"

"Gloria, let me finish. You know, I have to hand it to them. The machine is pretty impressive. They let people like you fire up the fringe of society, then watch them do something shocking. Once it's uploaded, they condemn it as loudly and broadly as possible to ensure that the inevitable copycat gets the message that they'll be famous too, and the cycle begins again. Fantastic business model. Really, it's fantastic." Colin paused and let his wry grin flatten into a sneer. "I mean, the only negative externality—you understand that phrase, right?—the only negative externality is that it wreaks fucking havoc on our society. People die for no reason except to increase ratings."

"Colin, please. I really don't know what to say to all that, but I think that we should wind this up. I assume that you know who it is, so is there anything you want to say to them over the air?"

Colin's hands were clasped together under his chin like a chess player contemplating a surprising move. "You know, I'd say just let it go. This isn't journalism, so don't play their game. Attention is oxygen for their fire. We can suffocate the violence by turning away."

Gloria turned down the corners of her mouth and nodded. "Oh, very eloquent. 'Suffocate the violence'—that's a nice sound bite. Well, I think that we should leave it at—"

"Gloria, I just want to say one last thing to your viewers, and that's, you know, just turn away. Every view, every click, every share, pours money into the system and encourages this type of behavior."

Gloria smiled at him. "Thanks, Colin." She turned to the camera. "That was Colin Harrington, and after the commercial break we'll meet the woman behind the latest fitness trend, so stay tuned."

Faye was shaking her head at the screen as the interview wound up. She tapped out a message: *Wow, he's upset.*

Her assistant replied, *Yes. Can't be fun at Magenta right now*

Ha, no. Who's working them?

Leon Mitcham

Don't know him. Send him a message from me personally. Tell him to keep up the great work.

Will do

And set something up. I'd like to meet him.

Will do

Thanks

Faye tossed her phone onto the desk, and it slid a few inches across the glass expanse.

Sitting on a couch she'd only left twice since she woke, Justine clicked the X in the top right corner of the laptop's screen just after the interview finished, and an advertising jingle for washing detergent evaporated.

A message from Leon popped up a moment later. *You watch it?*

Yeah.

That asshole.

Yeah.

I don't know if it matters, but I think you did the right thing. Someone was going to break this thing open. I'm glad it was you.

Had to happen sooner or later.

What are you going to do?

Justine paused for a few seconds before responding. *No idea. I'm going to sleep on it.*

Don't let him rattle you.

What?

Don't be fooled by that faux rage. Gloria's right. Those guys aren't more important than the truth.

You don't like him. I get it, but when did you become such a rebel?

Of course I don't like him. He just fired my best friend at the company for doing what's right. Don't let him win.

He won't

That's the spirit

Thanks dad

Ha. Sorry, didn't mean it like that, but if you need my support, just let me know.

Will do, bye

Bye

She typed *JD* into the search bar, and the predictive search added 04. She held her hands clasped in a fist above the keyboard before tapping Return and scanning past the first two headlines: "Who is JD04?" "What's next from JD04?"

The third headline was from the Current: "Fame Chaser?" She began reading.

Finding the true identity of JD04 will be an obsession for many in the coming days, but I'd prefer to ask, what's next? The frenzy will soon fade, and now we know that the curated media can't be trusted. The burden of bringing light to the truth belongs to the Current. There's hope that Colin and his media empire crumble as his deception is exposed, but of course this could all be for naught. If JD04 disappears now, they will have done little more than fan the fire while chasing their fifteen minutes of fame, and squander the opportunity to serve the greater good.

Justine slammed down the cover of her laptop as she rued the simple act that gave her the megaphone she'd lusted after but left her too scared to use. The vitriol of the keyboard warriors could easily be shrugged off, but she knew that the truly unhinged were peeling the security from the screen name to connect JD04 to someone at Magenta. She imagined an assailant clambering up the fire escape and wondered if any of the neighbors would come to her aid, even though she'd never managed more than a brief smile as they shared an elevator.

Her phone vibrated, and she jumped. The message was from Colin.

I'm sure that you're upset, but don't do anything rash

She shook her head like someone that couldn't believe the joke and wrote, *Don't text me.*

I know you don't want to hear from me, but leave this alone.

You're giving advice now? After ignoring me for years? It took me too long to realize that you guys are dinosaurs.

Forget the Current. The story will fade soon enough and no one will get hurt.

Seriously? I'm not taking advice from the guy that stole three years from me. I understand, but trust me, the Current will just keep wanting more. That's their business model.

Their business model? Yeah, it's just business. Come on. Don't bother writing again. I'll just block you.

Justine waited a few seconds, but when a speech bubble failed to appear, she tossed her phone onto the couch and thought back to her first day at Magenta. The responsibility of journalism had seemed so deeply engrained, and she had desperately wanted that myth to be true, but she wondered if the raw documentation of the Current was true reporting now. Her gaze drifted to the shallow drawer under her writing desk, and she tugged the handle. She pawed around until she found the white card hidden at the back. Staring at the string of digits printed on one side, she turned it over in her fingers and rubbed her thumb along the text, marveling at the ink's permanence. It had come from a friend of a friend, and he'd convinced her it was safe, but purchasing a drone was a felony. She entered the code into her phone with shaky fingers.

A moment later the words *How can I help?* appeared on her screen.

Papering over her doubts with haste, she typed, *Need drone, can you help?*

A few seconds later a bubble popped up. *Of course.*

I'm new to this, how does it work?

You transfer credits and I give you a drone.

How do I get it?

You come and pick it up.

Justine put the phone down. The room felt smaller, and the door seemed like the flimsiest of barriers protecting her from the outside world. The screen on her phone went black after a few seconds, and she took a quick breath before picking it up again. The screen flashed on, unchanged from the last message.

She tapped out, *Ok, when?*

The reply came quickly as though the delay between her messages were expected. *As soon as you need it. I will send invoice and pickup instructions. Don't come before the credits are transferred.*

Ok thanks

As Justine entered the credit information, she reminded herself that she didn't even have to use it. The bubble popped up, and three pulsing dots began their cycle as though a reply were coming, but the bottom left of her screen remained blank. She waited thirty seconds, then tapped the blank screen, but no keyboard appeared. She tapped again, then tried the buttons on the side, but the phone didn't respond. She laughed to herself in an attempt to smother the welling regret, and another twenty seconds passed by before a message arrived.

Find pen before pressing accept, message will only appear for ten seconds

Rifling through the drawer, Justine found an old keepsake pen and tested it on the card, drawing a crooked circle before she tapped her phone.

1645 Westwood. Between 10pm and midnight

She'd written "1645 Westw" when the message evaporated, and she continued with "ood" a little more carefully.

It was almost eleven. Justine walked briskly along a street that felt like an underexposed photograph, the streetlights barely highlighting the edges of houses that blended into the shadows. Even though she'd committed the four digits to memory, she double-checked the piece of paper in her hand every couple of minutes. Only a few of the houses still had numbers, and after passing 1637, she counted out four more. After a fruitless search for a number on the weathered facade, she scurried to the next house but had to pass two more before she saw the number 1651 on a lilting mailbox. Swiveling on her heels and counting back, she took a furtive glance along the street before taking the steps two at a time to an unmarked door. She knocked three times, more delicately than planned, and strained to hear any movement during the advised thirty-second wait before knocking again. Her knuckles only hit the wood once before the door was pulled back a couple of inches and the light from inside cut across the porch. It was extinguished a moment later by a man's silhouette.

"Justine?"

She squinted, trying to pull features from the dark mass. "Yes, that's me."

The man opened the door a little farther, but his face remained in shadow. "Please come in."

Justine nodded obediently and stepped over the threshold as the man gestured toward a room crowded with paperback-sized boxes, each marked with a collection of numbers and symbols. As the light found his face, he folded his mouth into a smile and waved toward the box on the counter. "Well, dear. I'm not sure what you have in mind, but I hope it's worth it."

She frowned as she picked it up. "Yeah, I hope so. Is this it?"

"They say good things come in small packages."

She glanced at him without softening her expression.

"It has to be that small to avoid detection."

"Ah, of course. So no one will ever know about this, right?"

"Look, dear, this might be your first time, but I wouldn't still be here if I were sloppy. Your secret is safe with me."

"Okay, so do I get a receipt or anything?"

The man shook his head, smiling. "No, no, there's no returns. Just take it."

She nodded once and thrust the box deep into her bag. "Okay, thank you."

"Good luck."

Justine nodded. "Yeah, thanks. Bye." She didn't wait for a response before turning toward the door.

As she entered her apartment, Justine dipped her shoulder to let the bag slide onto the kitchen counter. She sat down at the table and slid open the box, pinching the drone in her fingers and extending the blades. They snapped into place with a satisfying click, and she stepped out onto her balcony, cradling the machine as though it were a wounded bird.

Nervously holding the illicit object, she glanced left and right, almost hoping that someone would be out on their balcony so she'd have a reason to stop, but she was alone. Only a few squares of light broke the black facade, and the closest was a dozen apartments away, so she flipped the tiny switch and delicately placed the drone on a small round table. A light flashed orange before turning solid green, then winking out. When her phone vibrated a second later, she slotted it into the controller and pressed the green triangle. A second later the view from the drone's camera filled the screen. She let her thumbs fall to the joysticks and gave them a gentle nudge.

The drone rose from the table, and as she applied a little more pressure, the ambient noise absorbed the whine of the drone's rotors, and it merged with the night.

Stepping back inside without taking her eyes from the screen, she used the familiar tugs and taps to push the drone toward the dark territory. Soon the drone was flying over the eight lanes of asphalt that were considered the edge of safety, and she slowed the drone as it passed the merchants that braved this part of town, their carefully arranged displays mocking the decay on the other side.

Justine tapped the right joystick, and the drone spun lazily before she nudged it forward over the dark corner. The world below seemed to disappear until a car's headlights flickered and flared as it rounded a bend, momentarily lifting the alleys from darkness. She began patiently, remembering to swivel through a full loop at the end of each pass as she'd been trained. An occasional vehicle was the only break from the monotony, and an uneventful hour had stretched to two when she noticed a man ambling down the middle of the street in a puffy jacket zipped to his chin. He was holding a phone aloft as though looking for a signal, and when she lowered the drone to head height, he swiveled around and pointed his phone directly at the camera. She pulled the drone backward with a quick tug of her forefinger. The man glanced at his phone before beckoning the drone closer, and Justine nudged the right joystick, bringing the drone close enough to see the patchy flecks of stubble on his chin. He beckoned again, and she shook the drone from side to side to mimic a shake of her head.

He looked at his screen and shrugged. "You looking for Asha?"

Guessing that was the girl that she'd first seen, Justine wiggled the controller, and the drone bobbed back and forth in a nod.

With a broad grin, the man said, "Well, follow me," and turned around.

As he disappeared around the corner and she pushed the drone forward, the low-battery alert sounded. Justine was guessing how long 5 percent would last when she saw Asha crouched over her phone like a teenager waiting for a friend. Asha sat up when the man approached, and he nodded, prompting her to look past him at the drone.

"You're back? Didn't want to be a one-hit wonder? I have to say, that's a great decision. And is that your own drone, a secret one? I can barely see it. Great to see you making things happen so quickly."

Justine's thumbs were perched above the joysticks, but before she could decide between nodding and shaking, Asha continued, "A lot of views, huh? But you know, they'll be on to the next thing tomorrow. We'll have to keep turning it up, right? Gotta give the fans what they want."

Justine didn't respond.

"Are you still listening?"

Justine wiggled the right joystick, and the drone gave a little nod.

"You know, that feels great. No one really listens to us. Sometimes I feel guilty about what we have to do to be seen, but that's the problem with the system. It's too easy for you to tune us out…"

Asha took a step forward as the wind drowned out her speech, and Justine pulled back a couple of feet. When she beckoned the drone again, Justine tapped the joystick, and the drone moved from side to side in an electronic no. Asha sighed and held up two fingers in a pinching motion, prompting Justine to nudge the drone forward a fraction. A second later her screen went black.

Asha laughed. "Yeah, we got you now."

Justine tugged on the joystick and could hear the whir of blades through the microphone, but the blackness didn't shift. She screamed, "What the fuck?"

The muffled voice continued, "Pushing that joystick won't help. We got your boy, and we ain't letting go. There's no point wasting the batteries."

Justine pulled her hand from the joystick, and the whirring stopped.

"Cut the motor, cut the motor."

A gruff voice said, "Why don't we just turn it off?"

"I want them to hear us."

Justine jabbed the joystick again, but this time nothing happened.

Asha asked, "So what is it?"

"It's Ian's. It's one of Ian's drones."

"Does he have anything to do with this?"

"Nah, I think he just sold it to someone, but I'll lean on him."

Asha raised her voice. "Hey, JD04, did you hear that? We'll know who you are soon, but sit tight. You keep doing great work and there's no reason for us to pay you a visit."

The man said, "Should we let it go?"

"Let me get a photo of the serial number first, then you can let it go. This kind citizen can't continue their valuable work without it."

The drone was down to 3 percent, and the battery warning flashed again. A blurry image filled the screen as the camera fought to focus. As it resolved into a close-up of a puffy jacket, she tried the controls again, but there was no response as the man clumsily aimed the camera at Asha. The same crimson bandanna was wrapped over her mouth, but her hair fell in waves this time.

"JD04, I know you stumbled into this, but be sure to be back here same time tomorrow for another installment. It's the only way to keep the fine people of this town safe."

The man asked, "That's it?"

"Yeah. Don't forget to plug in the rotors."

"Okay, I got 'em. JD04, you'd better turn this thing back on; otherwise, it's going to hit the ground hard, and without it, you're not much use to us."

The screen blurred as the drone was thrown skyward. Justine grabbed the joystick and pushed hard with her thumb as though she were propelling the drone with the pressure of her hand alone. The image steadied as the rotors stabilized the craft, and she swiveled the camera around.

When it faced Asha, she tapped her chest with a fist. "You and me, we're a team now. Now run along. There's nothing more to see tonight."

Justine was too numb to move, but when Asha gestured as though shooing away a fly, she tapped the home button and fell backward on the couch. The screen flashed *2%*, then a blue dot appeared over a map of the area and moved toward her apartment. It was a few blocks closer when the batteries dropped to 1 percent and the signal disappeared in a final effort to conserve power. She ran outside and leaned over the balcony, squinting into the darkness even though she knew she would never be able to spot it. The phone beeped again, and she winced, picturing the only tool she could use to appease Asha smashing to the ground, but instead the word *Home* glowed on the screen. She swiveled around to see the drone sitting lifeless on the table. It was already well past midnight, and Justine scooped it up and stepped inside, locking the door before lying back on her bed and closing her eyes.

When her phone buzzed, she jerked upright and grabbed at it, but smiled ruefully when she saw the alarm clock icon under *2:00 a.m.* As Justine switched it off, her mind turned to the small room that had been her destination at the same time a week earlier, and she pictured a young, eager recruit staring at the screen in her place, oblivious to the fact they were there merely to mark territory. She rolled over and tugged the covers up to her chin, but as she weighed each minor decision over the last couple of days, it took another hour for her to fall sleep.

Blinking against the light as the midday sun painted bright stripes on the carpet, she reached up and closed the blinds. The sunlight was cut to a soft glow at the edge of each leaf. She reached for her phone and typed *JD* into the search bar. It still auto-filled to JD04, but the newest time stamps were ten hours old, and it felt as though her fifteen minutes of fame were waning. Half an hour later, sitting at the kitchen table and shoveling cereal into her mouth, she was scrolling through the news on her laptop when a message slid out from the right side of the screen.

Are you coming tonight? We have a show for you.

She watched it slide back off and shook her head with her eyes squeezed shut.

You listening? We want you.

Justine wrote, *Who are you?*

Seriously? There's no point in games. You know who I am. And more importantly I know who you are.

No you don't. You just have my number.

Justine, you know that isn't true.

Justine stared at her name in the speech bubble and slumped backward.

Thirty seconds later another message arrived. *Now you know it's real, but you knew it would be when you bought a drone. That was a risky move. You can't really turn to anyone now, huh?*

What do you want from me?

To do a little more recording. Your fans haven't heard from you since your first video, and it's getting stale.

No. Please no. This whole thing is a mistake. I just wanted to show what my boss was hiding.

That's perfect. That's exactly what we want.

No. Not your way. I don't want to broadcast your brutality.

Brutality is in the eye of the beholder. Some might call it justice.

Not me

Maybe I can change your mind. This one's not a job for a drone. We need some of that handheld shakiness. The little touches that give it the authenticity we need. We want the viewer to feel part of it. You know what I mean?

Justine didn't respond.

I know what you're thinking. But give it some thought. You won't be in danger. Your voice is too important. You'll come out with some amazing footage. You're going to be huge.

Justine's fingers hovered above the keyboard when the next message arrived.

Am I taking the right angle here? Or are you just another voyeur? I was hoping you'd be different.

Justine just stared.

A little stage fright. We'll be waiting for you at 2 am. Did I mention that we know who you are.

Justine slammed the cover down and screamed to no one. It was midafternoon, but she found a bottle of wine, filled a glass, and took a deep gulp. Then she texted Leon.
Call me right away. Urgent
She stared at the phone.
Thirty seconds later she wrote again. *Drop everything. Call me* She stared at the screen, willing a message onto it, but the phone winked out a few seconds later.
Where the hell are you? Do you have any idea how scary this is?
The phone vibrated, and Justine snatched it from the table. Leon's smiling face filled the screen, and Justine desperately wanted to punch it.
She answered with "Thank God."
Leon responded, "Justine, what's wrong?"
"She fucking found me, Leon. That's what's wrong."
"Wait. What? Who found you?"
"Leon. Do I need to spell it out? Who's the last person I'd want to find me?"

A few seconds later, Leon mumbled, "Well. I guess the woman in the video, but how could—"

"Leon. How she found me doesn't matter. She just has, and if I don't do what she wants, she knows where I am."

Leon paused for a few seconds, then spoke quietly. "You should call the police."

"I can't."

"Why not?"

Justine exhaled slowly. "Well, they won't have a lot of sympathy for someone who bought a drone, found trouble on the wrong side of town, and wants them to bail her out."

"Wait, what? You bought a drone?"

"Ah yeah. I was going to tell you about that. I—"

"Are you fucking crazy? How did you even—"

"Leon, that doesn't matter. Let's talk about that later. What matters is that there's a fucking psycho that knows who I am, and if I don't do her bidding, I'm done."

"Justine, slow down. Give yourself some time to think about this."

"That would be nice, but she wants to meet me tonight."

"Damn. Seriously? Anything else you haven't told me?"

"No, Leon, that's it. She wants me to meet her at two in the morning on a street corner."

"You can't go."

"Leon, I don't have a choice. I can either play along and hope that she keeps her part of the bargain, or I can cower in my room until someone knocks on my door."

"This is too much for me. Is there anyone else you can call?"

"No. No, there isn't. You're the only one that knows the video was mine. Well, you and Colin, and I'm sure as hell not calling him."

"You haven't told anyone else?"

"No. Maybe if I had, I wouldn't be in the mess, but I listened to you."

"Try to put it off. Just one night. We can think of something."

"That's it? That's all I'm going to get from you?"

"I wish I knew how to help. If I think of anything, I'll call right away."

Justine paused. "Yeah. Thanks. I appreciate it."

"And I'm here if you want me. I'll stay by my phone."

"Cool, thanks."

After hanging up, Justine tapped Asha's message and typed, *I can't come tonight. Tomorrow?*

She stared at the bottom right corner, willing a speech bubble onto the screen, but it remained blank.

Please. We have to work together on this.

She waited another minute.

Don't do this to me

Justine tugged the message pane to refresh every couple of minutes until the sun retreated behind the horizon. The darkness closed around her until the blue light of the screen was the brightest thing in the room. After setting the alarm for one and ordering a car for one fifteen, she typed, *Asha. Are you there?* and stared at the screen until it went black. Lying back, she squeezed her eyes shut and let the phone fall from her grasp.

A couple of miles away, Leon sat forward with his arms folded in a broad leather chair. A glass table with four carefully splayed magazines on its surface was the only thing between him and the receptionist on the other side of the lobby. With a faint smile etched on her thin face, she called across the expanse: "She's ready."

Leon nodded in a little stuttering motion but didn't rise.

The receptionist flicked her hand dismissively. "Yes, yes, go in. She doesn't have much time."

He pulled himself to his feet and scurried toward Faye's office but turned toward the receptionist before he reached for the handle. She sighed as she gave him an affirmative nod. When he cautiously poked his head in, Faye looked up, and her face cracked into a smile.

"Oh, you must be Leon. Come in, come in. Please take a seat. Would you like a drink?"

Leon shook his head as he lowered himself into a chair. "No. I'm fine, thanks."

Faye folded her hands together. "I really must congratulate you. Fantastic work. Have you seen the numbers?"

"Yes, yes, of course. I appreciate you taking the time to meet me, but—"

Faye tilted her head. "Just so you know, I'd hoped it would be you flying the drone when something like this happened, but it sounds like we got the next best thing. Great editing, don't you think? So, how much do you know about who did this?"

"Well, I know her. We've exchanged shifts for a year."

"Do you think she might be the one?"

Leon blinked. "I'm sorry. The one?"

Faye leaned forward eagerly. "The one that gets this story out— the bold, independent voice we've been searching for."

"I'm sorry, I don't understand."

"Leon, you know how everyone's skeptical of 'big media,' but someone like this, somehow they're more believable."

"Okay, I'm sorry, I understand now. I guess when you said 'the one,' it sounded a bit like we're looking for a superhero."

Faye laughed. "No, no, of course that's not what I meant, but sometimes thinking about it like that makes it more exciting, don't you think?"

"I'm not—"

"Do you think that she'll post more videos?"

"Faye, I'm sorry, but that's not top of mind right now. I actually spoke with her a few minutes ago, and she claims that the girl in the video knows who she is. She wants to meet her in person."

Faye leaned back, bringing her palms together and intertwining her fingers. "Wow. She wants to meet her?" She paused for a second. "You'd be flying, right?"

"What?"

Faye tapped her fingertips together, and the diamonds in the gaudy rings on most of her fingers sparkled in the soft light. "You'd take her shift, right?"

"I'm sorry, I haven't really thought about it. I'm more interested in how we can stop it."

Faye gave a shadow of a shrug. "Stop it? Unfortunately, we'll just have to let this one play out."

Leon made a show of gazing around the lavish office. "You know, by the looks of things, you're not the type of person that lets something play out. Unless it's what you want."

"Leon, everything's different in there. I hope that you don't think I can just blow a whistle and stop those people, do you? Now, I don't want the girl to get hurt, but—"

"It's Justine. Her name's Justine."

"I'm sorry. I don't want Janine to get hurt, but that's not up to me. She took this on."

"Justine, not Janine, and she did this because of us."

"Now Leon, you can't be sure of that, so don't blame yourself. And who knows? Tonight might be a dud."

"A dud? I hope you're not implying that you want something else."

"No, of course not. I'll be hoping for the best."

Leon leaned forward. "That's it? 'Hoping for the best,' that's all we're going to do? You must have some connections. If it wasn't for the Current, no one would know anyone in there existed. They owe you."

"Leon, you misunderstand the relationship. No one owes anyone anything. We simply allow people to share events, and we don't pass judgment."

Leon exhaled. "Faye, you can save the lofty platitudes for an interview. Justine might get killed because of us."

Faye planted her elbows on the table and leaned forward, allowing her head to rest on the backs of her knuckles. "Leon, I understand your concern, but she's not really in danger. Those people, they need this girl. They won't let anything happen to her. And she'll come back with a great story."

Leon was gazing over Faye's shoulder where the last blip of the sun's disc was disappearing behind the horizon. "Well. Okay then."

"I know you wanted more, but she'll be fine. In all this, I don't want you to forget how much I appreciate the work that you do. It can't be easy dealing with those self-righteous assholes each day."

He nodded as he rose, mumbling a "thank you." He had already opened Faye's door when she spoke again.

"Leon."

He turned.

"They're not the good guys, you know."

"What?"

"Magenta. You don't think that they got the drone contract due to their esteemed reputation, do you? We outbid them by a lot, but they'll sweep what's happening under the rug. Their whole dignified silence stance is a sham. It's not about the danger of giving extremists a voice, it's for a mayor that wants the city to seem safer than it is."

Leon let the door close. "Really?"

"Have you ever wondered why the drone ban's so strict? A few more might show everyone that the police aren't doing quite as good a job as the mayor claims."

"Why does she care that much?"

"Her policies are soft, but that bleeding heart doesn't want to believe that her choices lead to this. Don't you think that it's our moral duty to show everything that happens?"

Leon nodded. "Yeah. Yeah, I guess." He let the door close behind him as he left.

As he walked past Faye's assistant, she asked, "Did she want a follow-up?"

Leon responded, "No, no." He loped toward the elevator without slowing. After jabbing the button, he stared at the stainless-steel doors while twirling his phone in his hand. A ding signaled the car's arrival, and he eagerly ducked in as soon as the doors were wide enough, then hit the button for the first floor. In the lobby, he jogged a couple of steps to time the revolving door, and called Justine as he burst onto the street.

Justine answered on the first ring. "Some good news, I hope?"

"Umm, well, not really. What did you think I'd come up with?"

"I don't know, but—"

"I was thinking about it, though, and they don't have a voice without you. They'd be crazy to hurt you."

"Seriously? You do know that they are actually crazy, right?"

"I know, but that's a different kind of crazy."

"There's only one type of crazy, Leon."

"Justine, this is different—"

"Well, if you're so sure, why don't you come with me?"

"You know I can't do that. It's Thursday. I'll be at work." He paused. "Oh, but I'll have the drone. I can follow you. I'll call the police if anything happens."

"The police? Haven't we been through that? That woman's whole point is that no one cares what happens in there. Maybe she wants to prove it tonight."

"I wish there was more I could do. To be honest, I'm worried sick, but me being there just makes it more dangerous. I don't know what she'd do if she saw me. Maybe she'd think it was some type of trap."

"Okay, okay. Just keep that drone over me."

"I will, Justine. I will."

"Thanks. That's at least something."

When Justine's phone buzzed again a few hours later, she jerked upright and snatched it off the table, but instead of a message that might save her, the alarm icon was flashing on the screen. She stared blankly for a few seconds, turned to the clock on the wall to confirm that it was one a.m., then peeled off a blanket with a purposeful flick. Instead of lifting herself off the couch, she typed another message: *Asha, please, not tonight.* Her phone buzzed thirty seconds later, and she jumped. The message read, *Your car will arrive in fifteen minutes, please don't keep the driver waiting.* After willing herself to her feet, she stared at the bathroom mirror and brushed her hair with slow, deliberate strokes. She couldn't help wondering how important it was to look good in the movie of her demise.

Walking down the stairs in a daze, Justine slid into the back seat of a nondescript sedan.

The driver turned back to her after glancing at his GPS. "Are you sure you have the right address?"

Justine nodded solemnly, and the driver shrugged before tapping the accelerator. She stared vacantly as the city flowed past and still didn't move when he pulled over.

They'd stopped at a vacant intersection only one block away from the dark quarter, and the driver turned around without unlocking the doors. "You sure?"

"Yeah, yeah. I'm sorry." She turned to him. "I'm guessing that you don't drop people here too often, but a friend will swing by soon."

He narrowed his eyes. "At one thirty in the morning?"

Justine forced a smile. "It's a long story."

"It's up to you, but don't go west. A block that way"—he signaled over his shoulder with his thumb—"and there's a good chance you won't be seen again."

"Thanks. I know. I'll be careful."

"Yes, please do."

The driver unlocked the doors, and Justine stepped out into the cold, wrapping her arms around her chest as he accelerated away, the car's taillights flashing red as it paused at the next intersection. When they disappeared around the corner, only the fragile light of the moon was left to guide her as she walked timidly in the direction that her driver had warned her against. A defunct company's logo had been eaten by layers of graffiti on the billboard above her, the faded paint succumbing to wispy black letters.

Even in the desolation, Justine looked both ways before pulling out the drone. Comforted by the faint whir of the rotors, she held it out in front of her until the camera found her face. After tapping Lock on her phone, she launched it with a soft throw, and it wobbled into position fifteen feet above the ground. Checking that her face was in the middle of the frame before tapping record, she couldn't avoid thinking of the worst-possible outcome. She pictured the "She should have known better" comments from viewers oblivious to the events that had led to this moment and broke into a brisk trot as she tried to outrun the thought, counting out five blocks before turning right onto Eighth Street. It had been the main thoroughfare a decade ago, and she dashed along the wide-open street, squinting against the darkness for any sign of life. Arriving five minutes early, she stood in the shadows with her arms crossed for a few seconds, then sought relief in motion and walked away from the designated intersection.

"Where do you think you're going?"

Justine spun around. Asha was standing tall with her hands on her hips, the hound letting her prey savor the last moments of freedom.

Justine's gaze was drawn to the pistol sitting on Asha's hip like a gunslinger from an old western. "Sorry, I just wanted to keep moving. I'm a bit cold."

Asha laughed, her biting cackle cutting the night. "You're JD04? You know, I expected a little more from someone so bold."

Justine smiled wanly. "I'm not brave; I'm just the reluctant girl behind the camera. You're the star."

"Oh, but you are brave. You're standing here risking your life for the views. We're a great team, dear."

"I don't want to be a team. I don't even want to be here. I just thought I was doing the right thing."

"Oh, you are, you are. Sharing our story is the right thing to do."

"It's not our story; it's your story."

"Well, not entirely. You pushed us to it. The mayor that Magenta so eagerly supported swept our tents away, but after she rid your perfect world of those colorful nylon pimples, she thought that a roof and intermittent plumbing was enough to solve all of our problems. Once we were gone, Evelyn seemed to forget us."

"No, that isn't true. There's a proposal to—"

"A proposal? That's not much good to us. No one comes in here for anything. No police, no ambulance, no firefighters. It didn't take long for those on the margins to realize that unleashing their anger would go unpunished. Now our stunts are the only thing that remind you that this little experiment has been a disaster."

"Killing to remind people that you're still here doesn't help."

Asha's eyes narrowed. "You sound like someone who hasn't dealt with the pain of anonymity. Until I shed blood, there's not much point in telling our story because no one is watching."

Justine shook her head. "It's not the way. No one's going to listen when you do that."

"But if I untied this guy, you'd just turn around."

"This guy?"

Asha smiled, then waved her hands, and a car flipped on its headlights, tearing a hole in the darkness. Justine blinked in the glare, then opened her eyes to see a middle-aged man tied to a chair in the vehicle's path. Thick strands of rope bound his hands to the backrest and his ankles to the front legs. There was blood splattered on the lapel of his tailored suit, and his shirt was covered in sweat despite the cold. There were flecks of gray hair in his stylish businessman's cut, and a handkerchief was tied closely around his mouth. He squinted into the light.

Asha laughed. "You think this is crazy, but maybe that's just because he's wearing a suit. Maybe if he was in a sweat-stained T-shirt and soiled jeans, you'd be okay with it, because someone like that dies here every day."

Justine took a step backward. "There's no need for this. There are people that will listen."

Asha smiled, tilting her head in a way that might have looked questioning in another situation. "Oh, some more vague promises. We've certainly heard a few of those."

The driver revved the old car. It sounded like the roar of wild animal, and Justine jumped backward. Asha eased the pistol from her holster without any theatrics, then seemed to weigh the gun in her right hand.

"No—don't do it."

Asha raised her right arm and aimed the pistol at the sky. The car's headlights caught the glistening metal, and she pulled the trigger. A moment after the earsplitting crack, gravel sprayed from the rear tires and clattered into the brick wall behind them.

Justine screamed as the vehicle erased the distance to the man in its path. He jumped the chair, managing to move it a few inches, but the driver didn't even need to change course. Justine turned away as the car sped past and slammed into its target, but she couldn't escape the dull thud of a body hitting the windscreen. The car kept moving, and as the roar receded into the distance, Justine listened for a whimper—or any noise at all.

The silence was final and painful, and Justine refused to look up.

"Looking away? Your kind is pretty good at that."

Justine shook her head, her eyes glued to the pavement.

"Yeah, maybe you should just watch it at home. On a screen it will just look like a movie." Justine raised her head. Asha was pointing to the sky. "You don't have to worry; that thing got it all. Just think of the views."

The portly man who'd captured the drone the previous night waddled out beside Asha. "Should I take down Magenta's?"

"Yeah, they have all they need."

The man aimed what looked like a black pipe at the sky above Justine's head. His finger twitched, and a second later a drone slapped into the pavement.

Asha let out a dull little laugh. "Damn, that thing's not bad."

The man shrugged. "It does the job."

The broken drone's rotors buzzed like a wounded insect, and Justine turned to Asha. "Why did you do that? Don't you want them to hear your story?"

Asha's coarse laughter echoed off the walls as she raised the pistol and pointed it at Justine. "I've told the story we want everyone to hear, and you have to control the framing, right? There's no point in letting them see what happens next."

Back in the control room, Leon heard the crack, then watched the ground fill the screen in a rush before the monitor went black. In the sudden darkness, he wiggled the joystick in desperation, then fumbled for the switch on the desk lamp as his eyes slowly adjusted to the murky light. The moment he turned it on, the desk phone rang, cutting the silence with a high-pitched tinkle that was a comical throwback to an old movie. He searched for a screen to see who was calling, but the chunky plastic device only had a speaker and a red light throbbing in time with the ring. It didn't look like it has been used for decades. He carefully lifted the solid plastic handset to his ear.

"He-hello?"

A vaguely familiar voice asked, "Who is this?"

Leon paused for a second. "Who are you?"

"This is the guy that runs the place, Colin Harrington. So who the hell is this?"

"Oh, oh. Sorry, sir, it's Leon. Leon Mitcham. I'm taking over Justine's shift since she, she ahh—"

"Leon. I don't think we've met. What the hell's going on? I just got an alert that the drone is down."

"Yeah. That seems to be the case, sir. It only just happened, and I have no idea what it was. Everything was fine, then it just dropped to the ground. Some sort of power failure, I guess. Has this ever happened—"

"Anything unusual before that?"

Leon cleared his throat. "Well, yeah."

"Yeah? Yeah, what?"

"Umm. Justine's in there, and she was talking to two people. One of them—"

"What. Justine? She's there?"

"Yeah, but I'm sorry, I don't know why, sir. She told me she had to go."

"Are you fucking kidding me?"

"No, sir. I said that I'd keep an eye on her from here."

Colin laughed mockingly. "Well, you're not keeping up your end of the bargain, are you?"

"I was until a minute—"

"Come on, Leon. Why'd you let her go in there?"

"The woman in that video she made, she found out who Justine was. She threatened her."

"You're kidding me."

"No, sorry, I wish I was."

"Where was the drone when it went down?"

"It was at Eighth and Hutt."

"Okay, well, see what you can do about getting a replacement up there as soon as possible. The contact info's in the database."

"But what can we do—"

A click cut Leon's sentence short, and he slowly put the handset down and grabbed his phone. He called Justine, but her phone was off.

Justine shook her head without taking her eyes from Asha's pistol. "Killing me won't help anything."

Asha swung the pistol around, the streetlight catching its barrel with each loose wave. "Oh, it will help us. Controlling distribution is far more profitable than providing content."

"What?"

Asha laughed. "My dear, I didn't realize that you bought that sob story. I don't care about what happens in here; that's just the script."

Justine stared.

"I can't believe you haven't worked it out. We do these shows for the fucking money, all right?"

Justine shook her head. "What? Who pays you for this?"

"That doesn't matter."

"Whoever it is, they're just making it worse in here." Justine waved toward the body without glancing in its direction. "This is why no one helps. You don't get any sympathy doing—"

"Sympathy won't help. Money's more useful than some politician's empty promises."

"Until the money dries up."

Asha cackled. "That won't happen as long as people are still watching."

Justine took a step backward. "Why are you telling me? My drone's still on."

"Because that doesn't matter. I have this pistol in my hand, and soon I'll have your drone, so what it just recorded will be our little secret. Sure, you could tell people, but no one's going to believe a bitter voyeur trying to make a few bucks out of our misfortune."

Justine's gaze didn't waver from the gun's barrel still pointed at her chest, but she took another couple of steps backward.

Asha continued, "So hand me your phone, and to save us cutting your thumb off, could you unlock it? If you don't, the last thing your fans will see is you lying in a pool of blood. Remember that we can use your finger whether you're breathing or not."

Justine nodded and felt each of her pockets.

Asha barked, "Come on, there's no point in stalling. The cavalry isn't coming. This neighborhood belongs to us."

Justine nodded and dug into her jacket pocket to pull out her phone. "Okay then, you win."

"Unlock it."

Justine swiveled it around in her fingers, letting her thumb fall to the edge of the unlock button. "Sorry, it won't unlock. My finger's sweaty."

Asha waved the pistol. "Come on."

"Let me type in my code." Justine's thumbs flashed around the device as Asha scowled. She rotated the phone, bringing it to horizontal position.

"What are you doing?"

Justine held up her left hand while deftly pawing at the device with her right thumb. "Just a second."

The drone flashed past, crashing into Asha's cheek and knocking her backward. Justine spun and bolted into the darkness. She turned left at the first corner and sprinted as she strained to hear any sounds of movement above her rasping breath. Fear smothered the pain of exertion, but as her legs slowed in defiance, she sought safety in darkness. She skirted around a lone streetlight and spotted a sleek black car that seemed to have been dropped in from a different, glossier future. Justine glanced over her shoulder, then dashed toward it. When she was twenty yards away, an LED door panel lit up with Magenta Publishing's logo, and she swerved toward the familiar initials.

Thirty yards behind her, Asha yelled, "Getting across Broadway's not going to save you. Faye's long arms will find you."

Justine's strides were labored, but she was willing herself forward when the tinted glass of the driver's window lowered to reveal Colin's gap-toothed smile. Justine tried to stop herself and stumbled as her momentum carried her a few more steps. She teetered to a stop. Exposed and still a dozen yards from the vehicle, she spun around, searching for Asha.

Colin yelled, "No. Come on, don't stop now."

Justine turned to him, shaking her head. A shot rang out, piercing the silence. She crouched down and twisted around. A second bullet zinged past, and this time she felt the puff of air. She ran toward the car. The rear door opened, a clunky automatic movement that seemed to happen in slow motion. When it was wide enough to slip through, Justine shimmied into the back seat. She tugged on the handle as a bullet crunched into the door panel. Crouching forward with her head in her lap, she shouted, "Well, go! Fucking go."

"It won't move until the door closes. It doesn't understand bullets."

Justine tugged at the handle but couldn't speed up the mechanized closing sequence. Colin banged the steering wheel. "Come on, come on."

The latch clicked, and the vehicle eased forward. Justine raised her head and found herself staring into the gun's barrel. She ducked back down as the glass shattered. Asha wrapped her free hand over the sill, the glass remnants of the rear window tearing into her palm as the vehicle continued to accelerate. Screaming, she refused to let go as she staggered alongside. She fired another wild shot before her hand slipped. Her body thumped against the door as she fell.

Justine twisted around to see Asha aiming the gun at her. Then the vehicle swerved right, throwing Justine into the side of the car and putting a building between her and the gun. It eased along then next block, guided by invisible hands that were oblivious to the commotion. Colin was leaning forward anxiously, but neither hand was on the steering wheel.

Justine shook her head. "Really? You're going to leave this up to this fucking car? Just drive it. We have to get out of here."

"I can't drive, but it will get us out of here."

Justine turned around and squinted, but no one emerged from the shadows. The vehicle continued to accelerate, and a few blocks later Justine jiggled the door handle, then kicked at the door. When it didn't budge, she cleared the glass at the base of the window and flailed for the door handle on the outside.

Colin yelled, "Don't be stupid! We're going too fast for that."

Justine stared at the street below her, trying to follow the lines, then slumped back into the seat. "Okay. So you got me. Where are you taking me?"

"Home. I guess."

"You don't have anything to do with this?"

Colin laughed, a sound that felt wrong in the battered car. "No, Justine, I don't. I just—"

"How did you know I was there?"

"Leon told me. I got an alert when the drone went down and called the control room."

After a second of silence, Justine replied, "So why'd you come?"

"You know, it's hard not to feel partially responsible."

"Partially?"

"I tried to warn you."

Justine spat, "After you fired me."

"Okay, Justine, I get it. I don't blame you for being upset, but that shattered window should remind you how lucky you are."

Justine stared out the window as she absorbed her relief. "Okay then, if I'm safe, job done, Superman. You can just let me out now."

"It's a long walk home, and the drone's still following us, right? There's some pretty valuable footage in that thing."

"Yeah, it's mine. Don't forget what I risked to get it."

"I don't care who gets credit as long as it gets out."

"Yeah, yeah, I'll upload it as soon as…"

Colin let a few seconds pass by before asking, "As soon as what?"

"The woman, she said that Faye had long arms, so I guess I can't post it on the Current. It will be gone before—"

"She actually said Faye? Wow. Finally something concrete."

"So the Current pays them?"

Colin looked over his shoulder. "You laughed when I told you it might not be real."

"If you knew, why the hell didn't you tell me? Or anyone? You screamed about everything but this on Feedback. You didn't even hint at it."

"The gap between assuming and knowing is a dangerous one, and a lot of doors closed when we started prying into who's behind what happens in there. The Current has some powerful allies that wouldn't hesitate to shut us down."

"In the government?"

"Yeah. Of course, this is great for the mayor's challengers. Showing violent criminals roaming the streets might sway the election, don't you think?"

"It sounds like everyone's playing the same game."

Colin shook his head. "No. We're not here to shape public opinion. Sure, the mayor prefers that we err on the side of caution, but it's not for her. So often, the violence seemed too perfectly staged, and once the public sees bloodstained images, it's pretty tough to change people's minds, no matter what's happening behind the scenes."

"And the drone contract's pretty valuable."

"I probably can't convince you that we're innocent, but imagine if the Current had the contract. These stunts would be on their home page every night. Would you prefer that?"

"No, of course not."

"So, should we head to Magenta then? We could have it up by morning."

"Yeah, yeah."

They traveled in silence for the next ten minutes. As the vehicle slowed and angled toward the curb, Colin tapped the dash. "I hope that this gets me back to even."

Justine laughed as she pulled the handle and leaned on the door. "That's a discussion for another day. Let's take care of Faye first."

Thank you

Thanks to my family for providing so much support, and thanks to Belinda Gibson, Jonathan Sipling, Kristy Huffman, Damian Isla, Julie Farago, Seema Ramchandani, Cam Charles, Elysha Huntington, Alex Bruskin, Meline Toumani, Monica Cullen, Peter Birney, Cynthia Maletz, Danielle Restivo, Scott Green, Steve Herold, Ali Herold, Alex Malek, Bojana Duke, Stephanie Malek, Lynda Rimas, and Amanda Turner for reading early drafts.

www.ingramcontent.com/pod-product-compliance
Lightning Source LLC
LaVergne TN
LVHW011801060526
838200LV00053B/3652